Jeremy Akerman is an artist and co-produced *Active Genital* and at the University of the Arts, St currently curating *Wandering St Korean Landscapes* – an exhibiti show in Seoul in 2006.

Eileen Daly is a freelance book editor. She a board member of New Contemporaries and is currently working on *The Animate! Book*, a book about art and animation to be published later this year.

Contributors

Edward Allington, David Batchelor, Ian Breakwell, David Burrows, Brian Catling, Jake Chapman, Juan Cruz, Mikey Cuddihy, Polly Gould, Chris Hammond, Janice Kerbel, Balraj Khanna, Brighid Lowe, Gary O'Connor, Paul Rooney, Jon Thompson and Martin Vincent.

THE ALPINE FANTASY OF VICTOR B

AND OTHER STORIES

Edited by Jeremy Akerman and Eileen Daly

First published in 2006 by
Serpent's Tail, 4 Blackstock Mews, London N4 2BT
website: www.serpentstail.com

Designed by Untitled
Printed by LegoPrint SpA, Italy

ISBN: 1 85242 926 7
        978 1 85242 926 3

With thanks to The Elephant Trust for its support

CONTENTS

8   Editors' Note

11   Introduction
       George Szirtes

17   Chatterbox
       Balraj Khanna

37   Gypsy; Bonsai Man; Sistine Chapel
       Mikey Cuddihy

49   Heart of the Forest
       Brian Catling

57   Towards the Heavenly Void
       Paul Rooney

73   Breakfast at the Beauty Spot
       Polly Gould

83   SEDA – an Interesting Story
       Antonio J. Cruz de Fuentes
       Translated by Juan Cruz

101   Open Sea
       Martin Vincent

113   The Road to Nowhere
       Jon Thompson

127   Underwood
       Janice Kerbel

133   Bob
       David Batchelor

149   The Beginning of the World is Afar
       Jake Chapman

165   The Alpine Fantasy of Victor B
       Chris Hammond

179   Ghost Writer
       Brighid Lowe

191   Soft
       Gary O'Connor

199   Ex-Misters (A Catalogue of Sudden Deaths)
       Ian Breakwell

205   Mirror Travel
       David Burrows

221   The Drowned Boys
       Edward Allington

233   About the Contributors

EDITORS' NOTE

The idea for this book is simple. It struck us that no book had been put together to acknowledge the fiction writing of artists, which we perceive to be an increasingly popular phenomenon. Of course artists write. Some write highly influential art theory, many write art criticism and some leave their art practice behind to become full-time critics. Artists write all sorts of things: manifestos, plays and novels, film scripts and magazine journalism; they write statements and speeches, but we see this book as the first compilation to conspicuously acknowledge their fiction stories.

This collection of short stories has the advantage of being able to embrace an unlikely but fantastic selection of artists from different generations and backgrounds. It's a group that probably could not come together in any other way. Some of the writers included have written for years and are published and well known, others are not. This is new territory, a combination intended to challenge and expand ideas about what artists do. We hope this book will be surprising, entertaining and curious; something that is, indirectly, able to reflect on visual art practice from a new vantage point, and something that will allow this aspect of an artist's activity to be understood in its own right.

One of the first artists we called on was Ian Breakwell, a regularly published author. We spent a good afternoon with him and asked him to contribute a story. He was enthusiastic about our book, sharing his thoughts about artists who write and talking at length about his own writing. For him the medium didn't matter, it was always a case of which materials executed the idea best.

We would like to dedicate this book to Ian.

We'd like to thank the artists for their contributions, plus Sacha Craddock, Tony White, Ben Hillwood-Harris, Michelle Thomas, Marjorie Allthorpe-Guyton, Ruby Wright, Felicity Sparrow, Glenn Howard, David Hawkins, Arts Council England and The Elephant Trust for their help and advice.

Eileen Daly and Jeremy Akerman

INTRODUCTION

GEORGE SZIRTES

here are various arts but the relationship between them is uncertain now. They used to order these things better in the old days. The farther art moved from the purely sensory towards the intellectual, from the mundane to the spiritual, from the body to the mind, the greater the respect it inspired. So it was that writers, whose medium is the symbolic world of oral and written language, were thought to be superior to painters and sculptors, whose medium was the messy, tangible raw stuff of pigment, wood or stone. Writers, it was thought, fed the ear, the mind and indeed all the senses via the imagination – they got more of the world in – and, unlike painters and other manual workers, they never needed to get their hands dirty.

Visual art in recent times has, however, moved beyond the fields of painting and sculpture. There are fewer dirty hands and more acts, more words. The influence of theoretical writing particularly has created a framework within which the visual arts have tended to move and to which they often refer. Bodies of writing prepare the ground and supply the furniture. Few museums of contemporary art, few catalogues or articles, can press the claims to attention of this or that work without first locating it in a theoretical-historical framework. Once that is done, the ground prepared, the furniture supplied, the party can begin, and the money that is required to float the whole precarious enterprise may be invited in to wander nervously or brashly, as the case may be, through the hall with its exhibits and exhibitors. Words – of the appropriate kind – are the currency of institutions and investments.

Literature and visual art were long regarded as sister arts but visual art is now rarely concerned with literature as such. Literature is not thought to be an appropriate form of words. Artists may occasionally refer to this or that work of fiction or, very rarely, poetry, but in a slightly vague, grace-note fashion rather than as the keynote. That is because literature works very differently in the marketplace. Walter Benjamin and Richard Wollheim have compared autograph works that possessed what Benjamin called their own 'aura' to mass-produced material. Wollheim, in his *Art and Its Objects*, enquired into the physical objects that acted as the locus of this or that art. What is pretty certain is that literature – meaning the world of books – does not of necessity produce autograph objects or unique occasions. A copy of a book is just a copy. Institutions may support writers but they rarely invest in first editions. Books are easy, ubiquitous objects, the words transferable from one sheet of paper to another. Unless they are antiques, books – as objects – do not generally need a battery of scholars to support their authenticity. The market does perfectly well without them. People read what they want without the need for an edifice of ideas to justify them or to identify value.

To put it another way, literature has less need to be defended by theory. Visual art's investment in theoretical words has driven it away from literature. Furthermore, too close an association with literature as such might lay the artist open to the charge of mere 'illustration', illustration being considered a minor, somewhat corrupt art: heavy, sticky and plodding. Surely modernism was liberation from all that? Ironically, the idea of illustrating theory is thought to be cleaner, lighter, altogether more healthy. There is indeed much work in galleries and art schools that is essentially a kindergarten-level illustration of theory. The theorists then pat the artists' heads and everyone goes home happy.

So art and literature have gone their separate ways. But is it not the case that when it comes to the other arts participants are usually consumers along with everyone else?

Not exactly like everyone else, perhaps, since there is a certain coherence in the art process, in the modes of its engagement, that extends beyond theory or the marketplace. Somehow it was possible for Michelangelo to write poems, for Blake to paint pictures, for Dante Gabriel Rossetti, William Morris and David Jones, to take just a few examples, to do both from the inside, as it were. There was once a *violon d'Ingres*, an alternative craft, a road less travelled by the artist and yet not altogether neglected. Paul Klee, Kurt Schwitters, Jean Arp all wrote poems.

Eileen Daly and Jeremy Akerman, the editors of *The Alpine Fantasy of Victor B*, have thoughtfully provided a list of artists who made serious attempts to play that Ingres violin, to explore that less travelled road. They point to novels by Leonora Carrington, Giorgio de Chirico, Salvador Dalí and others. With the exceptions of Ian Hamilton Finlay, David Jones and Filippo Marinetti, however, the artists named would not normally be regarded equally as writers and artists. The *violon d'Ingres* remains something they picked up once or twice and made interesting noises with then put away.

It was natural that they should put it away because each art form is demanding of time and concentration and few people have the required overflow of time and energy to devote themselves successfully to both. And yet there are hybrid forms where writing of a distinctly literary kind is part of the visual art process and product. Ian Breakwell's diaries are clearly of this sort: the diaries were the art, and Breakwell's piece here shows a distinct feel for the fabular and grotesque, not so far removed from, say, the short stories of Donald Barthelme as to be unrecognisable in literary terms. In a similar way Gary O'Connor's story of observation, tracking and identity is related to the narrative nature of his installation practice, the style disciplined, the feel for written language highly refined and, well, literary, in the best way. Brian Catling is the author of several books of poetry: his practice is and for a long time has been adventurous and comprehensive.

For some artists, then, literary writing either *is* their practice or is an extension of it. For others it is parallel and distinct, the application of a sensibility to another area of experience. Balraj Khanna is a natural writer and novelist, indeed a prize-winning and highly successful one. His story capers and plays in a purely literary fashion. No one reading it would immediately think that it had to be the work of a painter. Painting and writing are simply things Khanna can do extremely well. They cater to different parts of his interest and experience.

Other artists here explore fantasies and obsessions, play with conventions of reality, or, in Paul Rooney's case, deliver a sprightly fantastical stand-up homage to the late comedian Les Dawson. For literature can be cabaret too. And philosophical enquiry. And delicately poised mystery or indeed the playing out of a balance of relationships, as in Polly Gould's perfectly pitched *Breakfast at the Beauty Spot*.

There are writers who write as though born to it, others who handle the form like a strange but potentially amenable material. The handling in itself is interesting, as are the connections, strong, weak or non-existent, between their visual practice and their writing. They all offer something new and unfamiliar, showing ambitions that can move beyond the conventions of the book market and the so-called 'common reader'. That can be very refreshing.

We live in interesting times in many respects. Boundaries often shift yet areas remain obstinately discrete. There is action everywhere. Borders have moved around so much in eastern Europe that a man may have been born in one country, gone to school in another, served in the army of a third and worked for the rest of his life in the fourth without ever once having moved. Versatility is a useful talent. There is overlap and overflow. A lot of the contributors to this book have been or still are in bands. Music perhaps is the great democratic pool into which we all flow.

And Paul Klee wasn't a bad violinist either. Talent will out.

CHATTERBOX

BALRAJ KHANNA

17

The doorbell proved to be a bombshell – BANG – as in a Lichtenstein painting. Five foot seven, 33, 22, 33, looking 35, 22, 33 with the backpack. The eyes were too big for the face Paul beheld. The lashes murmured a meaningful message. And those lips? They were crafted simply to be kissed. Hit for six, in that one split second Paul knew it had happened. His sister had vaguely mentioned that her new friend was 'sort of cute'. But...

'Please come right in.'

The panelled hall looked rather dark considering how light the rest of the house was and how sunny the Canons Park afternoon. The penumbra passage lit up as this apparition walked in.

'After you,' Paul said, holding out a hand at the entrance to the grand drawing room. Once inside, he smiled for no reason and said, 'I am my sister's brother, Paul K. Kapoor. Ready to provide my full CV should that be required.'

'No thank you. Where is Anjli?'

As the mouth-watering visitor said that, there came a shout from upstairs.

'Paul, is that Minna? Let her in. I'll be down in a sec.'

'Orders from High Command to let you in,' Paul said to his sister's new friend. 'Please take a seat. Sit where you like. Here, there, anywhere. Our house is your house. Indians, you know. We are different. Unique, even. Hospitable to a fault. Warm hearted and heart warming.'

The guest remained standing and didn't say another word. But she spoke volumes with those eyelashes and blue-mascara eyes, the gist of which was crystal clear to Paul: she was in the presence of a nutter of some sort. After a quick glance around the pleasant room filled with modern Indian paintings, she looked at Paul again and then looked away, resting her eyes on a bulbous Souza nude behind the soft leather sofa.

'F.N. Souza. B.1924, D. 2002. Dad bought it at auction for peanuts weeks before F.N.S. kicked the balti. Now his prices are shooting through the roof. Not because the guy was good, which he was, brilliant, but because the guy was crazy. An Ess maniac. You know he...'

Paul was cut short. The visitor's mobile rang in her backpack.

'Oh,' Minna said to herself. She peeled off the pack from her back and took out the mobile. Paul knew what brand it would be, that of his own. And it was Vodafone. Paul felt pleased with himself. 'Hello,' he heard her say, followed by, 'Oh, hi,' a smile spreading on her face. Then she tilted her head at an angle that made her chin look as if it had been chiselled by Canova, no less, Paul thought. Then he told himself not to ogle or appear too admiring, never a good thing.

'Just wait for the developments to develop, you fool.'

Less than a minute later, Minna said into her mobile, 'OK, OK. Ta. Speak to you soon,' and restored the gadget to its rightful place, her backpack. As she did so, something fell out of it, a pocket diary, thought Paul. In fact it was her passport. Quickly, she put it back.

'Ah! Have passport, will travel. Yes? *Moi aussi, moi aussi.* Someone just phoned me. Someone doing a survey of where people were on the day the world changed for ever. So where were you at 2.20 p.m. on 9/11? Me? I was right here that day, watching. All I did was cry long tears. I wanted to talk to someone. There was no one here to talk to. I telephoned everybody. Nobody was in. I wanted to hug someone. I went out of the house. I bumped into the cleaning lady next door, Mrs Frank Tyson Senior. I came right back indoors. Say something.'

The girl said nothing.

'You know this Laden Bin guy? He's got a problem. That pained look on his face means only one thing. And it's chronic. Bush should have aimed a big airdrop of a strong something at those caves. Senna. That would have flushed him out. Ha ha. Too late now. We all know where he is. But Mush wouldn't hand him over. He has his own skin to think of. Hasn't he? What do you think?'

The girl remained mum. She just looked around.

'Don't you speak? No speak?'

Paul was convinced of what she was thinking: that she was in the presence of an utter nutter, the sort you have to climb mountains, or dive deep into oceans, to find. And she had found one just like that, handed to her on a platter.

'As it were.'

The visitor successfully suppressed a smile and returned her gaze to the pictures on the walls. Sunlight from the large, three-sectioned window with lead casings fell on the right side of her face, lending a golden lining to her profile. Divinity had graced the 1920s drawing room overlooking a real pond with real swans across the road. The Kapoor house had become heaven on earth.

'You no speak? Me, I speak. Sis speak. Mum and Dad too. We all speak. A house of speakers, this. Any one of us can get the Speaker's job in the Commons, and shut up the Tories and Toothpaste Tone, the Ugh-bugh Brown and... Oh, God, do we get the leaders we deserve? Do we? Anyway, where was I? Oh, yes. SupaDupalax Dustbin Laden guy.' A little bird said in Paul's ear don't push your luck... Don't push your luck...

'OK, OK. I'll leave you in peace. Or Sis would kill me. Flatten me like a fried egg. Squelch. Squelch. All that yellow stuff. I love. Yum. Yum. I go. She come. See you later, crocodile.'

Paul bumped into his sister at the door.

'Minna, you look OOTW.'

'She no speak. What sort of company you keep, Sis?'

'Has he been a pest, my brother? Has he been a nuisance, this chatterbox? I am sorry, Minna.'

The girls kissed the air around each other's faces.

'Have I been a nuisance? What have I done? Only asked a few friendly questions.'

'What did you ask Minna?'

'Only asked what drugs she takes or what she'd like – we got everything here, I said.'

'Out. Out. I'm so sorry, Minna. He is such a pest, this boy. Eighteen and still a pest. A total pest.'

'I'm going to get on to the union and lodge an official complaint – these girls ganging up on an innocent bloke,' Paul mumbled on his way out. On the stairs up to his room, he began humming a tune from the brand new Bollywood blockbuster, *Lagaan*. His friend Mansu, short for his real Muslim name Mansur, had sold him the video for a fiver (it cost three times as much in the shops) and Jog, short for the Sikh boy Joginder, had told him how Mansu got it – it fell off the back of a lorry and Mansu, as always, was right behind it. Paul was only halfway to his room when he heard a volley of girlish laughter from downstairs. He had to get back and see that OOTW creature again.

Two minutes later, there it was again, that volley. And again. Then the house of sunshine began to resound with the girls' laughter and Paul desperately wanted to know what the hell it was that put them in such hysterics. He threw himself on his bed and thought of ringing Mansu to tell him what a wanker he was to have sold him an illegal video. But suddenly, he didn't want to speak to him. Or anyone. He wanted only to be downstairs. All he needed was an excuse. And an excuse was what he did not have to go down to the drawing room. Paul was dying; life was ebbing out of him. Then the phone rang. He let it ring. After the fourth ring, Paul jumped and lifted the receiver and saw from his window that the girls had now moved to the garden.

'Oi, wanker. It's me...'

'Mansu?'

Oh, no.

'...I had a fab dream early this morning. I was with guess who? That Sue. Boy, for once she was not talking because... I wish I could press Save and dream the dream again tonight...'

'Mansu,' Paul chopped him. 'Do me a favour. Put the cursor on the white cross in the red box on top right and press to exit.'

Paul hung up. A second later the phone rang again.

Paul didn't want to answer – he just did not feel like having a useless conversation with Mansu about his latest lay – but he did. It was Golly, his sister's best friend.

'Oh, Golly! How are you? Of course you can... She is in the *jardin* with a very strange girl who cannot speak. I'll give her a shout. ANJLI. FOR YOU. GUESS WHO? Golly, she's coming. Been a good girl or bad? It's good to be bad from time to time. Keeps you on the right rail... Oh, Sunita? Not interested. Not interested in no one no more from this day on. Madam prefers blond boys, anyway. She does, Snooty Sunita...'

Then Paul heard his sister pick up the phone in the drawing room and say to him, 'Get off the phone, Bruv. Now.'

'Anything you say, Sis,' Paul said, and got off the phone.

He knew he had his chance. Anjli and Golly, phone fanatics – could the two of them talk? It had to be seen, or heard, to be believed – them nattering away, giggling hysterically with streams of tears in his sister's eyes.

Paul had his chance.

'I say,' he shouted from his window to the beauty in the garden, now become a nature goddess surrounded by trees planted when Queen Victoria was still on her throne and all was well with the world.

Minna looked up.

'Would you allow me to do you a favour?'

The goddess's forehead furrowed in I-beg-your-pardon?

'No, I'm serious.'

I-beg-your-pardon?

'I'll come down and explain. Wish there was a balcony here, like in *Romeo and Juliet*. I'd have placed my life on the palm of my hand and leapt off it.'

Paul lowered himself from the window ledge and let go. He made a good soft landing. Half smiling, he glided across the well-kept lawn – Dr Kapoor, his father, liked his garden to look like a proper Mughal garden for which purpose he had part-employed a first-rate gardener shared by number 12 on the left and number 16 on the right.

''Tis Golly on the phone. And when Golly comes on the phone, Anjli is gone.'

'Can you speak English?'

'Honest. The two of them. And the phone. I should say the three of them. Boy, were they made for each other? Weren't they?'

Minna's eyes said what on earth are you talking about?

'Don't you see? They yap.'

Minna's eyes said – so?

'So you'd be stranded here on your own. Marooned, I should say. Maybe for hours. They have an arrangement with BT – cut-price long-talk. More you talk, more you save.'

So?

'So allow me to do you a favour. Save you from dying of boredom. Let me entertain you.'

Minna shrugged her shoulders: she was not bored.

'But you will be, left to your own devices, which are diminishing by the minute, I can see, and she's gone for hours. I'm already feeling sorry for you. Gosh, when Golly rings, Anjli is gone. Ha ha – Gosh and Golly. Ha ha ha. Seen any films lately? Go see *Lagaan*. First ever Bollywood movie to be put up for an Oscar. No, don't. I'll lend you my video.'

Anjli came right back, tiptoeing through islands of flower beds (though she could have walked on grass), a smile tiptoeing on her face, which made her look pretty as a flower.

'Oh my God,' Paul said. 'I shouldn't be here – she'll make scrambled eggs of me. I should do what I should do and make myself scarce, regrettably.'

'It was Golly. Just back from my favourite city. Lucky girl,' Anjli said to her friend.

'Which city?' Minna asked.

'Paris. My number-one favourite.'

'Mine too. But I've never been there,' Minna said.

Now Anjli turned to her brother. 'What are you doing here bothering Minna?' She glared.

'I wasn't bothering her. Ask her. Was I bothering you, Miss Maintained Silence?'

'Scram, Bruv. Disappear, Doggy.'

Doggy scrammed, muttering loudly, 'Not the way to treat your brother. Is it? Is it?'

Back in his room, he put a Michael Jackson on his stereo, turning the volume on full blast. Then he threw himself on his bed again and stared at the all-white ceiling.

The reaction came almost immediately.

'TURN IT DOWN.'

Paul became deaf to his sister's command.

'Are you deaf or something?'

Paul didn't hear a thing.

Next moment, the girls turned up at his door.

'The neighbours are calling the Noise Pollution Squad. They'll come and confiscate your thingybob. Arrest you even.'

'You'd like that, wouldn't you?'

'Turn the damn thing off.' Anjli turned the damn thing off. 'Honestly. Just look at your room.'

'Look at my room. What's wrong with it?'

'Looks like a tip. You live like a pig...' Anjli said, looking stern. Then she started to put things right, just like their mother, muttering, '...like a pig.'

'I don't,' Paul replied. Then he addressed himself to his sister's friend. 'Does my room look like a tip? Do I live like a pig, Miss Silence?'

Miss Silence said yes with her eyes. It was a resounding yes.

'Oh, God. I don't believe it. This sisterhood. You cannot be serious. There ought to be an impartial referee here. What old Mac asked for and was fined how much? He was brill, though. You have to acknowledge and admit. You've seen all them old clips, surely? OK, OK, my room is a pig and I look like a tip, so what? What does it mean? It doesn't mean I am a bad guy, or bad looking even. Ask your silent friend. I say, what you think? Am I bad guy? Do I look like a bad guy?'

Unanimously, the girls turned their backs on Paul and ambled out of his room, Anjli yelling without looking back, 'Leave us alone, will you? And don't put that damn thing back on again. Listen to your Walkman.'

'Anything you say, Miss Boss, sir.'

'And don't come downstairs either. We want some privacy.'

Paul put his Walkman on. But he couldn't listen to it.

Music had lost its sweetness. Sweetness was downstairs where he had been ordered to stay away from. But that was where he had to be, in the presence of that pot of honey, that amphora of it. Paul needed a genuine excuse to be downstairs or he would look a fool. Paul did not have even a lame excuse to be downstairs. He felt a fool. And miserable. Feeling the way he did, he rose from his bed and turned the pages of *Bridget Jones's Diary* (borrowed from Anjli's room). The entry he chanced upon was quite juicy. But Paul found it soulless. He flung it away and looked out at where his heart already was – on the plush grassy lawn of his father's Mughal garden where Sweetness walked and breathed. Realising he must look stupid – hanging in the window just like that – he came and lay down on his bed again. The bed had suddenly become a bed of nails. He abandoned it and plonked himself in the deep and cosy armchair. The chair had lost all its cosiness. Paul addressed himself to the only person in the world who could help. He looked at the blue rectangle through his window.

'Dear Sir, I know how busy you are running this big universe of yours, its countless stars and the rest of it, including us – some happy, most not – all made by your good self. So throw us a ray of hope. I like the girl down there, and you know it, Sir.

Therefore oblige. Now is your chance.'

Back came the answer by divine e-mail, 'You want attention? Then break a leg. Fetch you loads of it.'

'Sir, isn't there a less drastic way, less painful too?'

'Think of one yourself. You got brains. I gave them to you. Make use of them. Now is your chance.'

Paul felt kicked in his back garden by the very being he trusted above all beings – God. He felt let down, betrayed, abandoned. He realised that he'd come to a dead end, the cul-de-sac of love lane.

'But what if I just walked down to them and demanded to be included in whatever they are doing?'

That wouldn't do. His turning up would signal straight away his intentions: he was lusting after his sister's luscious friend (which must not appear to be the case even if it was, though so far it was only half a case). For the real thing was he had fallen in love. This was where the real problem lay – Indians do not understand love. For them love doesn't exist; only lust does. Bloody Indians. And they think they are the world's most cultured. What a joke!

If Anjli told Dad, which no doubt she would, Paul had had it. Dad would break every bone in his body.

Paul lost all hope. Just then, there came a shout from the garden:

'PAUL.'

Paul leapt like a gazelle and popped his head out of the window, his heart in his throat.

'Come down a minute, will you?' Anjli said.

Paul raced downstairs.

'Move this table in the sun. We can't. It's too heavy,' Anjli said, pointing to the big wrought-iron table.

'May I make bold and ask why?'

'We want to eat lunch in the sun.'

'I'll move it to Wandsworth Common if you like, but on one condition.'

'What condition?'

'That you invite me to eat with you.'

'We don't want to ruin our lunch with a chatterbox around.'

'Promise not to open my mouth. Only to tuck into the food.'

'Minna, shall we let him join us?'

'Oh, please. I beg on my bended knee. Please say yes.' Paul went down on his knee. 'See, Miss Mum doesn't mind.'

'OK, then. Behave yourself. OK? Minna, let's get ourselves organised.'

The girls ran away to the kitchen and Paul got busy with the garden furniture. A minute later, Minna returned carrying plates and cutlery.

'My sister pretends to be hard on me, but in fact she adores me. Everybody does. Except.'

Minna was too busy to answer – she had a whole table to lay. She did not even look at Paul.

'I know I've promised not to open my mouth. But that's when we are eating. Not when we are not. So talk. Say something. Anything. Or is it still no speak? Oh, please, do. I was only joking about the drugs and all that. Never touch the stuff. Never. I only drink. Champagne for breakfast. White wine at lunch. Red wine for dinner and cognac after. With a cigar, of course. A long one like that fat guy who looked like babies.'

Minna had laid the table. She folded the flowery Indian cotton napkins into equilateral triangles and placed them on the plates. That done, she turned her back on Paul.

'But we are only three. And you've laid the table for four?'

Paul didn't get an answer, only a devastating, over-the-shoulder-look. Weren't those eyes saying Me Too?

'Please answer, why four plates?' Paul pleaded, shading his eyes with a hand from the midday mad Englishmen's sun. Still he didn't get a reply. 'Maybe you can't hear. Maybe you are deaf. Are you? I have read somewhere that certain people can hear others very well, but some they can't hear at all. Not at all.

As if by arrangement. Like By Appointment to Her Majesty. Exclusively Deaf By Appointment to Mr Paul K. Kapoor Esquire. Or By Disappointment, should I say?'

Minna went away, giving him another lightning Me Too look.

But she was right back, carrying a large salad bowl with two carved wooden spoons sticking out of it.

'If you are really what you appear to be, then I can say what I like. Can't I? Oops...'

As Minna tried to place the bowl on the table, one of the spoons flew out of it. And Paul, in a moment so swift that it surprised even himself, caught it like a flash catch at first slip – he just scooped it up inches from the grassy lawn.

'...HOWZAAT!' he shouted, causing a pair of pigeons to flutter away from behind a bush. Then he burst out laughing like a lunatic. 'Did you see that? Did you see that? Not impressed? Tendulkar would have offered me a place in the next one-day against England if he were captain. Boy, he's something. Poetry personified – in runs. So was my catch.'

Minna wiped that bit of the table where some salad dressing had fallen. She turned to go back to the house.

'What are we eating?'

'What are we eating, *ji*?' Paul asked again when Minna came back, flatteringly using *ji* in his address to her. But it was useless. She had brought a baguette, a bread knife and a bread pannier. She started cutting up the baguette in elegant pieces.

'Man's got the right to know what man is about to eat. No? Of course, how can you answer if you can't hear? In which case man can say all the things man has in his heart. Such as, how man feels. Maybe I should help...'

Paul followed Minna to the kitchen. It was drenched in the basmati rice aroma.

'Sis, what are we eating? Who else is coming to lunch?'

'Take this, will you? And be ultra-careful, it's hot.'

'Ah, chilli! Chilli, bili, mili, my favourite. I hope it's hot hot hot.'

'You said you'd keep your mouth shut. Minna, you take the rice. And be careful.'

The telephone rang.

'I'll get it,' Anjli said, wiping her hands with a kitchen towel and picking up the kitchen phone. 'Golly?'

'Oh, gosh. 'Tis Golly again.' Paul laughed. 'Gosh, 'tis Golly again!' Paul laughed his head off at Gosh and Golly, hoping that at least for once Minna would say something or laugh or smile or something. He followed her out to the garden, laughing. 'I know only idiots laugh at their own jokes, but I do think this is funny – Gosh and Golly. However, since you cannot hear, you cannot have any idea how funny. How can you? Poor thing. I feel more and more sorry for you. I feel the world for you. They say those who can't hear with their ears can smell double with their noses. In which case you should be able to smell what my heart feels – roses, roses all the way from Canons Park to Hyde Park.'

Parking their pots and pans, they sat down across the table, Minna with a hint of a smile on her face and looking intently at the grass beneath her feet, and Paul looking up at the blue sky.

'Fascinating. Grass is,' Paul said. 'I've always regarded grass to be the most fascinating thing in the whole of God's bountiful garden. Cows eat it, horses too. Most animals do. If there was no grass, there would be no grass-eating animals and there would be no animal-eating animals – carnivores – either. There would be no animals at all then. Mankind would feel lonely...'

Paul was interrupted by a shout from the kitchen:

'You start eating. I'll join you soon.'

'And we know how soon that would be, don't we?' Paul yelled back, and Minna's mobile bleeped. 'Oh, no. The hostess with the mostest on the blasted kitchen phone to Golly and her guest the best on her mobile to...' Paul didn't finish. He sat back, 'waiting for developments to develop.'

'Hi, Mum... No, we are just starting... Yes, her friend's ringing to say she's late... Chilli and salad... Yes, I can talk. I am all alone in the garden. It's lovely here...'

So my presence doesn't count, Paul said to himself.
So I don't exist.

As the girl talked, Paul suffered, his cheeks hotter than
the fuming chilli, getting hotter by the second. Then a thought
crossed his mind: perhaps she said she's all alone because she
didn't want her mum to know that she, an Indian girl, was with
a young man in a perfumed English garden because that would
alarm her Indian mother, make her dispatch an army of sons
and nephews with pitchforks and spades to bury the bugger
alive 'in deep delved earth, tasting of...' nothing.

This was a cool thought, encouraging too. It sort of created
a bond between them, an illicit bond – she had said it was
beautiful here, so she must feel good about being here.

Meaning thereby she felt good being with him even if she
would not talk to him like a good Indian girl.

'...Yes, Mum... No, Mum... I love you, Mum. 'Bye, Mum.'

'She sounds nice, your mum. Why did you tell her you
were alone here? Do you think I don't exist? Maybe I don't for
you. In which case...'

Anjli came, looking mighty pleased with herself.

'How's the chilli? But you haven't tried it yet. Why didn't
you start? I told you to. Golly's on her way. She was speaking
from her car. Be here any minute.'

'That was a short conversation, Sis. BT must be
disappointed. But you are improving.'

'Has my brother been a pest again?'

'Didn't utter a word. Ask your friend. I sat here as if I
didn't exist – a poor church mouse in this lush garden. True or
not true?'

Anjli dished out the rice and Minna the chilli. Minutes
later, Golly arrived, looking hotter than any chilli ever
cooked. She wore something surely made of the Elysée Palace's
newest curtains. And, obviously, she had raided the Cartier
headquarters in Paris before catching the Eurostar.

'I say, just look at you,' Minna said.

'Where did you buy this heavenly *lehnga*?' Anjli asked,

pointing at Golly's OOTW Indian outfit. 'It's wicked.'

'From BK-KK in Ealing. Is that a Max Mara top you've got on, Minna?'

'No, Sonia Rykiel.'

'What a fab Hermès scarf, yaar, Anjli.'

'Sit down.'

'Paul, when do you go back to university?' Golly said. 'What are you doing with yourself anyway these days?'

'Just got a new job.'

'Oh, really? As what?'

'As a water sprinkler.'

'Where?'

'The Saudi Arabian embassy.'

'Inside the embassy?'

'No, outside it. In the garden.'

'Is it a nice garden? Must be. All that oil money.'

'It's special, as it would be. It's all sand, you see? Sand beds, sand dunes, sand designs and suchlike. You see, they miss their desert so much they made a proper sand garden in the heart of London. Had high-quality sand imported from home by the shipload.'

'And your job is to sprinkle water there. Sounds rather cushy.'

'Not as easy as it sounds, though.'

'Explain. We are fascinated. Aren't we, Minna?'

'You see, the water has to be just right. Not too thick, nor too thin. Or my boss brays at me like a camel.'

'You poor thing. How do you manage, then?'

'Very tricky. There are filters and things. A pain. But guess what I do?'

'Tell me. What do you do?'

'I cheat. I get it from the tap.'

'What happens when it rains?'

'I have the day off.'

'PAUL,' Anjli said.

'All right, Sis. I only answered Golly's question.'

'It's OK, Anjli. I find Paul's job fascinating. Not you? What do you do with your spare time, Paul?'

'I'm writing a novel.'

'Oh, really? What's it called?'

'*Flying Ducks Also Get Shot.*'

'What a title! What a title! Brill, Paul. Someone bright must have suggested it to you. A teacher or someone?'

'Gosh, Golly. You insulting me? Not very ladylike that.'

'Sorry, didn't mean to. But how?'

'Here I am trying to unfold my literary talents and here you are rubbishing me...'

'Sorry, Paul. Didn't mean to. But how much of it have you written, your bestseller, I mean?'

'So far only the title. Ha ha.'

'Not funny, that, Bruv.'

'Listen to this poem I wrote this morning. Listen:

"I was reading Geoffrey Chaucer
When from the corner of my eye I saw a flying saucer
Or thought I had seen one
But in fact there was none.
So I went on reading Chaucer
Drinking my tea out of a saucer."'

'Boooo. Not funny at all. Now eat in silence, Bruv. Total silence. Is that clear?'

From then on the world became a glittering emporium of clothes and fashion and films and CDs and Paul even more non-existent than before. He ate in silence, avoiding looking at anyone, especially Minna. Only at the grass under her feet.

After the chilli came watermelon, red and juicy like her lips.

Then came coffee, black and brown like her eyes. Paul drank a cup and rose – he had outstayed his welcome.

'Thank you for having me, Sis.'

'So glad you could join us at such short notice. I'm sure

I speak for my friends too.'

'Thank you all so much, the Three Graces of Canons Park.'

'Might as well make yourself useful, Bruv, and take the dishes in.'

'Of course. Silly me,' Paul said, and made a pile of everything like a seasoned waiter.

'Don't overload yourself.'

'No problem.' A mountain of things in his hands, he moved briskly towards the house. On a wet bit of the paved area outside the kitchen door he slipped and fell. Everything fell with him with a crash, glass and china breaking around him.

'Oh my God,' cried Anjli, running towards the scene of the accident. Her friends ran after her. 'Are you all right?'

'Yes, I'm fine.'

But Paul was not all right and his sister knew it. He couldn't move – his left leg.

'Silly boy. Told you not to carry everything at once. Sit up,' Anjli said, her forehead creased in pain at the sight of her brother lying on the floor like that. She sat down by him.

'Sit up. Can you?'

Paul simply couldn't move. Anjli cradled his head in her lap and the other girls sat down next to her, worried – it was clear to them that Paul had broken something.

'Your back all right, Paul?' Golly asked. 'Move it a bit.'

'My back is all right. It's my leg.'

Golly felt his left leg and shook her head sadly – she knew it was broken below the knee. 'Anjli, we better call an ambulance.'

'Don't be silly. I'm all right. Oooh!' Paul couldn't move.

'Call the ambulance. He's broken his leg,' Minna spoke at last, her voice tremulous, and Paul thought, did a man have to break his leg to be noticed? He thought of God and laughed as he heard her say with those eyes Me Too, and bite her red, red lip.

'How can you laugh, silly boy? You've broken your leg. Is it very painful?' Anjli said, her beautiful face distorted – her brother's pain was hurting her more than it seemed to be hurting him. 'I told you not to carry everything all at once. You never listen, do you, Bruv?'

'Anjli, he is in pain. Telephone for an ambulance,' Minna said.

'When in pain, go to Spain and ask for it to rain.' Paul laughed.

'Shut up,' Anjli said through gritted teeth. She was crying, tears rolled down her cheeks. She got a cushion from a chair and placed it under Paul's head. Then she went away with Golly to phone for an ambulance.

'Can you hear me now? Will you talk to me now?'

'Yes, I will. A lot. Sorry I was so beastly.'

'No, you weren't. You were wonderful. Oooh.'

'Does it hurt a lot?'

'No, it doesn't. You know what?'

'What?'

'From the moment I saw you, I wanted to wash your feet with milk.'

'Wash my feet with milk? Funny boy, why?'

'That's what they do to their goddesses in India.'

'But why?'

'Because they worship them. Ooooh.'

'Don't move and don't talk.'

Anjli and Golly came back, tears streaming down Anjli's face.

'Gosh, Golly. Your golden *lehnga*. Must have cost you an arm or a leg. A leg!' Paul said and laughed again.

'Shut up,' Anjli said, but couldn't help smiling herself even though she was crying. 'Don't talk. They'll be here soon.'

'Do you think they'll amputate my leg? They are such fools, these NHS guys. You know they've been operating on the wrong patients, taking out their kidneys and suchlike.'

'Stop it, Bruv. Don't talk. They'll be here any minute.'

The ambulance arrived within minutes.

'They're quick. And they've come to the right address,' Paul said as two men came into the garden from the side of the house.

'Which leg?' was all one of them said. He put a red blanket over Paul's legs and, with his colleague's assistance, transferred him to a stretcher. All the three girls went with him in the ambulance to the Edgware General in Burnt Oak near by.

'The NHS has become punctual at least.'

'Don't talk. It's not funny,' Minna said. 'Does it hurt?'

'Not at all.'

'Don't talk.'

'Why not? It makes me feel better to talk. Why haven't they got the siren on? Maybe you should take them right back. I'll fall again and break the other leg too and then they would have an emergency on their hands and turn on the siren to clear the roads for yours truly.'

'Shut up, Paul.'

In the A&E unit of the hospital, Paul was left alone for a minute. Then, while Anjli and Golly talked to the staff in another room, Minna joined him and he smiled.

'You know what I've been thinking of besides washing your feet with milk?'

'What?'

'That if I could run away from here now, would you come with me?'

'But you can't run, Paul.'

'But if I could, would you?'

'Where would we go?'

'Waterloo station.'

'Why?'

'To catch a Eurostar train and go to your favourite city you've never been to. I have my passport on me. And my cards...'

'Don't talk. You've had a shock.'

'...I'll phone Mansu to meet us at Waterloo with all the cash he has. The fool is always loaded.'

'Paul, don't talk. You are in severe shock.'

'Would you come with me if I could run?'

'But you can't.'

'If I could, would you?'

'Yes.'

Paul kicked the NHS blanket off his legs and leapt to his feet. He took Minna's hand in his and ran to Burnt Oak station five minutes away. So swift they were, no one saw them go.

'You are a fraud,' Minna cried. 'A total fraud,' she repeated. But she ran with him.

GYPSY

MIKEY
CUDDIHY

aria flees to Glasgow to visit her beloved sister, Lucia. Again a top-floor tenement, but the stairs are wide and easygoing; daylight filters down, bringing you up brighter as you ascend to a door scribbled and patterned with crayon, and a bell that buzzes like a muffled bee.

Her sister's flat, which she lives in with her husband, two children and a budgie, is tiny and spartan; shiny wooden floors, and almost no possessions. All social and work activities are carried out in the little kitchen, which has an improvised look about it – from the orange crate doubling as a seat to the piece of fabric pinned to the window as a makeshift curtain.

A chopping board is an unnecessary luxury; Lucia has devised a nifty way of cutting an onion in her hand; a tomato sauce is made in the bottom part of what was once a double boiler, stirred with a wooden spoon so old and worn it looks like a stick. It's as if she hasn't lived here for thirty years, as if this is only a temporary arrangement before moving on to something more permanent.

Paintwork is peeling and sad, but Lucia cleans and wipes the table fastidiously. Only food you'll eat now is there: half a loaf, a little hunk of cheese, one orange (all are too polite to take it). Two-foot piles of *Heat* and *Hello!* magazine line the edges of the kitchen floor, and are read vicariously. Lucia's husband, Alex, can keep coffee beans and a grinder, and grows geraniums, trained elaborately and high-climbing, in the bedroom bay window; they look startling and excessive. And there is a piano, for Manuella, her daughter, who plays it with difficulty as the piano's so old they joke it's almost a harpsichord. Luxuries shine like treasures, icons from another world: a washer-dryer gleams. An i-Mac on the kitchen table seems jewel-like, almost vulgar. Piles of novels (no need for shelves) rise from the floor in sculptural columns; boxed and ancient board games are stored under the budgie's cage by the window. Lovely drawings by Manuella and Jimmy – yellowed and dusty, with the crayon still bright – are pinned precariously to the wall, and remain there each time she visits.

Christmas-time, things are different – the i-Mac is cleared from the table; a platter is magically produced from a wooden trunk, which is suddenly revealed as furniture when the piles of magazines are removed from its surface, and the table is laid, with red tartan paper plates, napkins to match, and maybe, yes, plastic wine goblets for the cava. There are crackers too. The piano stool is brought in from the bedroom, a chair borrowed from the flat next door. They have a lovely feast; there is even gravy, and sweet potatoes done just like their mother used to make, with melted marshmallows on top. The budgie helps himself to turkey and cranberry sauce from their plates, which have gone limp from the gravy; nobody seems to mind.

The bathroom is like a gypsy encampment: a museum-grade bath along a peeling panelled wall; a Victorian clothes rack above, the wooden struts warped to semicircles, holds hangers of drying clothes. Looped on the other end are carrier bags, filled with bathly possessions. The worn enamelled bath is cleaned after use with great care, using a brand of bathroom cleaner she'd thought was extinct.

Again, gleaming and out of place, on a little wooden plank above the sink is a collection of luxurious beauty items, looking conspicuous and stolen. The ledge of the wooden panelling lining the wall to waist height is almost possessively coated with years of dust and flakes of paint ('don't you dare clean me'). And yet, all that is necessary is clean. Routine is important: the loo chain must be pulled a certain way to flush, and don't flush at night. And don't let the water drain out of the bath without inserting first a silver tea-strainer to catch hair.

But her sister is generous; with conversation, phone calls and numerous acts of kindness. To her son, Jack, she'd sent a delightfully received twenty-pound note for his tenth birthday, and there are other things Maria finds out about only by accident, like the time she phoned, and Alex said Lucia was out blind-dancing, you know, he said, 'She goes dancing with people who are blind, on a Wednesday night.'

And this woman, her sister, who has so little (not even an egg whisk), will produce, on request, a postcard, written twenty years ago by a witty and long-dead friend, or a letter from a much-loved uncle, with a dollar bill still attached.

Her life in London, Maria realises, seems luxurious, with her clock radio, electric kettle and living room. Her own random collection of pots and pans, interesting cups from junk shops, seems frivolous and extreme.

The tragedy that disrupted their lives when they were children has affected them differently. Maria is the reckless, extravagant one; Lucia sober and cautious. Uprooted and sent off to live in a foreign country with only the clothes they stood up in, it's as if at any moment her sister is expecting another catastrophe, to be left again with nothing; it's as if at any moment she might have to pack up and leave. And she'd be ready, carrier bag in hand, with everything she needed for the journey.

BONSAI
MAN

MIKEY
CUDDIHY

She knew the minute she saw him on the station platform that she'd made a mistake. He was smaller than she remembered, and even though she'd worn her flat-heeled boots, she towered over him. She tries to shrink herself as they kiss awkwardly, each aiming for the wrong part. Into a dirty, litter-strewn car they get, with her son and their luggage, and drive to his place (just a visit before she sees her family).

An Edinburgh tenement – they walk up and up a dingy stone staircase, greasy banister coiling beside it, metal spikes poking out at intervals, unkindly.

The flat: woodchip half-painted baby blue, leading to a hot living room; swirly carpet, coal-effect fire. Her eyes search for something ordered and beautiful in the bachelor darkness. Three fish tanks, unlit and teeming with silent fish; she can't see anything remotely friendly or familiar, no books to recognise and comment on (covered plastic containers under the fish tank held, she was sure, live bait or worse).

On the opposite side of the room there is a darkening bay window with a child's battlefield laid out in front of it on a large table; fake trees, moss and ruins. But she's wrong, they're real – seventy nurtured bonsais, and real moss, real water, with channels, a model railway, and Lilliputian soldiers in all manner of poses. Her son, Jack, is enthralled: 'Is this tank amphibious?' he asks hopefully of an army-green vehicle pointing its gunsights at a bridge.

He says the battlefield is for his nephew to play with, that the trees and irrigation are his hobby, but Jack's fiddling with the tank and the enthusiastic gun noises emanating from Jack's puttering mouth are making him edgy; she can tell these aren't real toys.

She tries again to see something pretty, something to latch on to. 'This sofa has lovely wooden arms,' she says, tracing one, which coils to a decorative spiral. The tea, in unflattering, squat pottery mugs, looks like washing-up water; she can only taste its milky sweetness.

A middle kitchen, cooker caked in black (clingfilmed broccoli in the corner stands out clean); dishes dirty, piled in the sink.

A back room, painted dusty pink, for the pristine computer; a Renoir print (busty women in high-necked dresses), the red bleached away long ago. Window looking over a deep back yard decorated with iron clothes masts; a scarily pretty dwarf tree in a pot on the dirty window sill. An old red mattress, a coverless pillow; they lie there together embracing. 'He's the collector, I'm awkward and anxious,' she remarks to herself. Her son comes in and says, 'Let's go home now.' She's glad to leave, to get some fresh air.

Days later, still in Edinburgh, she goes back; the flat looks cleaner – more painting's been done, though the washing up is still there, and the broccoli is yellow now. He gives her a watch, hastily wrapped in Christmas paper; it's gold coloured and weighs heavily on her wrist; she feigns delight, surprised.

They make love under a 'downie', he calls it, ugly-patterned in brown. The sex is good, but he's all-over small, a miniature of someone else, a man she can't forget.

SISTINE CHAPEL

MIKEY CUDDIHY

illie went to Rome when she was seventeen, with her friend Keith. They'd stayed up all the night before at her sister's flat in Edinburgh and watched the first moon landing, then caught the bus in the morning. She can remember almost nothing about the sights they visited when they got there, but she can recall every dress, every outfit she brought with her.

One, a second-hand dress from the 1940s (with the utility label sewn inside it), was a sort of cherry-red lightweight linen, patterned with white squares, spots of red inside them, cut nicely around the bodice, with short sleeves, just to the knee. She'd tied a white velvet ribbon around the waist, as it was a bit too big. Millie felt like Sophia Loren, or Audrey Hepburn in *Roman Holiday*, or maybe just an extra from *Bicycle Thieves*; anyway, it made her feel romantic. She wore it for sightseeing their first day there – she can't remember much about what they saw, the Trevi Fountain maybe, and the Colosseum – she remembers a lot of stray cats.

Millie wishes she'd worn the red dress to the Sistine Chapel – she remembers nothing about the painted ceiling, but she can recall exactly the two dresses she wore on her attempts to get in. The first, sky-blue voile, with puffy short sleeves and a bodice, fitting to the waist, gathered at the skirt, and sprigged all over with tiny white flowers – it had a printed paisley border around the hem which finished midway down her thighs. The dress was declared too short by the museum guards (they almost slapped her legs in disgust – the cheek of her).

Millie returned next day, wearing the wrap-over sundress

she'd made from a complicated *Vogue* pattern ('*plus difficile*'), using the green-and-yellow batik material her friend Janina's mother had given her. It was a sophisticated length, stopping on the knee; again the museum guards refused her entry – her shoulders (slap) were bare, and this was disrespectful. She went out to one of the stalls positioned around the steps, and bought a black lace mantilla to cover her modesty. It made her feel quite dramatic.

Given the choice between the chapel ceiling and her dresses, she knows which she'd rather see again; the dresses win every time. To feel the sky-blue voile, shake the dress out by the shoulders and be dazzled by its blueness would be wonderful.

And the sundress, sewn so carefully; she'd touch and examine it, savouring every seam; she wants to see the mango yellow, examine its hue; to check the skilfully hidden hooks and complicated under-bra – the elastic cleverly slipped through a strip of fabric, gathering it in such a satisfying way would bring her closer to her previous self than any photo or memorabilia.

Millie remembers floating through the streets in Paris a few years later, fresh from three weeks in the South, looking 'tall and tanned and young and lovely', she sings in her head. She's wearing a cheap red Indian sundress (ruched bodice with a frill at the hem); she'd bought it in a boutique in Nice with nearly the last of her holiday money, and people had remarked: '*Elle est belle.*' She felt divine almost; surely this was a kind of love? And if beauty could be projected, surely it could be inverted, making her beautiful inside? She glowed, basking in the warmth of people's gaze, and the sunshine; yes, she felt that she was truly loved.

HEART OF THE FOREST

BRIAN CATLING

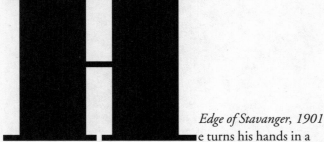

Edge of Stavanger, 1901

He turns his hands in a lapping rhythm, the wrinkles and veins folding and flexing. He looks down at his hands as he decides to think about the horror that overshadows his little death and the vastness of his life after it. He is a small man sitting on a simple chair, cut from the cylinder of a tree, hollowed by a patient axe. He twists his hands at the end of his sight, quietly wringing an answer from their constant prayer-like motion. In the upright back of the chair is a hole carved rigid into a heart-shaped gap. It fits his heart like a picture frame, a wooden X-ray lovingly open. But like all simple things a great secret of purpose broods in its design or in the ritual of its making or in the clenching together of those sacred deeds.

Teeth. Tiny grey-white nubs, albino nails, ring the seat beneath his thighs. A ring of teeth embedded into the rim of the chair. Milk teeth slipped away from children and planted in the still-fresh wood, oozing with carpentry. He should know, they were his once. His parents, like others of that most haunted vale of Norway, bejewelled their chairs like this to charm away pain, warding off the toothache of future years. Toothache was the least of his worries, so perhaps the chair had worked and held him away from that gnawing pain.

But not a single tooth had been pulled from the jaws of the vicious nightmares that tore at him night and day with constant durable ferocity.

He and the chair are outside a small wooden house. The house sits at the edge of a forest. An optimistic road to the nearby town runs past his door. He is surrounded by wood.

Piles of it neatly cut and stacked, dwarfing him, his thoughts and the intricate machine of his turning hands.

He is known as a fool. A respected fool who keeps his distance and makes visions of an improbable world. A woodcutter who used to be an artist; a craftsman painter who slipped unexpectedly outside the picturing of what there is, into what there could never be. He has grown from and is haloed by one of the most magnificent landscapes in the world. Tranquillity and breadth flow from its mountains to its seas. A pleasurable subject for any artist, engaging in the task of capture. God's own perpetuum of balance. The majestic and the stark pivoted by operatic weather and glorious isolation. A land without the need of embellishment, which in itself is an act of blasphemy, brimming with pride. But he is not proud; in fact he says nothing about his tiny fragile paintings which he exchanges for tobacco and food. Paintings made on emaciated wrapping paper, overused, glued together for scale, paintings that gleam with the light of translucent innocence.

Behind him the forest grows away from the paths and languages of men. Twisted tracks often lost, coiling as they grow deeper, set apart from greedy husbandry. A tunnel best described as wild, better described as indifferent to all else. Consumed in a passion of growth. Here a darkness is not named as light, or its absence, rather it comes channelled inside the stems and trunks; in the sullen focused weight of water, held, so that each leaf changes by the tides or darkness in its daily blood. The sky above held at bay, its nutrients ferried down to the dusk-glimmer of the forest floor. And this is just the edge.

When young he showed great promise in his school, where words and the world were scribed in sandboxes, for chalk and slate were exotic in those lands, and paper reserved for the gentry and the priesthood. During lessons he would cast terrible waves of answers long before the slow dribble of questions, so that his box was always in motion, landscapes and faces forming and dissolving. His diggings oft delayed or

foreshadowed the needed response. But this little strangeness
was forgiven, because he did not stare out of the narrow
windows into the wideness of his father's fields, but deep into
the shallow garden of spoken sand.

He loved that place deep in the hub of the wood. Where an
invisible wind embraced the constant twilight and turned, like
the heart of a genie, swallowing sensible space, like his hands
turn when thinking. He loved it when he and the trees shared
their breath. The woods were always safe, a haven until he went
to Germany.

His talent showed itself through his infancy. The ability to
draw anything that came before him. He would concentrate the
hours into his precious given paper. Filtering all other actions
and necessities to distil the line. Sombre portraits of townsfolk,
his parents and the few patient friends who squirmed while he
locked his body into forgetful slavery to his eye and hand. So it
was noticed and marvelled at, and agreed that he must now
leave the small town to gain a proper education as a painter.
So in early adolescence he was sent abroad with the help of the
community who then treasured his uniqueness.

In his small community he had never really noticed the
time slips. Those little trickles that divided the continual.
Those moments where *déjà vu* and its opposite bustled past
each other in the tight door frame of now. But in the great
European city it began to become, to disclose itself. At first he
believed it to be just an awkward reflection of his foreignness,
a kind of temporal misunderstanding, very like his stumbling
translations of language and custom. But as he grew into
Germany and his fear fell away with his rural mud he began to
notice the slips getting brighter.

One day while walking through the city he noticed a
baker's shop whose window was piled high with many different
types of bread. He stopped and made a brief drawing of its
tumbling composition. He conceived of a painting, where
biblical allegory and common display would come together in
a dramatic alliance. He hastily returned to his simple room to

gather a larger drawing book and a grabbed handful of pens, ink and pencils. He ran back to the shop that so inspired him. It was a building site. Confused but knowing, he stalked the streets and alleyways around, hoping to find that he had simply made a wrong turn. But no, it was as he knew it to be. He questioned the builders, whose thick dialects made nothing of the straw and clay of his enquiry. He talked to neighbours. There had never been a baker's here, never in memory. Not yet.

He worried about his isolation and about the thrill of these disquieting moments.

Were they symptoms of his shyness and constant imagination? Were they manifestations of a greater purpose or the onset of malady? He needed to think deeper. He would leave the city and find a forest, a deep one where he could really reflect. He took a train after talking to his fellow students. They directed him east, where the wooded countryside was at its thickest. A great excitement grew inside him as he began his adventure, rattling out of the man-made into the wildness and security of his understanding. He got off the train and into the trees. Choosing the station by its rightness, by the joy of its remoteness: just a halt and an inn. He took a room and unpacked. Reloaded his rucksack and walked into the forest.

The trees came to meet him halfway, wrapping their age and stillness around him with an intoxicating breath of earth and air. The sound of their leaves and the semaphore of their bodies unbound his anxieties in minutes. He became open, translucent and at home.

That night he slept with the trees in his room, whistling away any notion of a dream. The next day was even better. Bright spring sunlight sharpened by water poured through the dignified core of the forest. He stopped to draw again, finding that invisible place to think that can only be reached while the hands and eyes are passionately engaged in something else. Where words cease and our transaction with the world becomes permeable. Never wake a working sleepwalker or someone submerged in active reverie, the shock can splinter their contract with reality.

The silence changed and slapped him hard back into himself. The compound wave of sound that makes a peaceful unhearing was gone and in its place was a quietness of the void. Chilling and without reason. The birds were gone, the wind fell away. He had been sitting on a fallen trunk which now lost all its temperature. He stood up and looked around him, feeling his hackles rise. He walked mechanically forward into the forest, which had become unknown and unlike anything he had ever experienced. The only other movement was a distant blur of mist suffocating the trees. A fat heavy smoke that shrank all motion in its approach. He walked on.

There are no words ever. No words to describe what he saw. Only the words in his head which rotated the images, flocking to make sense, and deny that such a reality could exist.

He collected his clothes from the inn and found his way to the train like a sleepwalker.

Nothing of the journey imprinted. He fell into a fever and a pit of sleep, broken only by his landlady, who insisted on feeding him. It took her fifteen minutes at each sitting to wake him, shaking him back into the rubbery spilt world, where his life had gone aground. His studies ceased and he was gently steered back to Norway.

The man who came home was very different to the boy who had left. Most of his speech had fallen away; he was unfocused, fearful and distracted. He would be seen staring at empty spaces, examining inconsequential corners of the town, smiling at walls, shivering near the forest and unable to paint or draw. Eventually he was gently guided into hospital, where he would live for three years. Very little is known about that passage in his life. A few notes and some Chinese whispers of stories. But it was clear that he was seeing things that others did not. Especially on his weekly chaperoned visits to town. There he would wander into saturations of incident and image that should have been fenced by temporal boundary. The reason why he was expelled from High Protestant care was understood, but his reasons for promoting it were mysterious until 2002. He had been watching the mumblers and self-talkers. Those that roamed the corridors and the day rooms locked in the cycles of their own conversations, lips always moving, heads nodding answers. One day he had corralled them and given them gifts to aid their communication. It must have been planned; he had been collecting bootlaces and scraps of string for months. Each had been given a limp cord with a knot tied in one end and another tied farther down. The eight gathered with patience and sat together wearing their string. One end plugged into an ear, the other hanging loose. The second knot was close to their mouth. All were talking, all listening. The artist was delighted, grinning in triumph. The authorities were not.

Set loose, he started to make experiments in saturated light. Landscapes that shone in the last rays of the sun. They became brighter as his hope of being taken seriously dimmed.

He fell into poverty and freedom. He began his life as a woodcutter to stay close to the forest and turn a few coins of survival. He would stare for hours into the movement, longing for its heart, but never daring to enter its dark enclosure. The wood had to be brought to him. They all said he was mad. The generous said his little intense paintings were visions of an over-sensitive mind. In fact they were blindfolds, bandages to the fear of his rotting soul. What he had seen those years before told him about hell, without doubt. He told very few about it. Nobody understood or believed him. Such a thing was impossible. His guilt and witness clad his heart in lead and as the years passed it got thicker. Destined to carry him to the bottom of the pit, in a gulp of bleak overwhelming gravity. The paintings were set against this; kites of light, rising above, stabilising and cleansing his fall. They were never fantasy visions, but prayers to all that he loved through his eyes: the sensuous forests, the radiant waves of cloud and sky, the mirrored waters, the eternal stone of the mountains, the wind. In these he might wash and purify the weight of the stain that suffocated his paradise, here and beyond.

It was known that he glimpsed our time. A few fragments of action or picture showed through, but how much he saw or what he understood of it is a mystery. Details out of context or the pressure of the time that conceived them curl into enigma, dangerously swaying between the profound and the comic: our great achievements dislocated into foible or cant. He must have also seen past our moment and scooped something from there back into his vision. Colours and moods beyond our recognition. Invisible incident and object. Perched woefully outside of reference.

It is not known whether he ever wandered into or passed by the museum that holds his few remaining works, gathered together. If he had peered through its windows to see his furniture paintings gleaming back. Landscapes written on doors and panels. Or the tiny frail pictures, priceless in light, that modestly ignore the solemnity of the building; skies and forests, beaches and fjords impossibly alive in a fusion of spectre and paint.

Even after dark, like hope, they hold on to the last particles of glowing air. Energy smouldering benediction along time lines and the grey wiring of normality and guilt.

On his way home he walks past one of the grander wooden houses by the shore. He stops, takes off his long-serving hat and runs his questioning hands over his head. It has never been necessary to ask why he sees more. Most things he sees are wonderful. Perhaps the quantity of those might balance against the pitch of the other. Perhaps those paintings hiding in the museum could be made by him, if there was enough time left. The sea breeze sings above his head, its voice proclaimed across a white metal disc, high up the building's wall, gazing at the sky. He looks at this unknown thing as the sun catches its rim and knows that there are angels.

TOWARDS THE HEAVENLY VOID

PAUL ROONEY

There seemed to be an amorphous glowing form hovering in the centre of the white room, like a transparent jellyfish in a brightly lit aquarium. Immediately before the levitating shape appeared, I had been staring blankly in the dressing-room mirror. I had noticed that one light bulb in the far right corner of the mirror's edge was brighter than all the others. Probably a hundred-watter, I'd thought; the warmth was coming off the bulbs on to my cheeks. And then it came. The floating form gradually appeared in the mirror, as if conjured up by my distracted gaze. At first I thought it was a smear or some misting on the surface of the mirror itself, but the form eventually defined itself into a human face. And though the face looked as if it was in the centre of the room, when I turned round it was nowhere to be seen.

If it's not one thing it's another, I thought. I knew I was having another turn, another visit from the 'other place'. I was calm, but I couldn't stop myself from being a bit worried as well. It's only natural, isn't it? I'm no expert at all this, but it can take a lot out of you, because of the strain involved, the strain of staying in touch with the presence, of keeping it there. Like coaxing a shy animal to come closer, patiently earning its trust. There had probably been hundreds of faces that had looked into the depths of that glass over the years. Maybe this was one of those faces, I thought, left over like an after-image which had floated into visibility again, and only certain people can see them, people with special gifts. I looked at the flattened, thickset face. It was much clearer now. I was certain, it was... was it? I was sure it was him. The fat face looked as if it had absorbed more than a few punches in its time, it was drained of colour and a peaked military cap of some sort was perched above it.

'Who... who are you?' I said. It simply raised its eyebrows as if to admonish me for even attempting a conversation. Was its mouth moving? Yes. It began to speak.

So this was a different kind of turn. Usually I had to channel the voices through my own vocal cords. And I don't often remember the turns, but this one is still as clear as day. I pressed the record button on an audio cassette player I had with me, normally used for recording ideas for melodies and that. As I pressed RECORD, the voice was saying:

'Please pay heed, Dermot, good man, to what I am about to say. Many years ago, in the dark days of the early 1950s, I was sitting staring out of the window of a dingy and cheerless hotel room in the city of Paris, which is like Oldham with onions, looking as gormless as you are now, gazing up over the city lights towards a darkened river bank, and then down to the alleyway at the side of the building. I'd noticed what looked like flattened, sparkling white flowers splattered all over the cobbles, flowers that glinted in the orange street light like constellations of loosely painted stars. It was pigeon shit.'

With this, the podgy face announced itself, and then continued in its serrated Mancunian accent: 'I'd been in Paris for almost a year. As I'd wandered the streets on one of my first nights in the city, I'd bumped into an American tourist who'd taken me for a meal after I had admitted to him that I was desperately hungry. This encounter became a crucial turning point for me. I recall the bounteous meal, the tender meat, the rich sauces, the exquisite wine, and as the man imbibed some of the ruby-coloured liquid, he talked about seeing Lenin's tomb in Red Square in the city of Moscow, which is like Rochdale with fur. He said that every ten years or so a look-alike fresh corpse replaces the previous body on public display in the mausoleum, because the Kremlin mortician's attempts to preserve "Lenin number one" had failed years ago. There are

certain men in the Soviet Union who are chosen to be in on
the secret, the man told me, and these party members, loyal
Bolsheviks every one, grow beards and pluck out their hair as
they approach the age Lenin was when he died, each hoping
that he will be the chosen one. The chosen man is then snuffed
out and stuffed, achieving the highest reward for his loyalty:
he will literally embody the cause. As I finished my coffee I'd
thought of the foggy breath of old women with ragged gloves
on a Russian winter morning, of how their breath slowly
dissolves as it rises up towards the snow-covered minarets
emerging out of the blankness of the sky, and how the women,
stooped to face the ground, spit their black-streaked phlegm
on to the freezing cobbles in front of them.

'The man's story reignited the embers of an idea I had in
my head – my own plan to find somebody willing to embody
an ideal. As I sat in my hotel room that evening, one year on
from that restaurant meal, nervously staring over the rooftops,
I was about to set the plan in motion. A few months before,
via a telegraph from Paris, I had placed an advertisement in
the *Manchester Evening News* and after some correspondence,
I'd eventually asked a man to meet me at my hotel. The ad
had read:

> 'Young man! As you reach the top of the marble stairway
> of decision, now is the hour for you to walk through the
> enchanted bronze doorway of aspiration and enter into the
> gold-pillared and crystal-chandelier-bedecked hallway of
> ACHIEVEMENT! If you are intrigued, send a photograph
> and return address to Room 17, Hotel des Astres, Paris.

'There was a knock on the door and I opened it to reveal
a thickset, shabbily dressed man. As he entered the room the
man seemed unimpressed by my accommodation. Not that
the room was incommodious, but the mice were throwing
themselves on the traps and you had to spray the place with
DDT before the flies would come in. Anyway, I was very

pleased by the man's striking resemblance to myself, which
was even more apparent than in the photograph he had sent.
He had a face with all the charm of a bag full of ratchet
spanners, and he was obviously built when the meat was cheap.
His eyes were pits of desperation, with just the right sort of
frustration in them, the kind that you see when a hedgehog
realises it's been mating with a yard brush. Sorry, I will try to
keep to the point, indeed I will...'

The voice paused, then said: 'I asked the man, who was a
native of Macclesfield, which is like Bogotá with chimneys, to
read out some literary scribblings I'd sent to him. We chatted
away and I tried to interest him in the little idea I'd had.'
The voice stopped. I looked over at a small, domesticated
jungle in the corner of the dressing room, some potted palms in
tarnished brass pots. One of the fronds seemed to have moved.
Or was it me, seeing things? I looked at my tape machine on
the black marble-topped dressing table. The table reflected the
tape recorder in the limitless depths of its surface. You could see
the ghostly reflections of my hands as they struggled to reattach
the microphone, which refused to stay in its socket. The marble
also reflected some of the lights on the dressing-room ceiling,
smudging them in the greasy smears on its surface. There was a
folded and laminated notice at the far end of the dressing table.
It said, NO SMOKING PLEASE.

The last time I had seen this room was with my previous
band, Rooney. We played here in 1999. After the gig I was
sitting in a similar chair, staring at the same mirror. Then
something made me wander back onstage. There weren't many
folk around, no more than four people were still in the venue,
including me. The full attendance that night was less than
fifteen; and we were really bobbins that night. I can't remember
what happened after I got back onstage, but the barman told
me afterwards that I had stared straight ahead, slightly above
where the audience's heads would have been, and chanted a
list of nonsense words and sounds for at least three minutes.
I apparently followed this up with the constantly repeated

chant of 'Nellie, with an IE', 'Nellie, with an IE'. In the glare of the house lights, and with the ringing sound of bar tills being emptied in the background, I then sank to my knees and sang the lyrics to 'You're The One That I Want', from the musical *Grease*, in a distorted and tuneless voice. 'I got chills, they're multiplyin', and I'm losin' control, 'cause the power you're supplyin'... it's electrifyin'.'

A few weeks later Sergio, the Rooney drummer, told me what I had mumbled in the dressing room afterwards. He recalled that I had mentioned the name Hylda Baker – the Northern comedian, or comedienne, as they were called in the old days. I had rambled something about her 'coming through' after the performance. Hylda had asked me to take her on to the stage. She seemed happy to be back in front of footlights again, I had said.

Any road, apart from these occasional improvisations I was usually a reliable performer. It was just that my 'turns', as the band called them, became more common, often happening during the actual gigs themselves. I never remembered any of the gigs that involved these incidents, in my memory there are just black holes, framed by the unloading of our equipment from the van at the start of the night and the reloading of it at the end. Now here I was back in St Helens Art Centre as a solo performer, listening to the low rasping voice of a gurning spectre before the gig had even started. The face in the mirror was now staring at some fixed point straight ahead. Occasionally it would pucker its lips up into its nose, a kind of visual punctuation, at significant points. The mouth formed an inverted U as it did this and the whole face seemed to collapse in on itself, as if it were being squeezed in an invisible vice.

The voice resumed its tale: 'I told the man I'd come to Paris to be a writer, to enter a tempestuous love affair with the ravishingly beautiful maiden, Mrs Muse, and to fly a literary glider into the blue infinitude of art. But I came to realise that I may never make it as a writer in the conventional sense, and when I was at the bottom of a sombre trough of woe during this wretchedly bleak period I was even driven to disparage some of my favourite novelists. An American I'd met asked me if I liked Emile Zola. I said I didn't eat that foreign muck, and even as I said it, I cursed myself. After months of staring into the murky depths of my brimming tankard of failure, however, a judicious plan to give my art a new life started to form itself in the gloom. The shape of the idea was this: that the material I had written, wrought out of the unspeakable suicidal despair and dreadful poverty of my early life in north Manchester, which was like Stalingrad with clogs, would be adapted to be performed in comedy routines. Routines with jokes about desperate poverty and emotional misery, along with longer lavishly verbose monologues that would set an idyllic scene, only to undermine it with a comically prosaic ending that would ground the audience in brutal reality once more. Monologues that sum up our mortal experience: that we are born, and hardly have we time to glimpse the powder-blue sky and smell the sweet pollen before our face hits the mud at the bottom of the grave. Monologues like life.

'Partly because of my deprived early experiences, cowering in the shadows of gaunt factories severing the skyline with their dissipated profiles, I'd decided to concentrate on the revolutionary struggle for the liberation of the oppressed peoples of the world, a commitment that would place my life at risk. So a career in show business was out of the question, and besides, I was not a performer, I had all the stage presence of a catatonic gnat. I felt that someone else, the right gurning mouth for my gurning words, would perform the work better and I suggested to the Macclesfield man that he should be that person.

'This may all have seemed quite reasonable, as many writers wrote material for actors or comedians, but there was another level to my idea, an absolute, supreme, indubitable commitment. I proposed that he would literally *become me*, occupying my identity, taking my passport and birth certificate, and resuming my life where I had left it in sunny Manchester some months before. I would give him enough writing for innumerable years of comedy routines and he would try to establish a career as a comic on the Northern working-men's club circuit – those dismal depositories of human flotsam – braving the clash between my darkly flowery texts and the audience's expectations. After a few years of this he would reveal his identity and our elaborate and mischievous japery. I asked him to think seriously about my humble plan and come back the next day with a decision.

'Macclesfield man came back to tell me: yes, he would be honoured to be part of such a noble project. We both went out that night, on his money, and painted the town iridescent rouge. Macclesfield man agreed to try out his new persona and I coached him in personifying a much exaggerated version of myself. We ended up at a club, where, after being spotted fooling about on the piano, the man was promptly offered his first gig. The club was a front for a brothel and my man later claimed that he invented his trademark style of out-of-tune piano playing during his residency at the club: he was always being plied with drink by the madame, which affected his playing. He gradually worked my texts into the gaps between musical numbers and then his comedy career was truly on its way. He never looked back. From then on he was Les Dawson, and I left him to it.'

As the voice was speaking I had been looking out of the dressing-room window at the night sky. As the seconds passed my eyes drifted up to the ceiling. I looked at the plastic water sprinkler above my head. It was white but slightly darker than the whiteness of the painted plaster. Some of the lights were recessed into the ceiling; others were covered with large round frosted-glass lampshades. I found it relaxing to look at the different shades of whiteness. It was as if all of life's meaninglessness was associated with colour and detail and could be left behind by staring at blankness. If only for that fleeting white moment.

The Mancunian voice continued its monologue: 'Our physical similitude had to be convincing, though, and as I had a broken jaw from a boxing injury, making me look like a gastric bulldog in a gurning competition, we agreed that I had to punch him to unconsciousness until I dislocated his jaw. After he had recovered he left for Manchester as me.

'So we swapped lives. I moved to Macclesfield and was careful to avoid his friends and family as I had advised him to do with mine – they might recognise us for the impostors that we were. Eventually, as the relatives and friends of Macclesfield man – by all accounts an infinitely noxious gaggle of wastrels – gave up trying to see me and drifted away, I was able to totally disappear and immerse myself in the intellectual stimulation of historical and political texts. I did venture out to go to Spanish language classes, however, and it was there that I met a large-girthed woman who was as loose as knicker elastic...'

For the first time the eyes of the mirror face met mine, peering at me through the creases of a concertina of flesh. He addressed me directly: 'The stork blessed us with a baby-shaped bundle of human joy in 1966. But not long after the birth the baby's mother had had enough of my all-consuming political commitment, my accompanying deteriorating and unsteady grasp on immediate reality and my lack of worldly goods. She said she'd married me because she thought I had collateral: I said no, it's just the way my legs are crossed. She eventually insisted on a divorce and we decided to leave the baby somewhere, to be found by a stranger. She put him in a holdall and before abandoning the kiddie to the precarious vicissitudes of fate, I persuaded her to let me place an old black-and-white photograph in the bag beside him. The image was of Macclesfield man and myself taken in the Paris hotel room. We faced each other in the photo like corpulent mirror images, the light shining on our shirts dappled by the shade of the trees directly outside the window.

'A few months later, in the summer of 1967, I left Macclesfield for the wild and restless jungles of South America, which is like Lancashire with mules. I had become fascinated by Che Guevara years before and was determined to track him down and join his hearty band of heroic revolutionaries, inspired as much by the physical beauty of the man as by his politics. I'd hoped to be bathed in the glow, to have my unlovely gormless mug tanned by the golden rays of his image. As a man of the left his credentials were extraordinary. That was why he walked bandy. I had also read his speeches in Spanish and was particularly taken by a term that became synonymous with Che: "New Man", a term which struck me partly because it was the name of a fine gentlemen's outfitters in Bridlington. But to Che, it meant that each person must be the veritable architect of his or her own new human type, working for the benefit of the collective, driven by a supreme revolutionary moral consciousness. A medical doctor himself, he spoke of his concept almost in the same terms as the unfortunate Dr Frankenstein in Mary Shelley's monstrous story: as the attempt to conquer nature and history with reason. I think my wife was one of Dr Frank's; his name was embossed on the bolt in her neck... But enough of this pathetic drollery. In a speech to a group of medical students and health workers on the theme of "revolutionary medicine"....' The gruff voice then assumed a slightly higher key: '...Guevara had said, "And we will then conclude that almost everything we thought and felt in that past epoch should be filed away and that a new type of human being shall be created."'

After a short pause, the voice continued, 'In the mid-1960s Guevara had taken his commitment to the extent of leaving Cuba, which is a bit like the Isle of Man with cigars, to return to the guerrilla struggle. This involved his complete disappearance from the face of the earth, the notorious and renowned rebel travelling the world under false identities. If you can find any dust-blanketed historical tomes featuring Mr Guevara, look for a photograph of a sober-looking bald-pated man in a V-neck pullover, sitting with a cigar in his mouth, holding a camera between his legs and taking a picture of himself in his hotel room mirror in La Paz, Bolivia. La Paz is a town very much like Wigan, but with sombreros. There are some floral curtains to his right. He looks like my old bank manager on a cheap holiday. The man is, or was, Che. The transformation pictured in the photograph required a prosthesis in his mouth to give him a puffier look, and his hair had to be painfully plucked out, in order for him to look convincingly bald. The poor pitiable wretch. His eyes watered during the ordeal, just as they did that time when he was in bed with his wife and she'd dreamt that he was a piece of loose machinery and had tried to tighten his nuts.'

I looked away, down at the beer-stained dressing-room floor. I did not want the mirror face to see any involuntary cringe of embarrassment that might have drifted across my face; my squeamishness at the smell of ancient jokes, half decomposed. The voice continued:

'The last example of my base clownery, I assure you. So back in 1967 I had read some news reports of a guerrilla commander called Ramón who was establishing a presence in Bolivia. It had to be Che, I thought. And with no more than this vague hunch I set out for South America and spent three months in the untamed Bolivian jungles searching for Che, or La Paz Ramón as I will now call him. But to no avail. Luckily I was helped by a bandy-legged peasant farmer called Gordo, who looked like a wishbone in a poncho. Gordo took pity on me. I told him I was from Manchester and Gordo started calling me, affectionately, "Manchester Ramón", after I forlornly and endlessly chanted "Ramón?! Ramón?!" to him in the hope that he may have heard rumours of the whereabouts of La Paz Ramón and his gallant band of men.

'One night, when I was chewing on a cheroot, waiting for Gordo to return with supplies, a nightingale acclaimed the crescent moon and with pincer fingers I pulled away the damp clothes from my sweat-stained torso. I tried to suppress my hunger by admiring the beautiful surrounding vista, a quiet gully that Gordo called Quebrada del Churo, and I looked up at the starry sky. As I stubbed out my cheroot and crouched down to defecate into a brook, I remember wondering how many fraudulent fortunes had been deciphered from the planets spinning in that black canopy, and I suddenly felt myself levitating towards the same dark emptiness above me. I then looked down from a great height to see myself slumped in a heap with my arse still half immersed in the cackling stream. I had died instantly, shot in the back by Bolivian government troops, who had been waiting patiently on the ridges above me.

'They buried me two hours later in an unmarked communal grave under a vast star-filled sky and because of a stroke by the ruthless sword of a warrior called "Cruel Irony", I was buried with La Paz Ramón and six of his comrades. I was barely yards away from where the last of them were captured and shot that same week. As I speak to you, I can't help recalling to mind my first attempt at journalism, back when I was still Les in Manchester, a report of the funeral of a local councillor that the editor had rejected for being too long winded: "Gone now, that common clay that once so noble trod with purpose..." The paper had the circulation of a flea's foot.

'You may or may not have heard of the week-long period of celebration in the Cuban town of Santa Clara, in 1997, to welcome back the remains of La Paz Ramón and his comrades after twenty years. It was a bit like the Stockport Fish Festival but with palm trees. The cherished remains of the revolutionary saint, the man who used to be Che, were brought back to bring a moral polish to Fidel's cause – it had needed a right buffing by then. But because La Paz Ramón's body was burnt after he was shot and left smouldering and bubbling in the Bolivian sunshine for two days, there was little left of him in the grave to bring back to Cuba other than some blackened stumps of bone. So the Cuban archaeologists, working in the sorry pit near the town of Vallegrande, which was like Accrington with moustaches, decided to box up the thickset bones of my good self to stand in for the bones of La Paz Ramón, in order to have a skeleton substantial enough to weight the coffin, and to cradle a rifle next to its ribcage. My bones were certainly stocky enough – you could've made a monkey's canoe out of my thigh bone. So it was none other than yours truly who was at the head of the procession of coffins in Santa Clara, and I was given final rest in a mausoleum covered with bronze reliefs of jungle fighters, casting the pointed shadows of rifles and raised fists in the Caribbean sun. As I talk to you now I can hear the noise in the streets of Santa Clara, the sound of birds singing above the grumbling of forty-year-old Cadillacs' exhaust pipes. It sounds like... er, Warrington with... rhythm. And it really is bloody hot. There used to be air conditioning in here, but the bat died.

'But enough of this tatty comedic dross. Back in Blighty, after returning from Paris and spending years on the Northern club circuit, Macclesfield man was eventually an unexpected success as Les Dawson. He became a legend of British comedy during the 1970s and 1980s, famous throughout the land, but contrary to the agreement we made, he never did get round to revealing our conceit. In order not to run out of my texts, he'd worked more and more of his own wife and mother-in-law jokes into the routines, but some of this material was of dubious distinction and compromised the purity of my initial concept. My art was given some kind of life, but a limited one, I now realise, because Les Dawson is fading from the collective memory. Who will know who he was in twenty years' time? Will he eventually be forgotten, and my material along with him? He was a cracking comic, though, the lad, yes indeed. Marvellous.'

There was a short pause and then the voice said: 'Dermot, if you ever visit Santa Clara, the Clitheroe of the Caribbean, and want to say a few words to me through the six feet of stone and bronze, please do. And just call me Manchester Ramón. Son.'

The voice stopped. The face froze. It then faded out of sight. I was left with my own reflection. And a lingering dank-smelling coldness.

I've got a bit of a reputation, you see. People now expect the paranormal to linger around me. Like a bad smell. 'Unstable' behaviour is nothing new for me, as I've already explained. Onstage I'm well known for displays of what people have called 'Northern English working-men's club shamanism'. Though I often have to rely on other people's unconvincing descriptions of these events. Fanzine writers mostly. But all this isn't an act. I'm kind of... chosen. I guess. I don't know. I wish I could understand it all. The 'father's voice' I've transcribed above, the voice of Manchester Ramón, could easily have been my own voice or a voice in my head. That's what folk will think. Talking to himself again. But I know. I know.

As I sat there in front of the mirror my judgemental faculties felt buggered. They couldn't quite organise themselves to digest what I'd just witnessed. It never gets any easier and this was not the usual kind of visitation. Even now, as I write this, I still feel like a benumbed boxer trying to get through the final round. Back in the dressing room on that strange evening, I listened to the distant voices of the stagehands in the corridor. Their conversation had begun to leak quietly into the dressing room. The voices were comforting to me: I needed the safety of normal life as it's lived.

But the bloated face in the mirror gradually bobbed to the surface of my thoughts again. In a way, I'd always known. Kind of. I knew that my stepmother, Anna, found me as a baby, in 1967, in a holdall. I was left in a room in the Station Hotel, Macclesfield. She'd worked there as a maid and that. The woman who'd abandoned the holdall had given her name as Bucknall, falsely, I guess. She'd written Bucknall in the hotel ledger. My stepmum called me Dermot, she'd always liked the name Dermot. So, Dermot Bucknall. There I was. And in the holdall, apart from a sleeping baby, was a photograph. There were words written on the back: 'Your dad (on the left) in Paris, 1952. *Su padre siempre*'. There were two stout men staring at each other in the image. Apart from the cigar in the mouth of the man on the left, it was difficult to tell them apart; looking as they did like Tweedledum and Tweedledee, or the clowns Grik and Grok with their mirrored faces.

According to the mirror vision, my dad was the man on the left in the photograph. I'd always known that. To his right was a young Les Dawson, the popular comedian, the famous Les, who we all know and love. But now I knew something else, that my dad was *also* Les Dawson. He was more Les than Les was. He was the original Les Dawson but gave it up; he gave up his entire being to the flowing currents of a final heroic purpose. My dad! He *gave* himself. But it was weird, you know. I don't know. After the vision in the mirror I felt... I felt strangely consoled. Was this a chance to make some contact with my old man? Maybe now there was a way of knowing him? A way of knowing myself? I could make a connection with my dad by listening again to the comedy of Macclesfield man, Macclesfield Les. Maybe then my dad's voice would seep through. Between the lines of those elaborate monologues, those overblown sentences that seem to be about to explode with poetic imagery and the wonder of language, but which always deflate at the end, expelling their air with a sloppy rasp.

Since I was a kid, I've collected Les Dawson videos and tapes. Practically the only thing I knew about my dad was that he knew Les Dawson, so I guess I'd been trying to construct some kind of tenuous connection between my dad and the fat-faced drollery of Les. Now I knew there was more. I got my notebook out of my vinyl bag, which was filled with jottings of material taken from TV and radio appearances by Macclesfield Les. I then walked over to the dressing-room window. Looking out on to the large car park outside and up to the limitless black sky, I recited these words, by now committed to memory:

> Last evening, I was sitting at the bottom of my garden, smoking a reflective cheroot, when I chanced to look up at the night sky. As I gazed, I marvelled at the myriad of stars glistening like pieces of quicksilver cast ceaselessly on black

velvet. In awe I watched the waxen moon ride like an amber chariot across the zenith of the heavens, towards the heavenly void of infinite space, wherein the tethered bulks of Jupiter and Mars hung forever festooned in their orbital majesty. And as I stared in wonderment, I thought to myself, 'I must put a roof on this outside lavatory.'

Back at the dressing table I stopped my tape recorder. I quickly rewound it to check that it had recorded. I pressed PLAY, but there was nothing, just the sound of the condenser microphone's automatic compression of silence. The hum of nothingness swelled like an aural tidal movement, filling the gap left by the absent voice.

BREAKFAST AT THE BEAUTY SPOT

POLLY GOULD

e lays out the table mats with their pastoral scenes. The large one in the centre of the wooden table takes the hot coffee pot and the pair of thin china cups and saucers. He sets them out: one, two, three cows by the watering hole, watched by the rustic cowherd who is playing a tune on his flute while the animals graze. He pours himself a cup of coffee and drinks it while he takes up the newspaper and settles himself into his chair. He takes a red Biro from the breast pocket of his shirt, stained from previous leaking pens, and deliberately circles a column. Sitting at the table, with the two cups and the coffee pot in front of him, he pours himself another cup of coffee and spills a little milk from the jug as he replaces it. Unnoticed, colour white against the green.

'Come on, your coffee is getting cold.'

She is in the bathroom, standing in a thin green dressing gown in front of the basin, looking into the bathroom mirror and casually trying to comb the tangles out of her hair from the night before. She twists it up into a lazy knot. Her fingernail catches. She tries to bite at the snagging nail and tears it a little. In trying to make things better, she thinks, she makes them worse. She pulls open the bathroom cabinet door to see whether there's a pair of nail scissors or a nail file in there. As she opens it a small glass bottle of perfume falls and shatters against the porcelain.

'Bugger.'

He hears her call out and wonders what has happened, but without looking up asks, 'What is it?'

'It's that bloody Chanel No. 5,' she replies.

Listening now, he lifts his head and slowly answers.

'Well, throw it away if it's still bothering you.'

'It's not that. I just broke it. There's glass everywhere.'

She pulls a length of toilet paper from its roll and gathers up the shards of broken glass. Lifting the sodden tissue paper from the sink, she drops it into the bin then swills a small stream of water around with her bare hand to flush away the last of the glass, and finally dries her hands on the bathroom towel.

She walks into the kitchen to find him sitting at the table, his back to her. He is halfway to being dressed, wearing his jeans and a white shirt; a funny pair of slippers by the chair. His hair is short against his neck and she smiles to see him like that. She walks up behind him and strokes him under the ear as if she is scratching the head of a faithful dog.

'God, you smell a bit strong.'

'It's the perfume,' she says, still caressing his neck.
'I suppose you liked it once?'

'In small quantities maybe. You smell like a tart's boudoir.'

He takes her wrist in his hand and pulls her around to face him.

'In that case,' she says, rubbing his cheeks with both her hands now, 'I'll have to make you smell like one of the clientele.'

'No, really,' he insists, 'I don't like it. I think it might set my chest off.' He pushes her away and she moves towards the kitchen sink.

'That kind of smell just catches in my throat.'

He pulls at his shirt collar. 'I can feel my chest getting tight with it.'

She squirts a line of washing-up liquid on to her hands and rinses away the smell of a sophisticated Parisian lady.

'It is nasty,' she mumbles to herself. 'You're right. I don't know what you were keeping it for.'

She takes the kitchen cloth in her hand and wipes down the already clean stainless-steel sink and then sits down. With the cloth still in her hand, she picks up the jug of milk to pour a little into her coffee. She wipes the base of the jug and cleans away the pool of spilt milk at the foot of the little cowherd, before returning the milk jug to its place.

'Listen. I've found something for you.' He looks up from the paper to see whether she is paying attention.

She looks over and sees that he has already red-ringed something.

'What is it?'

'"Dead woman ate nothing but air."' He looks up again with a slight smile on his face and then returns his gaze to the article.

'It's not going to spoil my appetite, is it?'

'Put the toast on, won't you?'

'In a minute. I'm listening now, go on.'

He tilts his head back a little to get a better focus.

'"A woman in an isolated beauty spot in the Scottish Highlands may have died while trying to convert to a New Age movement whose adherents claim not to eat or drink."' He looks up at her to gauge her response, but she's staring at a space somewhere in front of her.

'Anorexia?' she says, a little absent-mindedly.

'Well, not really. It's more odd than that. It seems she was following the recommendations of some guru. She was trying to follow her twenty-one-day conversion course. It says here that: "Followers eschew all food and drink for seven days and then take only sips of water for a further fourteen days. After that, Jasmuheen claims" – that's the guru – "adherents to 'breatharianism' need never eat or drink again."'

'Well, she's not wrong there. Dead women don't eat, do they?' she says.

'Can you believe what some people will believe in? Stupid cow.'

She looks up at him, startled. The scene is becoming a little more vivid in her mind: the dead woman, pale and still, a lonely spot. She watches him, sees his dark hair and broad face, the

shadows of an older man growing in the jowls, the strong jaw
and the hairs that grow up from his chest around his collar
bone. She watches him while he reads, his strong and tender
hands gripping the flimsy newspaper. He doesn't see her
and continues reading, with a little smile playing on his lips.
She is struck by the vehemence of this last comment.

'How long can you survive without water, anyway?
I thought it was only about three or four days?' she says.

'It says six days here. According to nutritionists. So she was
only one day off from having a drink. She was just unlucky
that seven is a more aesthetically pleasing number generally
preferred by mystics and gurus. She was found by a nature-
loving tourist. Imagine that, you are out to enjoy the
countryside and you come across that sorry scene.'

'Other people do so spoil a pretty view,' she says
sarcastically.

'Don't suppose he expected to find her when he set out
for his walk.' He laughs to himself.

'I don't expect she meant herself to be found.'

She wonders about how they always seem to take different
sides.

'And then the police enlisted the help of a local shepherd
to lead them back to her.'

'It's funny, I imagine her naked.'

He gets up to make the toast, and shuffles his feet into the
slippers. He slides them along the floor to keep them from
coming off.

'One slice or two?' he asks, as he opens the bread bin.

'One.'

'I'll make two or you will only be wanting some of mine.'

He puts the loaf on the breadboard, and puts his hand
around it. He squeezes the bread tight, until all the air seems
to go out of it, and cuts slices from it. When he releases the
loaf, it slowly expands to its former shape. He bends down
to the fridge to take out the butter and two pots of jam.
Crouching down, he needs to search for a while among the

disorganised shelves.

The toaster clicks the hot toast out for buttering. He puts the two pieces of toast in front of her but she doesn't seem to notice. She is looking into middle distance again. Like a lovely soft animal, he thinks. He remembers how his thumb sometimes presses into her thigh as he holds her to him; he always expected it would leave a dent, like a fist kneading dough.

He sits down and takes a bite of the toast. The noise in his head is surprisingly loud and he looks up to see whether she has heard. She is still preoccupied. He sees that she still hasn't started to eat her toast.

'Breakfast. It means "breaking the fast", did you know?'

'I had heard,' she replies.

'It's the most important meal of the day. Get a good breakfast and you are set for whatever the day demands of you.'

She has been staring at the brown and green of the table mat as he talks and only now registers the image that she is looking at. It is a pastoral scene from the eighteenth or nineteenth century. The little cowherd is reclining on a hummock of grass to the side of the river and playing a tune on his flute as he attends the herd. He has breeches to his knees and thick socks on his lower legs, which are daintily crossed at the ankles. More like a milkmaid than a burly country lad, she thinks, with those feet in dainty slippers. A painting of three cows at the riverside, big heads bent down. They look extraordinarily muscular in their haunches. She thinks they look more like beef cattle than dairy. It occurs to her that they are kept for meat not milk. A distinction these beasts are ignorant of, their only purpose being to tirelessly chew the cud. Does the cowherd appreciate the bovine gentleness of the creatures he is commissioned to watch?

She looks at them again, the three eating away at the grass to fill each of their four stomachs. Poor cows. She reaches over abruptly to take the paper from the table; sees the red Biro marking the place and, scanning the article, picks out a line to read to him.

'"With 'breatharianism' we free ourselves from the very basic primordial fear which is if you don't eat you are going to die." She wanted to be free, I suppose.'

He is concentrating on spreading jam on to another slice, and comically tries to catch a globular strawberry as it slides from the toast. He is embarrassed and she enjoys his continuing awkwardness in front of her.

Something is bothering her about the story. Or perhaps it's reminding her of what it is that bothers her about him. Something is sticking in her flesh and she feels compelled to go on. To worry at it until some result is manifest. To ask a question that might get an answer. She wants to know what he was keeping it for.

'What are you keeping me for?' she asks while she watches him wipe the edges of his mouth and lick the jam from his fingers. He doesn't respond. She watches him and wonders, 'What kind of a cow am I for you? What do you keep me for? Is it for milk or meat?'

She tosses the paper back to where she found it.

'Was it like that, do you suppose?'

'Was what like what?'

'The beauty spot that she chose. Do you think it was like that picture on your great-aunt's hand-me-down place mats?' she says as she leans forward and pushes the cups and coffee pot from the mat to make the cows and cowherd visible. He half-catches the jug as it tilts.

'Be careful. And they are not my great-aunt's. Those mats are there for a reason, you know.'

He pointedly lifts the coffee pot from the table, revealing a dark-ringed watermark, and replaces it on the mat. He obscures the view of the cows and the cowherd. All that remains to be seen is his delicate shoes.

'There can be no good reason for having such absurdly trite images of old England on your kitchen table. Not in the twentieth century anyway.'

He seems not to have heard her, so she persists.

'But really, do you think it was like that? Like that picture on your mat?'

He replaces his glasses and lifts the paper to read it again, looking over the top of his glasses as he answers her. 'It says here that she was found in the Scottish Highlands. So that would suggest a far more harsh and austere type of beauty, closer to the sublime than the picturesque.'

'Closer to the sublime than the ridiculous, you mean.'

'Hmmm, very good.'

He looks at her over his glasses as he discards the newspaper and its odd little article about the disaster of someone else's life. She sees him looking at her querulously.

'What did you want me to think?' she asks.

'I thought you would find it funny, that's all.'

'Your amusing little story is someone else's catastrophe.'

'I just thought it might make you laugh. You are always going on about the high-minded pretensions of these self-styled thinkers.'

She is not looking at him.

'I thought it would amuse you.'

She doesn't reply. She's rubbing at her finger with the snagged nail, and thinking that it is hurting more than seems right. She feels like biting at her nail again but knows that it is a habit that makes her seem nervous, so she resists the urge. He sees that she has not touched her toast yet.

'Eat your breakfast,' he says.

Suddenly there is a sharp piercing pain in her finger and she brings it to her teeth to bite it, despite herself.

'Ouch.'

'What is it?'

'I think I have a piece of glass in my finger.'

'Glass?'

'Yes, from that bottle of perfume. I just smashed it. I told you.'

She doesn't look at him but adds quietly, 'I don't know what you were keeping it for.'

'I wasn't keeping it. I just hadn't thrown it away yet.'

She looks across at him now, and says emphatically,
'It hurts.'

He chooses to believe that she is talking about the pain in
her finger and not his souvenir.

'Let me have a look.'

'You won't be able to see anything.'

'Let me try.' He stands up from his chair and moves round
to her side of the table, taking her hand in his.

'Is it this one?' he asks as he pulls her hand towards him
and kneels down at the foot of her chair. Her sore forefinger is
extended. 'Let me hold it in the light.' He turns her hand a
little to let the light fall on it from the back window. 'I can't see
anything obvious.'

' Well, I can feel something pretty obvious.' She tries to
pull her hand away as he presses on the slightly reddened skin,
but he has her wrist in a firm grip.

'Hold still. It does look a little sore. I think I can get it if
you will just hold still for a moment.'

She lets her body go limp under his ministrations.
He squeezes the skin around the bright splinter of glass. As he
presses her fingertip between his nails, the shard is slowly
released amid a tiny beauty spot of blood. In its place he puts a
little kiss.

'There you go,' he says, as he presents the offending
item for her approval. 'You have your very own St Jerome.'
He makes to move away.

'Don't get above yourself,' she says, bringing her near leg
around his waist, pressing her bare foot behind his calf, locking
him in place. 'Perhaps you are only a lowly cowherd like our
friend on the mat.'

'Well, that would be a demotion for you too, my love, from
lioness to cow.'

He is still kneeling in front of her with his finger pointing
towards her with the offending shard on display.

She says, 'Touché,' and moves slowly, bringing his hand to

her mouth to blow away the now innocuous fragment of glass. Hand on thighs, he slumps down as she pulls him against her, then puts his hands around her. She pulls him to her, her hand on his neck, her legs around him, his back knocking the table; the sound of crockery shifting. Face in breasts, ear against her chest; the jug has tipped over. She feels his warm breath on her skin through her thin gown and the rise and fall of his breathing against her. Head against her chest, eyes closed, resting above her left breast; he can hear her heart beating. She is caressing his head again and the smell of perfume is powerful now. With his eyes closed, her body beneath him and the smell of Chanel No. 5, he sees his last lover's smile; hard and bright, her body sinewy and strong, and the clear glass of her laugh which would shatter his silences.

He hears the sound of something dripping on the floor and opens his eyes to see a line of milk trailing from the table, splashing upon her left foot. The whiteness of the milk makes the paleness of her skin seem even more astonishing. He watches as the remaining flow lessens to a few drips, adding to the little puddle of spilt milk on the hard kitchen floor. He stays there, looking at her foot, the milk seeping between her toes. She says nothing, holding him to her.

'The milk,' he says, but she is holding his head to her chest, still stroking his neck, not letting him go.

SEDA– AN INTERESTING STORY

ANTONIO J. CRUZ DE FUENTES

Translated by Juan Cruz

I t's more than likely that you, kind reader, who lends his work or his capital to this firm, have asked yourself more than once about the origins of SEDA. What were the beginnings of this workplace? Who are the men, many of them already deceased, and what are the motives that have led to the circumstances whereby our chimney has not ceased billowing smoke for a single day in the fifty-five years that have passed between that distant 14 July 1940, when the factory started, and the present day.

It is legitimate to feel proud of belonging to such an old firm, which has had and still has, as its guiding light, the desire to do things better every day. To feel it also in considering ourselves an essential piece of the team that achieves it, without which – as happens with the chain that is missing a link – everything would be useless.

To reinforce that legitimate sentiment, which all at SEDA feel, I am going to answer the question that you asked me about the origins of all this.

It was around spring 1939 when, after a forty-month campaign, my battalion arrived in a Madrid that had just been occupied and which was full of desolation. I was twenty-five years old and had the honourable rank of private. As soon as I arrived I began to search for those relatives and friends who had spent the cruel war in the mousetrap that was Madrid in those interminable years. Among them was my teacher and dear friend Francisco Grande Covián (Paco Grande to us), who has died recently. I met Paco Grande many years back in the

Residencia de Estudiantes, and we also lived together for many years in the Fundación del Amo in the nascent Ciudad Universitaria de Madrid. Paco was the professorial assistant to Dr Negrin (who would be the republican prime minister in the civil war), and hence I had him as my physiology teacher for two successive years. Our friendship, alongside this academic relationship, was constant and sincere.

When I found him again at the end of the war, Paco Grande was living in the house of Dr Francisco Jiménez, on the Calle de Torrijos, where we spent many hours together.

Towards the end of April of that year of 1939, Grande and I went to have lunch in the home of Virginia Vighi; Virginia was the only sister of the great Paco Vighi, one of the Palentinos (born in Piña de Campos) most enamoured of Palencia that ever there was. Over coffee after lunch, the conversation fell on the paucity of medicines that the country was suffering and on how we were exporting many of the raw materials from which medicines were manufactured, which we then had to import at exorbitant prices. Paco gave me the example of ephedra, from which ephedrine was made, and also that of blue fin tuna livers, which Spain exported to Germany and Norway and from which was extracted vitamin A, which we then had to import.

The large blue fin tuna were fished, almost exclusively and in fabulous quantities, on the Atlantic coast of the Straits of Gibraltar. The fishing was monopolised by a semi-nationalised company, which was called the Consorcio Nacional Almadrabero Español. The livers of these tunas constituted a source of vitamin A five hundred times more concentrated than the classic cod liver oil. They were carefully prepared with salt in chestnut barrels and exported to Germany and Norway at the price of a dollar per kilo.

The Consorcio Almadrabero itself had tried to exploit this raw material before the civil war. To this end it had contracted Professor Juan Negrin, great politician, average physiologist and poor industrialist. Their efforts failed to achieve any significant ends.

I was at a crucial moment in my life. The war had interrupted my medical studies for three successive years, and I was due to resume them that autumn at the age of twenty-six, and to finish them on the verge of becoming thirty. My situation was complicated by my desire to get married, and so it's therefore not surprising that the substance of my conversation with Paco Grande should generate, in my mind, the idea of dedicating myself to the task of obtaining vitamin A in Spain. I expressed it thus to Paco Grande and I convinced him, in the days that followed, that we should collaborate to this end. I was confident that my father, Juan de Dios Cruz Valero, who was a doctor in medicine and a pharmacist, would help us economically and with wise council.

The idea was very impulsive and as such could, in principle, have been ludicrous, because the principal ingredient was missing: the Consorcio Almadrabero selling us the raw material, without which everything would be useless. Also, it was necessary that my father, or someone else, should stake the requisite capital. As for the possibility of successfully resolving the complicated manufacturing technicalities, such was our youthful improvidence that it was never discussed. My father agreed. The prestige already enjoyed by Dr Grande and a desire to help me encouraged him to embark on this improbable adventure.

In the first week of May 1939 I rented an abandoned bar in Madrid, which was situated on the corner of Francisco Silvela and López de Hoyos. Hectically I installed a basic laboratory there, and during that spring I went to Barbate several times, accompanied by a soldier from my regiment named Diego, who was from the area and through whose mediation they gave us five kilo tins full of the livers of freshly caught tuna. I worked long days on these, during which I managed not to show my face in my barracks.

Paco Grande had been sidelined from the university because of his dealings with Don Juan Negrin, despite the fact that during the war he had held no political office and dedicated his time solely to completing an invaluable scientific study about the effects of hunger on the civil population of Madrid. He needed to find, more even than I, a job to make a living. The possibility of spending a long period of time working on a project uncertain of success, such as our vitamin A venture, and assuming also the joint responsibility of spending my father's money, ended up filling him with doubts about the wisdom of continuing our collaboration. In the month of July the Ibys Institute offered him a post as scientific adviser and he came to tell me that I should consider him free of his commitment to the vitamin A project. His understandable desertion could not divert me from my trajectory, which had already gained considerable momentum.

I decided after little more than a month that, in order to spend fourteen hours a day in the laboratory, it would be better to move somewhere I could work, eat and sleep. I took an interior-facing flat on the Calle de Garcia de Paredes 66 and I converted the kitchen and the larder into the laboratory. I slept on a camp bed and cooked with the Pyrex glassware that I used for my work. Around the first fortnight of August I believed I had reached a conclusion to my experiments. It was time carefully to develop an industrial project, for which it was no longer necessary to have a laboratory; nor did I need to stay in Madrid following my discharge from the army in August 1939. I moved to Palencia, with all my utensils in a travelling crane, which my battalion lent me as a last favour. On 15 October I married Guadalupe Picallo Diez, my lifelong sweetheart.

From the time of my wedding in October 1939 until February 1940 I dedicated myself to studying medicine and to passing some of my outstanding academic courses.

In February 1940 we began to bring to fruition the vitamin A project. We set up a company called 'Antonio J. Cruz y Cia, Sociedad en Comandita'. My father invested 150,000 pesetas. My brother-in-law, Jerónimo Arroyo Alonso, came into the project with another fifty thousand that his father lent him. After a series of refusals from the city council about alternative locations, we chose a plot for the factory called del Rosal, on the way to the Monte. The name Rosal is a corruption of the word Osar, which designated the site of the old cemetery of Palencia. The plot belonged to Doña Pilar Calderón, from whom I bought it for 30,000 pesetas. Building work started there on 14 April and we began manufacture on 14 July of that same year of 1940. Demetrio Paramio was a lad who worked with the building contractor, and before the building was finished he became our first employee.

Our contacts with the Consorcio Almadrabero were completely negative. Juan Negrin had failed to resolve the problem of the extraction of vitamin A for them, and furthermore he had fled Spain at the end of the war. The Consorcio Almadrabero, adhering to its mistaken criterion that the most qualified person to set up a vitamin factory was a professor of physiology, contracted the successor to Dr Negrin's chair, Professor Garcia Valdecasas, to replace him. With the excuse that they were going to obtain vitamin A 'straight away' they refused to sell us a single kilo of tuna liver (which, meanwhile, they continued exporting to Germany and Norway). The alternative raw materials (Canary Island tuna, northern bonito, etc.) were of much lower richness, and therefore very uneconomical. But we had no alternative but to accept them. We established a warehouse in Las Palmas de Gran Canaria and we began to harvest tuna livers there. The flight of our representative there to America, with our funds for the purchase of the raw material, was one of many anecdotes from that phase.

By November 1940 we had managed to produce a vitamin A solution that was entirely homologous with all the foreign products that Spain imported, and through the intervention of Paco Grande the Instituto Ibys became our first client. We sold them consignments of 25,000 pesetas and with this, and the odd export to France, we got by.

There were no profits to distribute to the shareholders and what was earned was invested in improving installations. At the beginning of 1941, with a loan of 500,000 pesetas from the Banco Mercantil (later to be the Banco de Santander), we ordered the construction of a very technological and modern plant, which was finished and operational in the autumn of that same year of 1941. It was providential that we took the decision to spend that sum of money because (perhaps I had a premonition) the Consorcio Nacional Almadrabero Español caved in in February 1942.

The economic policy of the then government was based on what has since been called self-sufficiency, and on the state bureaucracy's intervention in the economy and its central organisation. Each industry had assigned to it a rigorous quota of provisions. The tuna livers from the Consorcio Almadrabero were granted to half a dozen laboratories which, without having the appropriate installations, claimed a portion of the precious raw material with which later to achieve some manufacture or other benefit. The important thing then was to get quotas, to be used later, or to be sold at black-market prices. We were assigned a quota of 20 per cent of that raw material, in spite of the fact that we were the only established manufacturers.

The Consorcio Almadrabero reacted by sending 3,000 kilos of livers free to each of the designated laboratories. In order, it said, to donate the resultant vitamin A to schoolchildren. This stunt was designed to demonstrate, through the ministry's controls on the vitamin A obtained, that there was no industry capable of adequately exploiting this raw material, and that therefore the Consorcio Almadrabero should hold on to it for its own production (when they had it). Things went well for the Consorcio with the other laboratories. But we delivered the appropriate quantity of a vitamin A concentrate of international quality to the ministry, and they had to recognise this, sending no less than Dr Bootello, chief of the department, to Palencia to receive it.

The Consorcio then proposed buying the factory from us,

a tempting offer which I declined, because I had a firm vocation and nothing and nobody could wrench me from my destiny, which was then full of potential, and which has taken me along unforeseen and difficult paths to the SEDA of today.

As an alternative, the Consorcio proposed, and we accepted, a contract whereby they provided free raw material, we did the work and we shared equally the income from the sales of the resultant vitamin. Once the contract was signed for three years, we began extraction that summer of 1942 using more than 40,000 kilos of livers. The same amount was available in 1943 and 1944, so that, even though we organised sales to all the Spanish laboratories, with the help of José Nogués Caiz (an agent from Barcelona who collaborated with me for many years), the truth was that an enormous quantity of vitamin A was being stored in the factory refrigerator. Finally, all of it was sold in 1943 and 1944 to the German government. Both the Consorcio Almadrabero and Antonio J. Cruz y Cia, S. en C., made a fortune during those years.

Alongside those massive exports to Germany, our vitamin was exported to France, Switzerland, Hungary, Denmark and Belgium. Coinciding with this, we had to take some spare plant to Lisbon, where an affiliate of Ibys named Laboratorios Victoria had finalised an agreement with the Portuguese state to produce vitamin A there. They had no plant, and they didn't know how to do it. Paco Grande asked me to get them out of a pickle and within a few days Enrique Madrigal, our factory manager, and Demetrio Paramio were in Lisbon, together with all the machinery we had dismantled in Palencia. Laboratorios Victoria were able to demonstrate, within a valid time limit, that they were ready to exploit the tuna livers from the Portuguese tuna fisheries.

The anecdotes relating to the memorable transfer of the machinery and people to Lisbon, under the care of the factory's official hauliers – the celebrated and unforgettable brothers Angel (Bigotes) and Pedro Fuentes Guerra, would in themselves fill a humorous tome.

Following my vocation and the lodestar of my actions, our profits were invested in a new factory. The purpose this time was the production of chemical products by means of fermentation – for the time being ethyl alcohol, acetone, butilic alcohol and yeast feeds. A new company was set up, Bioquímica Española, S.A., we bought more plots adjoining ours, and work on the new factory began in April 1943, exactly three years after work on the vitamin A factory had begun.

In August of that year my father, irreplaceable counsellor and mentor of my actions, passed away.

The acute lack of materials, aggravated daily by the prolongation of the world war, resulted in the building work developing extremely slowly. We had to wait almost a year until we were assigned a quota of cement and the steel plate for storage tanks, and the rest of the machinery was delayed by about four years.

By then the war had finished. Following many difficulties, we began normal production in 1947, extracting very pure products and with good levels of efficiency. At the beginning of 1949 there were already tenders from the USA, at much lower prices. Not only did they have much larger factories there, but they also used mouldy or damaged corn as their raw material, which they obtained at very low prices, while we had to use black-market barley and molasses, which the state sugar monopoly sold us at punitive prices. Caught in the snare of corruption, which facilitated the import of finished products and impeded the purchase of agricultural residue from the USA, Bioquímica Española began immediately to experience difficulties. It was our first contact with the endemic problem of Spain: absence of the competitive spirit.

Between engineers, chemists, technicians, administrators and labourers, some fifty people worked at Bioquímica. I believed it was my duty to protect those jobs, and we worked towards the sale of the company to the Calvo Sotelo, an INI organisation. Of the 15 million pesetas we had invested, we obtained, after settling our debts, 2.8 million pesetas as a reward for seven years' work. My industrialist zeal had cost my family almost all the profits obtained from 'the Vitamins' (as the business was then called in Palencia). We were technically ruined.

Fortunately, Bioquímica and the Vitamins were two different companies, so that while Bioquímica took a new course as a public company, which it continues to follow after forty-four years (now as Repsol Derivados), we concentrated on the usual, and no longer brilliant, exploitation of vitamin A. There were no great exports, because the Japanese and American products, which were cheaper, began with great facility to find their way around the world. The beginnings of a flourishing national market compensated, in part, for this loss, however, and we patiently began our economic reconstruction. The termination of our contract with the Consorcio, which had been prolonged for several years at a diminishing level, was replaced by purchases of livers from North Africa and later by the establishment of our own factory in Lisbon, so that we could use the livers from the large tuna of the Algarve fisheries (1958). By this date, Laboratorios Victoria had abandoned this manufacture. Our factory in Lisbon was in the Quinta do Rio, in an industrial quarter called Sacavem, and my agent there, the inestimable Juan Marquez Chicharro, is, still today, SEDA's agent for the sale of instant coffee in our neighbouring country. The man in charge of production – I remember him affectionately – was called Portela, and his trade was that of *fadista*, or singer of fados. The factory in Sacavem went by the name of Materias Primas Para las Industrias Farmaceuticas (Farmaprima), a name later inherited by our decaffeinating plant in Palencia.

Towards the end of the decade of the 1940s, F. Hoffman La Roche in Switzerland and Eastman Kodak in the USA simultaneously discovered a useful method for the synthetic manufacture of vitamin A. The development of this synthesis was a warning to me that the life of an industry that had fed us for many years was nearing its end. We would have to do something else or shut down. I visited the synthetic vitamin A factories in Basel (Switzerland) and Rochester (USA) and discovered that it was a procedure requiring a very large investment, which was not justified by the modest size of the Spanish market. I also discovered that we were threatened by insurmountable competition. The million international units of natural vitamin A that we sold for ten to twelve pesetas per unit cost only three pesetas to manufacture by synthesis.

During my stay in Rochester (USA), in the winter of 1950, I was working in the Kodak laboratories to learn the technique of 'molecular distillation'. This consists of distillation in a microscopic layer and a very rarefied atmosphere (a pressure of 0.005 millimetres of mercury) which enables the separation of very heavy molecules, like that of vitamin A. We acquired a small plant which arrived in Palencia in September of that year of 1950. Unknown then in Spain, it was designed to allow us a notable extension to the time during which it would be possible to exploit the business profitably.

In 1952 we began to work in the field of amino acids, for therapeutic applications in stomach illnesses. In order to research them, and to produce them in powder form, I bought a laboratory atomiser (NIRO) and later, for their production, a semi-industrial model of the same make. This material was also used for the separation of lactose from whey in dairies, a process inherent in the production of penicillin. Until then penicillin factories had employed pure lactose, which was very expensive, and it was our idea to introduce deproteined whey, which was very much cheaper.

My brother-in-law Jerónimo Arroyo then proposed leaving the business, so I bought his share, and my mother and I became the sole shareholders.

The work that is required to create a profitable industrial activity in order to replace another that is faltering for reasons beyond one's control is extremely exhausting owing to its urgent character and the anxiety that it generates, considering that the chances of everything going well are very low (perhaps 20 per cent). By May 1956, pressured by this anxiety, I found myself exhausted. I rented a caravan and went for fifteen days to Galicia, with my wife and three of my children (Manolo, who was ten years old, being one of them). To take on the journey, we made powdered coffee with milk and sugar in the NIRO laboratory atomiser. Espresso coffee plus milk and sugar, passed through the atomiser. The results were so good that the children ate it by the spoonful without dissolving it. I began to think about instant coffee, because the other projects in which we were involved did not hold much promise.

The only brand of instant coffee available on the Spanish market in 1956 was Nescafé. It was sold in 50-gram tins. The label announced that the product contained 50 per cent carbohydrates to preserve the aroma. Needless to say a considerable amount of dextrose was introduced to lower the costs of the product.

To establish production in a market that has only one supplier might seem like a reasonable proposition. It wasn't entirely so for two reasons: first because the market had emerged from nothing and the consumers identified the product with the brand. (When we began to sell instant coffee under our brand Khedive, people called it 'Nescafé Khedive'.) And because of the prestige and strength of Nestlé. But I didn't have much time left to think about it, so we worked in the laboratory to establish a competitive product, we registered the distinctive brand 'El Khedive' (Khedive was the title of the ancient Turkish viceroy in Egypt) and we ordered an eight-unit extraction plant from Barcelona. With this plant (which worked at 2 kilograms of pressure) and with coffee roasted with sugar to compensate for the load of dextrin that Nestlé added, we began to work with a 42 per cent yield of instant per kilo of green.

During 1958 our sales grew to such a level that we struggled to meet demand – we were very pleased with ourselves. But Nestlé, alarmed by the figures it was seeing, increased the publicity for Nescafé to such an extent that it didn't take us many months to learn a wise lesson: that we couldn't compete with them in the same market. That is to say, with our own brand.

It was at the beginning of that year of 1958 that we put decaffeinated Khedive on the market – the first decaffeinated coffee on the Spanish market, two or three years earlier than that of Nestlé. It was not a success precisely because people didn't know what it was, or what its advantages were. It was demonstrated that we didn't have the power to create a new market, despite having the technology to manufacture the product.

In September 1960 the firm Tasada y Beltrán, a very important food distribution company (Maizena, Flan El Niño, Müller Chicory, Knorr Soups, etc.), came into our world. They wanted us to make a product similar to Nestlé's 'Eco' and Gallina Blanca's 'Afin' for them very urgently. They offered us the technology of the German firm Quieta Werke of Augsburg.

By then the sales of Khedive had descended to uneconomic levels, so for us the skies were open. I made two journeys to Augsburg, one with my wife and another, with more time, with my son Juan Antonio, who was finishing his degree in chemistry. In November of that year we allowed Tasada y Beltrán to invest in my company on a 50 per cent basis and we built a drying tower, a small malt and enlarged packing plants (the ground floor of the current SEDA office). Carmelo Eguiguren, president of Tasada y Beltrán, became president of the company, which changed its name from Antonio J. Cruz y Cia, S.A., to Kafix, S.A. (Kafix was the brand name of the product we were to make).

I remained as managing director. This business was of paramount importance for us because the T. and B. organisation was thinking of moving Müller Malt, which they manufactured in Pamplona, to Palencia, and also to use

Palencia for other future activities.

The year 1961 was dedicated exclusively to the construction of buildings and the installation of new machinery. The vitamins, which in a residual form continued to operate, were passed to Farmaprima, a Spanish company created by me and housed separately because this activity did not form part of the agreement with Tasada y Beltrán.

In February 1962 Tasada y Beltrán held its sales conference in Palencia, to show the salesmen the production of the product they had to sell. Subsequently, with great publicity, the sales activity began. Initially, until every shop in the country had a box of Kafix, activity in the factory was intense. But in the summer we began to get the impression that the product was not leaving the shops. In October the factory stopped production and by January 1963 it was clear that we had failed. Tasada y Beltrán proposed that we should go into receivership, which I opposed because I could not do such a thing in Palencia. I proposed that they should decide whether to sell their share or buy mine. The price was 30 per cent of the nominal value. They chose to sell (January 1963).

Don Jerónimo Arroyo Alonso (the father of our current director), who, as I said, had spent nine years away from the business, came back into the concern at my request, buying from Tasada y Beltrán a large number of the shares these gentlemen were selling. I bought the rest of the shares with credit from the bank. I changed the name from Kafix, S.A. (which, since the product had failed, had no validity) to SEDA, S.A., and I set about the task, almost impossible now, of changing our production and our market for a third time.

The new objective was to sell instant coffee to industrialists and wholesalers who had openings into the market, albeit localised and of little consequence. I meant in this way to achieve large volumes, through the accumulation of many small markets, instead of creating a single large market, which would be like jumping off a tree and exposing us to being eaten by a lion (which is what had been happening to us with Khedive and Kafix).

We started, around March 1963, to offer instant coffee to coffee roasters. First to Cafés No.12 of Valladolid. Our task was difficult. Private labels and white labels were unknown, and the roasters had a visceral hatred for instant coffee, because Nescafé took sales from them and nothing could persuade them to sell such 'muck' with their brand name.

Miguel García Abril, of Cafés No.12 (a great gentleman of business), had vision. Not only did he embrace the idea with enthusiasm, but he also placed in me an unshakeable faith which did not pale in the thirty years that remained of his life. We owe him inestimable gratitude.

I then visited many coffee roasters in Catalonia, Levante, Andalusia, Madrid and the north of Spain. I managed to obtain agreements with fifteen of them by virtue of which they would contribute money to SEDA in exchange for an exclusive supply within their own market. We were also joined by a new associate, Jaime Roure Bou, a constructor of machinery for the coffee industry, a man with great prominence in the sector, who accepted the mission of accompanying me on my visits to coffee men, and was decisive, in many cases, in getting them to accept my proposals.

On 24 February 1964, in the Hotel Wellington in Madrid, the first general meeting of the society, transformed now into Sociedad Española de Alimentos, S.A. (SEDA), was celebrated. At the said meeting it was agreed to raise the capital needed to grant entry to these new members, and the new administrative council was named. I proposed Miguel García Abril as president in gratitude for the help that he had given us, and I remained as managing director, agreeing, following a proposal from Jorge Soley, to raise my salary from 18,000 to 25,000 pesetas per month.

With these fifteen client-shareholders we set to work in the spring of 1964. It was a very slow business preparing the labels for all of them, and their initial sales were similarly all slow.

But at least we now had some clients who had invested a sum of money in SEDA and who, because of this, and because they were convinced about the idea, worked with great commitment on the sale of instant coffee. Having started late, sales in 1964 ended at 28.33 tonnes and, for the only time in our history, we made considerable losses. Not so in 1965, when sales rose to 34.36 tonnes. The target was, in those days, to reach a million 50-gram tins per annum (50 tonnes).

Naturally, this group of coffee makers, who had representation in the administrative council of SEDA, wanted to retain exclusivity for the business, since there was no other supplier of instant coffee in Spain for small retailers. But the emergence of other large brands, and the many requests that we were receiving, finally convinced them that the going concern was now SEDA and not the small section of the market that each of them held. And so the existing list of clients gradually expanded.

In 1965 a new extraction plant was installed and the sale of decaffeinated instant coffee was agreed. Even though I had developed a decaffeinating technique by active carbon absorption in 1958, the technical focus of this operation had changed greatly. In order not to complicate things too much for the time being, it was decided to reach an agreement with Cogesol (later to become General Foods) for them to supply us with green decaffeinated coffee. With the aim of packaging the resultant instant coffee, a Hamac-Hansella 2-gram sachet-packing machine was bought in Veert (Netherlands) and later another made by Wolkogon.

Given the substantial purchases of decaffeinated coffee that we made from Cogesol, we researched a new process to decaffeinate it ourselves and established an integrated plant (which was on the site currently occupied by the steam boiler that was in operation until the previous summer). This decaffeinating plant started up at full capacity from its first day, with no mishaps.

Already in the sixties, the help of my son Juan Antonio had made possible, not a lesser effort on my part, but a fuller and more efficient operation. This beneficial effect was multiplied in the seventies and eighties with the incorporation into the business of my sons Juan de Dios and Manolo, and that of my nephew Jerónimo. To these and other decisive human contributions is owed the maintenance, over more than thirty years, of the exceptional rate of growth of our market and our industrial facilities. My twenty-five years of solitary work found, at last, some reward.

Gradually a generational change was felt in the company – not only my retirement from the management in 1978, but also the renewal of board members, directors and personnel in all the working strata. The workforce has grown threefold in the past twelve years. SEDA became a strange place for those who had struggled in the difficult early years. People like Román, Leocadio, Senorio, Demetrio, Fermín and many others could not understand what was happening in the company. Many of those who were there at the beginning, or who joined us later, like Tomás Salgado and Leocadio, left us. They have the remembrance and gratitude of all of us.

The bases and the principles, as much technical as moral, which I impressed on the company since its foundation have been followed faithfully by those who slowly took over the helm of SEDA from my own hands. This has allowed me, with the collaboration of all, to see SEDA rise to its current level of importance and prosperity.

Many years have passed. Many efforts have been made. The majority of the profits have been regularly reinvested in the factory. We are strong in our sector. We sell half the amount of instant coffee that Nestlé does and yet... we still have a long way to travel to reach the technological level of the best.

Looking back at the very many good and bad times that the factory has granted me in this long half-century, I have to confess that the experience has been fascinating for me.

I would, if I could, do it all again. But since my eighty-two years now impede it, I want to ask something of you, dear reader, who comes here to work, or to invest your savings each day: that you should do it for me in the future, without giving the least opportunity to despair.

SEDA is the future of everyone. No one has the right to put their immediate interests before the future prospects of the firm. And when I say no one, I mean those who manage, those who do the work and those who have their savings invested here. Because the current climate is showing us that it is better to have enough for today and for tomorrow than to have a lot today and nothing tomorrow.

To make of SEDA a firm that is ever more competitive must be not just a simple duty for you, but an honour. And above all a very wise personal investment.

Antonio-Jesús Cruz de Fuentes
PRESIDENT
Palencia, June 1995

OPEN SEA

MARTIN VINCENT

And so without turning her head too much to the left she raises her eyes to acknowledge him. The sun has just set, perhaps three minutes before he came in, so he missed it. She was trying to find a way of arranging blocks of text so that the narrative would run in every direction. Like a magic number square, where each line of figures adds up to the same total. She drew out a grid to arrange the texts on a sheet of A0-sized paper on the table, and then printed out outlines of pages as she wrote them. She set herself a six-hour limit and the deadline passed with the end of daylight.

'Do you mind that I regress into a drooling idiot in your presence?' he says. 'I could hold myself together better but I enjoy the pleasure of surrender. Please let me know if it's becoming tiresome and I'll be a bit more suave.'

'Suave is for twats who induce brain spasm with their dull and relentless intelligent observations,' she retorts. 'I spit on your suave.'

Jane's flat from memory. It is on the sixth floor of a council block. As you come in the front door of the flat there is a poster on the wall facing you. It is a picture of Curtis Mayfield when he could still walk. He has a small child on his shoulders. The hallway turns to the right and the first door off it to the left opens into the bedroom. There is a double bed, from Ikea probably, against the wall to the right. On the far wall there is a rail with clothes on it, and next to that is the window. There is some sort of bedside table or cupboard on one side of the bed, which almost certainly has a lamp on it and a radio alarm. Back in the hallway, the first door to the right is the bathroom door. Inside the bathroom to your left is the washbasin, white porcelain. In front of you is the bath, along the wall, and to the right the toilet. They are both also white, the bath enamelled metal. Resting on the side of the bath is a thing for scraping the hard skin off your feet.

Opposite the bathroom door is the door to the second room, which Jane calls her study. Against the right-hand wall as you enter is a table from Ikea, with an Amstrad computer on it. To the right of the table is a filing cabinet and to the left a bookshelf. The room invariably has the look of somewhere that is in the middle of being used, rather than a place where everything has been tidied up and put away.

The door next to the bathroom takes you into the kitchen. The work surface is an L shape starting to the right of the door (there is a cupboard here where there was a fire that started when the water heater was left on, which for some unknown reason was dangerous) and then running along the wall in front of you to the sink. Next to the sink is a bit more work surface, and then a cooker. At the end is the fridge, which is tall and white, and has something magnetic stuck on the front. On the work surface to the right of the sink is an orange squeezer with six handles like a satellite. Opposite the fridge is a cupboard. There is a window at the far end, and there is a folding table attached to the wall opposite the work surface. Opposite the kitchen is the living room.

They get into her car and she drives. The guest house has been booked but it is hard to find. There is a low fake stone wall and a fake rustic sign, but Yew Tree Farm is not a farm. She hesitates, stopping the car in the road by the entrance, and looks at him.

'Have you got the fear?' he asks.

'Yes. I don't think I like it.'

'We can go somewhere else if you like...'

She turns into the driveway anyway, and drives slowly

towards the house. It is a bungalow. She stops the car. 'It's not right.'

'Shall we run away?' he asks. A woman appears outside the bungalow. One hand rests on her hip; with the other she beckons them on. It is too late to run. They continue to the house. The fake farm offers two double rooms, one of which is occupied by a fat salesman. The other is freshly made up for them.

'We're going to have to kill her,' he says, and she nods happily. 'We'll have to kill him as well...' She smiles with delight. '...and make it look like they killed each other.'

'Give us a squeeze,' she says.

The following morning they speed away from the crime scene and stick a Bruce Springsteen tape on to make it feel like a movie.

He tells her a story.

'It was five a.m. and we had just got into the early morning bar, after sitting out on a bridge over a canal for three hours playing stupid word games and drinking grappa like saps with nowhere else to go. Then Richard said, "Let's go to San Marco, there'll be no one else there, it'll be great, completely empty." We followed him out into the dawn sunlight. As the square came into view we saw some people in the centre. There were three women running in a circle, they were naked and waving colourful translucent fabric. There were lights and cameras, operated by men with beards and ponytails. Any other time I would be happy to see naked people cavorting, but on this occasion the idea of seeing the square free of tourists had been withdrawn, corrupted, besmirched, and I turned away. Then Richard walked towards the circling figures like he was hypnotised. It was the last we saw of him that day.'

'That's a funny story, lover,' she says, 'but I missed the ending. You would have been happy but what?'

Paul's house from memory. Paul lives on a large suburban housing estate close to a medium-sized town. The front door has glass panels. To the right as you enter is the staircase; passing this you enter the main living room, which is also the dining room. You see the back of the sofa; there is a fireplace to the right and a television next to it which can be viewed from the sofa or one of the two armchairs that face it. The stairs go above the dining area. On the left-hand wall is a sideboard. The room is carpeted, and there is almost certainly some sort of pattern on the carpet. The far wall has French windows leading on to the garden. If you turn right as you enter through the front door you can go into the kitchen, and beyond that is a spare bedroom. It is attached to the garage.

As they drive back towards the city that evening the sun dissolves and the lights of potential stopovers become increasingly inviting. They circle the car park of a shitty hotel – for reps and practical people – and he hops out to enquire, returning a couple of minutes later unhappy with the expense and the attitude. They do not have many chances and if it is not right then the night is squandered. Their crimes are following them. Pursuing them.

They stand outside a guest house and she telephones to book a room, giving them time to think before returning half an hour later, when they are greeted by a middle-aged person who was once a boy and would now, perhaps, like to be thought of as a woman, but mainly does not care what others think. They pay the thirty-five pounds between them, feeling very conspicuous, and are shown up to the room. They take in the heart-shaped pillows and teddy bears. He collapses next to the bed, resting his head on the orange covers.

'I think they deserve to live,' she offers. He raises his head and nods and smiles and they embrace.

She has been reading his text messages when he was not in the room. She found out about the lunches in secret restaurants, and the tokens of affection he had plundered from their past to nourish his new liaison. She made a note of the name and number and discovered the address.

'Helen?'

'Yes...but, I don't believe I...'

'I'm Jane, Paul's wife. Don't worry, it's not what you think.'

'Well. This is unexpected... Will you come in?'

'Thank you.'

'Please, sit down. Would you like a drink? I have gin, some not very nice port, whisky...'

'A small whisky please.'

'Scotch or Bourbon?'

'Bourbon for a change.'

'Good choice.'

'Sorry, I should explain.'

'Please...'

'Paul has told me about you. I was curious to meet you. Do you mind if I smoke?'

'Not at all. Just curious?'

'Yes. Paul has many affairs. Mostly they don't last long. This one is special. You are privileged.'

'And...you don't mind?'

'No, no. I'm not a girly girl. I don't believe in monogamy. Paul and me, you see, we have an arrangement. We are free from each other. We tell each other everything.'

'Well... That's quite a relief. Thank you for coming to see me. It's always a concern, with a married man. I do worry about families and people talking. I don't want to cause trouble.'

'How long have you been seeing him? Do you have a light, by the way?'

'Sorry, no. I don't smoke at home anymore. Not so long. Three weeks maybe.'

'How did you two meet? You don't mind me asking?'

'I can't really object. It was quite simple. I went to a movie, a matinée. He sat near me. I sensed a kind of... availability. The film was a bit shit, we both moaned about it afterwards.

We went for a drink, and then we came back here. It wasn't complicated. Happens all the time.'

'Yes. I see. And it's going well?'

'What, you mean...?'

'You're pleased with him?'

'Well, he's lovely, of course. You know what I like about him? His softness. He's not at all angry or tense. I see why now, you haven't cultivated his sense of guilt.'

'No, no. Not at all. We've been married for eleven years. We have a son.'

'Yes, he told me. You're very lucky. I was married to a horror. A total bastard. Paul's a good egg. Another drink?'

'Thanks. This is a nice flat. A good size.'

'Yes. There's this room with the kitchen. The room through there is for guests. A bathroom, lots of cupboards...'

'Could I see? I like to see where things go on.'

'Are you a bit pervy?'

'No. It's just for my own amusement?'

'You can see this bedroom is not huge. I'm not in love with Paul. I don't fall in love easily. Do you like that? Paul gave it to me.'

'We bought it in Antwerp. But why give it to you?'

'Just to please himself? He said you'd forgotten. Will we go back through?'

'I can't do this anymore.'

'What's that? Are you alright?'

'It's just my head.'

'Is it the whisky? Do you want to sit down.'

'I'll be OK.'

'Do you want an Aspro? You look terrible.'

'I know.'

Helen turns to get a painkiller. Jane's eyes find the tall ceramic duck standing on the floor. She picks it up and brings it down heavily on the back of Helen's head. And again. Helen falls to the floor without emitting a sound. Blood puddles.

In the restaurant they drink happy-hour champagne and eat a plate of oysters. On the next table a mother and daughter are talking about them. They order some more seafood and the waitress asks whether they had a nice time the previous day. They hesitate and nod and smile. Then they remember it is 15 February today. They gouge out shellfish with the special implements and shove it into one another's mouths. After a minute he says:

'I should have told her I was at home with my wife and family.'

'We might as well have a big sign that says "We are on the run".'

'But we're both going home after this.'

'Tell me a story.'

'I saw a beautiful woman in the Czartoryskich museum. She was small, with brown eyes. I kept her in sight for a while, and later she was standing in front of me buying postcards. I followed her out and wanted to tell her I loved her, but I was called back into the museum as she walked away. I used my clearly distressed condition to excuse myself from the afternoon's activities, but instead of heading home to rest I set off in pursuit of the subject of my transference. I walked breathlessly down Ulica św. Jana towards Rynek Główny, dripping sweat from the heat and humidity, and the glowering confusion in my brain. The clouds thickened and I scanned the crowd for a familiar movement. I heard birds singing on the other side of the square and walked in their direction. A woman was selling ceramic bird-shaped whistles; filled with water, they imitated birdsong, till the water dripped out like tears from their eyes. My ersatz lover was buying one and the woman made her try it, gesturing and grinning and a bit crazy. Slow drops of warm rain began to splash on the ground. The crowd ebbed from the centre of the square to gather beneath café canopies and arcades. Lightning flashed above the cathedral and I gawped at the silvery trails for too long before turning back to look where my love no longer was.'

'That's a lovely story, my sweet,' she says, 'but I missed the ending. You looked at the lightning and then, what?'

Helen's flat from memory. The flat is maybe on the fourth floor of the building, which is a converted warehouse. The door opens into the hallway. To the right at the end is the bathroom. In the bathroom as you enter in front of you is the toilet and to the right of this is the washbasin. Next to that the bath, occupying the right-hand wall. On the wall above the washbasin is a large mirror. Behind you next to the door and above the bath is a towel radiator with one small towel on it. Back in the hallway the next door is the door to Helen's bedroom. Then there is a room which Helen says is for guests, it has sliding doors to connect it to the living room. The hall also leads into the living room, which includes a kitchen area where food can be prepared while looking out into the room, when entertaining guests. In the fridge there is only soya milk, no dairy milk. There is herbal tea and some instant coffee. In front of the kitchen area is a sofa.

'Hey, sweetheart, is the sun shining into your heart? I was drunk last night and seemed to be almost as tired as you were. It began to numb my feelings a little, which at least made the pain of leaving a fraction easier.'

'But what were you going to explain to me later?'

'I don't remember, I'm sorry, did it seem very important? When did I say it?'

'Shortly after the rendition of marsupial sounds. You came over all forlorn, said that line then squeezed me so hard I didn't dare pursue it. Later I was enjoying you too much to ask again.'

'Maybe you read more into my shallow utterances than I can live up to. I have nothing profound to contribute to the understanding of our predicament. I'm hanging on to my life by the fingernails. If I fall I'll try not to land on you. I'm sorry,

I don't think I can be very useful to you.'

'People are not meant to be useful, you fucking idiot! Plumbers... getting your car fixed... you can always pay to get that stuff done. But the people you know are not for being useful. That's not why you want to hang around with someone.'

'Hello.'

'Hello, this is the police station. There's been an incident; we need to speak to you.'

'Erm, what is it, I mean, where did you get my number?'

'Your number is in the mobile phone of someone we are looking for. A woman called Helen Pegala. A writer.'

'Helen Peg... I don't really know her much.'

'When did you last see her?'

'Well, I mean, we met at an opening, exchanged a few texts... But that was weeks ago, I haven't seen her since.'

'I'd like you to let us know if you hear from her again. She's missing.'

'Missing? Do you think something has happened to her?'

'We don't know at the moment. If you can help us...'

'Of course, if I hear anything I'll let you know.'

He goes back to the room where he left her putting together her narrative squares.

The campsite is not how it was described to them. There are lots of families with children. The farmer who owns it says they have some spaces because of last night's storm, which blew away some badly pitched tents. They find a space next to a family who, they conclude, are descended from a long line of root vegetables. Leaving their tent they tread cautiously down the steep path to the beach, where they drink whisky and play snakes and ladders on a giant board they draw in the sand. The ladders are made with sticks and the snakes with seaweed.

'They can never leave this place,' he decides.

'I was thinking the same.'

They kiss and go back up to the campsite.

In the morning no sounds come from the next tent. They leave hurriedly, knowing this trail cannot be covered as easily as last time. In the car they listen happily to the Shangri Las tape she bought at the charity shop.

'One more story?'

'We went into the Bar Las Vegas, a hexagonal shack a hundred metres from the roadside, on the route south out of the city. It was late afternoon, and we were tired from walking all day. We drank Cinzano and cherry soda. There was loud music on the jukebox, and outside the local urchins began to dance. We went out to join them, hoping they might teach us the steps. One of them took Alessandro by the hand and they started to dance together, Alessandro following easily as the boy showed him where to put his feet and how to swing his shoulders with the right movement. Then a bus appeared on the road. It stopped to let someone off as the boys scrambled to pick up their belongings and run towards the stop. The bus began to pull away, kicking up dust in the hazy sunlight, into the faces of the pursuers. We wanted to run too, but our legs wouldn't carry us. The bus slowed and, one by one, they jumped aboard, leaving us alone and bereft.'

'That's a sweet story, babycakes, but I missed the ending. The bus started to leave and then what?'

She screws up the sheets of paper on the table and stuffs them into the bin. The story makes no sense, it has no satisfying arc; the characters, though there are few, all seem to meld into one when set out in this configuration. She phones him to see whether he has scouted the next liaison.

'It's hideous, like a service station only without the promise of adventure.'

'Then let's sack it, sugar.'

'Will we run away soon?'

The cave from memory. You have to climb over the rocks on the beach, and then you see the cave. It is not endlessly deep, but as dusk begins it is dark and a bit forbidding, and provides a lot of shelter. As you walk in you can see there is light from the top at the back, where a crack opens up to let in water and sun. The water trickles down and through. You sit on rocks and with driftwood and dried stalks you can light a fire which, because of the shelter and the draught from the opening above, flames up swiftly and easily. The smoke impregnates your clothes and the light outside dims to a dangerous level before you are prepared to forsake this temporary haven. But this is no hiding place; in the morning children would quickly find you.

He closes his eyes. Next morning she opens the curtains and the pale sunlight hits his eyelids. There is a knock on the front door.

'I have to go away for a while, my love,' she says. He opens his eyes and looks into hers, and knows what she has done.

THE ROAD TO NOWHERE

JON THOMPSON

Each day Fabian watched over his father's goats, grazing the scorched, ashen flank of the great grey bull. From the doorway of the small stone shelter, which had protected generations of his family from the blistering Andalusian sun, he could observe the whole sweep of the Campo la Indiana stretched out below. Today, he was watching for Marie José going to work in her battered old blue Fiat. If she turned left at the river crossing when she set out from the Venta el Puente she was heading for the clinic at Grazalema, if she turned right then her destination was the hospital in Ronda. Left and she'd be gone all day, the coast would be clear. Right and she would be back by lunchtime and at home for most of the afternoon. Fabian peered into the shadows under the distant olive trees, already shortening as the sun climbed clear of the hunched shoulders and highest point of the old bull's back. Marie José was late. He could see the car parked between the bar and Concha's new bungalow, but still there was no movement, no visible signs of life. Fabian looked at his watch. The time was coming up to eight o'clock and across the valley a steady stream of cars were climbing the zigzag road into town, the sunlight flashing on their windscreens at each turn. On a normal day, Marie José would have been ahead of this daily procession of commuters; would already have crossed the Moorish bridge high over the Guadalavine and entered the old town. On a normal day she would already be threading the dark labyrinth of narrow streets looking for somewhere to park. The boy's attention was suddenly taken by a disturbance in the herd which sent the goats spilling upwards out of the arroyo where they had been feeding contentedly for the last half-hour.

Fabian picked up his thick herdsman's staff and set off with a loping stride across the hillside, stooping from time to time to gather up pebbles as he ran. Experience told him that it was the lead male, Hechicero, up to his old tricks again, and sure enough, when he reached the dense knot of bushes at the edge of the dried-out, stony gash in the hillside, the scene confronting him was all too familiar. His aficionado father had named Hechicero after a legendary black bull that had killed three men in the ring in Seville in the 1930s, and the animal never failed to live up to its *nom de guerre*. Today, in his usual brutish fashion, the old buck was doing his best to mount a two-month-old *cabrito*, and persisting even though the kid had already collapsed under his weight. Bleats had summoned the angry mother, who was furiously biting at Hechicero's neck in a futile attempt to drive him off. Fabian's first stone was perfectly aimed, striking the tense muscle of the buck's rear end with all the force the boy could muster. But it produced only a brief pause in the old man's onslaught. One resentful sideways glance at Fabian from a baleful red eye and Hechicero resumed his frantic thrusting. Moving swiftly round to the front, the boy took aim again, this time for the crown of the old goat's head, between the horns, the place that bullfighters call the *cuna*. The first stone missed, but the second, a viciously whipped underhand, struck home with sickening force, causing the buck to rear up and scramble unceremoniously backwards on its buttocks, a bloodied, distended member still unsheathed. Now Fabian went in for the kill. Moving swiftly into the arroyo with staff flailing he made a full-frontal attack, beating the upper parts of Hechicero's forelegs, driving the buck relentlessly backwards until it turned tail and headed off across the open hillside with several of the females in hot pursuit.

Despite the urgent entreaties of its mother, the kid was still flat to the floor. Slipping his hand between its hind legs from behind, as he had seen his father do, Fabian raised it into a standing position and held it there until it began to feel its feet again. He then checked it for injuries, feeling its pelvis and running his hand along its spine, before returning it to its mother's teat. By the time the boy had reclaimed his vantage point, the blue Fiat had disappeared. Looking left and right from the old bridge he could see nothing. Already the heat haze was thickening into a golden soup swallowing up the town and turning it into a greenish-brown silhouette with uncertain edges. Fabian cursed Hechicero long and hard. He'd already marked this day down as the beginning of the worst week of his young life. Now the one promised moment of pleasure had been snatched away from him. He knew very well that they dare not risk a meeting in Marie José's place if there was any chance at all of them being found out. Five days more and Manolo would be formally engaged to the shy, rather plain girl from Arriate. Six days and his friend would be enlisted in the army and stationed at Bilboa, in the far north of the country; he had looked it up on the map. Bilboa was still in Spain, it was true, but as far as Fabian was concerned it might as well have been the far side of the moon.

Manolo was light-hearted about the prospect of their enforced separation. Then Manolo was light-hearted about everything, including the marriage deal his father, Antonio, had struck with the rich farmer from Arriate and the square-faced girl soon to become his *novia,* his wife-to-be. Manolo was even light-hearted about the sacred estate of marriage. Despite the regular chaperoned meetings with his intended and the long family discussions presided over by Concha and the sharp-featured future mother-in-law who spoke only of money, despite the solemn admonitions of the dandruff-ridden priest from Setenil, Manolo continued to laugh it all off. Glancing in Fabian's direction, he would wink and touch his nose. Like all first-born sons of the *campina* he thought himself indestructible; as enduring as the Andalusian earth upon which he trod. But Fabian knew differently. Fabian knew that marriage had the power to subdue even the most carefree spirit. He had watched his own brother change from a smiling, irrepressible, sometimes wild young man into a grave-faced, anxious adult, in the space of two short years. Marriage was only the beginning. Children would quickly follow. It was the way of things among families whose heritage was to work the soil. Children, especially male children, were as important to their existence as the land itself. An extra pair of hands. More work done. More produce to sell at the market in the Plaza Ruedo Alameda on a Saturday morning. But beyond the daily necessities of life a son represented continuity and the prospect of a comfortable old age. Fabian knew that all the rowdy old men who spent their afternoons in the shade of the great willow trees by the Venta playing cards had sons who worked the small parcels of land handed down to them by their fathers. Just as he knew that the old men with stooped shoulders, scorched, deeply fissured faces and grey crusted hands that gathered there in the evenings to drink their quarters of red wine were without male offspring. They were condemned to work the powdery soil of the *campo* until the day they dropped down dead.

Unlike Fabian, Manolo would never have to work the fields because his father had been lucky. Five years earlier, quite unexpectedly, Antonio had sold the strip of land by the banks of the Rio Guadiaro gifted to him on his marriage day by Abuelo Manolo José and bought the almost derelict Venta del Puente plus the grounds and orchards that went with it. The word on the *campo* had it that he had paid cash. A lot more cash than could possibly have come from the sale of family land. No one knew where the extra money had come from, but rumour said that Antonio had won the lottery. For a time he certainly behaved as though he had. Within a week of his registering ownership with City Hall, workmen moved in to refurbish the place. A new, stridently orange roof presaged a much grander establishment, one that was more in tune with the times. The front door opened on to an American-style bar with licked-around chromium trimmings and high stools where Antonio could hold court in the evenings with his cronies. The dining room was enlarged and what had once been the family sitting room was turned into a professional-looking kitchen for Conchita. When all this was up and running work began on an extension with a separate entrance, the subject of a great deal more speculation by the denizens of the *campo*. Most mysterious of all, after the builders departed, a pantechnicon full of black boxes and a small army of electricians had arrived from the coast. The mystery was finally solved when, one afternoon, a puce-pink neon sign was put up proclaiming to the Campo la Indiana and the world at large a brand-new entertainment venue called 'The Discotech Saigon'. Inside, a blacked-out, air-conditioned, magical world of whirling mirrors and flashing coloured lights, wrap-around sound and softly intimate furniture greeted the army of *campo* teenagers who managed to buy tickets for the opening night. An event that quickly took on all the gaiety of a small-scale carnival. Whole families arrived, from aged grandparents to babies in arms, to camp out in the grounds of the old Venta for most of the night. Prowling mothers and fathers keeping a watchful eye over their sons and daughters.

Antonio's intention for the Discotech Saigon was to ensure the future of his two children. In the case of Marie José, by providing a livelihood for her grossly over-fed, pathologically lazy husband, the ironically named Paquito. In the case of Manolo, by helping him avoid the tyranny of manual labour and an accelerated passage into the next life, a fate that had overtaken so many of the male members of Antonio's family. But more than anything else he wanted to find Manolo work suited to his outgoing temperament to prevent him high-tailing it for the coast.

For Manolo, it was not an ideal arrangement. Although he revelled in the role of host and DJ, as the first and only son he had for a long time felt oppressed by the suffocating attention of his mother. The advent of the Discotech Saigon had tied him even more closely to home. By now he had begun to think of military service as his first realistic chance of escape and marriage as a way of making escape permanent.

Some days, seated outside the stone shelter high on the hillside, Fabian had the illusion that he could see and know everything in his past and his future existence. It was as if the limits of the *campo* were the limits of his life. If he looked north towards the Seville road he could see the bleached, crumbling façade of the church in which he was christened nearly sixteen years ago. If he looked south he could follow the Algeciras road, the road to nowhere as the locals called it, until it disappeared out of sight to plunge in company with the single-track railway line down through deeply cut wooded valleys heading for the coast. It was the same route that Manolo and Flauta had taken in the Englishman's big green Mercedes that very morning, and were probably just now returning along with a boot stuffed full of contraband pornography from the coast. Fabian had been that way only once to swim in the Englishman's pool while the car was being loaded with foil-wrapped slabs of the brown stuff from Morocco for the run to Córdoba. Across the valley was the tiny schoolhouse that he had attended for six years of his life before going to the big school on the hill, and beyond that, climbing the old mule track into town, was Flauta and Maria's house, where sometimes at weekends they went to smoke *chocolato* and play cards. A little to the left was the dark and tangled mass of the old thorn tree in which each year the golden orioles came to nest and where one very dark, burning-hot, August night he'd first given himself to Manolo. Both stoned, neither of them quite knowing what they were doing or why. Wanting... wanting like mad, that is all that Fabian could remember, and the pain and the exhilaration afterwards. Faced with the knowledge of who he really was, Fabian had grown up that night. The unreal, adolescent dream of a normal life foisted upon him by his family had suddenly taken flight, leaving him split apart and raw, but strangely at ease within himself.

But Fabian's moment of self-discovery had been something quite different for Manolo. Beneath the fun-loving, the devil-may-care and the risk-taking he was just a simple Catholic soul. For him acceptance of what had occurred was not so easy.

Resurfacing from his drug-induced sleep the next morning, he was unable to shake himself free of the idea that somehow he had transgressed his true nature. Remorse had begun to eat away at him. And self-disgust quickly followed. He had taken advantage of Fabian's feelings; experienced something close to ecstasy through the younger boy's body and in the process the seed of a most disturbing confusion had been sown and was already beginning to germinate. Intense physical pleasure had brought an extraordinary sense of release, as if all the pent-up frustration of his teenage years had been dispelled in a matter of minutes and seconds. This new feeling of well-being would not be denied. He was not – he felt sure – that unspeakable thing which, according to the Christian Brothers who had schooled him, meant swift and certain damnation. He remembered well, however, the venom with which the otherwise liberally minded Brother Thomas had spat out the word sodomite. As he recalled, there was no offer of redemption for this. At best an infinite emptiness; at worst the harrowing of hell. Like so many young Catholics, he found the idea of moral jeopardy both terrifying and exciting in equal measure, but on this occasion it was the fear which got the upper hand. Manolo had made the decision to freeze Fabian out; to treat him with complete indifference until feelings had cooled and reason could prevail.

Fabian allowed his gaze to sweep the far side of the valley past the long, white-painted, almost ship-like silhouette of the Estanzia Gonzalez de Los Rios where they bred the high-stepping silver Arabs and trained them to perform in the riding schools of the southern sierras. Following on from the line of its roof to the ridge behind, he allowed his eyes to rest for a moment on the single-storey house where he lived with his mother and father, two older sisters and his younger brother Rafa, before following the steeply meandering track down the field to the grounds of the Venta, where Manolo lived with his family. Contemplation of this faint but freshly trampled umbilicus joining their two lives together brought mixed emotions. For the past five years the field had been planted with sunflowers. A nodding congregation of tall stems and flat, yellow-fringed faces in early summer which turned into a brittle, spiky black and burnt-ochre forest for harvesting in late August. This year, once ploughing was over, it had lain fallow, exposing the spot where what Fabian still thought of as his 'thorn-tree week', his season in purgatory, had reached its emotional climax. For a week Manolo had barely spoken to him – had avoided meeting his gaze even – and as they worked the bar together on the Saturday night, with Manolo acting the coldly superior boss-man, an angry exchange had taken place between them. Lashing out wildly, Fabian had thrown a half-full beer can at his friend, drenching him in beer, striking him in the mouth and drawing blood. Manolo had chased him into the sunflower field; flooring him violently from behind, pushing his mouth and nose deep into the dusty Andalusian soil. Their tearful, night-long reconciliation had happened somewhere there, among the scratching, snapping stalks. They had never before felt the need to confess their deepest feelings to each other and that night, squatting down among the sunflowers, each was desperately seeking reassurance from the other. Finding the right words had not been easy, but gradually Manolo had managed to convey something of the panic and fear that had overtaken him, and Fabian the urgency of his desire. By dawn each had been able to grant some kind of halting absolution to the other.

Somehow they arrived at a very grown-up arrangement. They would have sex with each other but there was to be nothing beyond that. Manolo was insistent. There was to be no emotional commitment other than the sex itself, and certainly no mention of the future. Outside the time they spent together they would each pursue their own lives. Manolo was free to continue his futile efforts to get one of the good Catholic daughters of the *campo* into bed and Fabian was free to look wherever his fancy took him. Except that for the younger boy there was nowhere else to look: not close at hand anyway.

Manolo revelled in the arrangement from the start. He was

not, as he put it, when communing with himself, sinning in his heart. But for Fabian it was more difficult. Naively, perhaps, he had started out imagining that he was in love with Manolo and as long as that lasted he had been forced to pretend otherwise for fear of scaring his friend off. By now, though, the love thing had gone away and only the lust remained. But that still fired up his blood like a drug. Giving himself over to the burning presence of another's body, their sweating limbs moving into and against his, and the ecstasy he experienced in the other's climax produced in him a feeling of completion and a sense of wholeness that he could achieve in no other way. The thought of Manolo gone from his life – Manolo far away, in Bilboa, or afterwards married and living in Arriate – on occasions such as now, when he allowed himself to think about it, filled him with a feeling of utter despair and dread. The overwhelming force of his desire could still scare him, but as long as Manolo was there he had some means of release.

Fabian's attention was caught and held suddenly by a movement in the valley below, just before the rising ground leading up on to the first ridge of the sierras. Squinting into the sunlight, he could just make out the shape of a horse and rider traversing the deeply shadowed scrubland, heading for the old mule track that wended its way through the mountains to the coast west of San Martine. It was a favourite morning ride for the stable lads from the Estanzia. Once on the plateau they could give the horses their heads before bringing them helter-skelter down the scree slope on to the Algeciras road for a brisk gallop home past the Venta del Puente. But this was no stable boy. As the horseman emerged from the valley's shade, outlined against the whited-out landscape beyond, Fabian recognised the haughty carriage and elegant dress.

For more than a week now, following a chance meeting on the old road into town, Eduardo, the youngest son of the Gonzalez family, who was mostly away at school and appeared at the Estanzia only in the summer months, had been in Fabian's thoughts. He had even wormed his way into his fantasy life, where nightly he performed prodigious sexual feats. It had started with a sideways glance and an unmistakable moment of mutual recognition. Fabian and Manolo had been zigzagging their way up the steep and loosely rutted road in the Venta's antiquated open-topped Land Rover with its snarling, clapped-out diesel, when, rounding the bend beyond Flauta's house, they had come face to face with Eduardo Gonzalez de los Rios mounted on a big and very lively grey stallion, standing some sixteen or seventeen hands, heading in the opposite direction. At the sound of the engine, the horse started to bridle and prance sideways across the road, threatening to throw his young rider. Manolo pulled over and turned off the engine to let them pass. When horse and rider came abreast of the Land Rover, Eduardo had halted the horse and raised his hat in salute. The gesture was directed at Manolo, but he had been looking at Fabian. There had been something electrifyingly open, even blatant, about that gaze. In an instant, the Gonzalez boy had undressed Fabian with his eyes and Fabian had returned the compliment. He felt the tug of the other boy's desire as surely as he knew that Eduardo Gonzalez had felt his. Fabian watched the horse and rider's progress along the ridge, at last seeing him pause and genuflect to the shrine of St Ursula at its summit before dropping out of sight.

He looked at his watch. It was gone midday. Glancing around, he saw that the goats were spread out across the mountainside and grazing peacefully. Soon he would be relieved by Rafa coming from school, and then he would be free to go in search of Manolo, who had promised to be back from the coast by the time he reached the Venta.

Fabian heard the seesaw sound of the police sirens at the same moment that he caught sight of the bright yellow-and-green school bus speeding along the Seville road. It would stop to set down the *campo* children in the usual place, just out of sight. By the time he had identified Rafa in his red T-shirt moving along the track across the widow Patracinia's field, the police cars had emerged from the built-up part of the town.

Three of them travelling at speed with an ambulance trailing along behind, threading round the hairpin bends to the floor of the valley. To his great surprise, at the bottom of the hill where the main road divided east and west, they took the small loop back on to the Algeciras road and headed in the direction of the *campo*. Once off the main road the cars were swallowed up in a cloud of white dust like a miniature whirlwind which streamed down past the Venta at breakneck speed to disappear eventually where the valley swung sharply away to the left. It was the route that, all things being equal, Manolo and Flauta would be driving at that very moment, and Fabian experienced a sudden pang of unease; an inexplicable chill, which sent a shiver through his body and raised goose bumps on his bare arms. He scanned the distant grounds of the Venta for a sight of the green Mercedes, but it was not to be seen. There was no reassurance to be had there. With some difficulty, he tried to push the dreadful thought that had just entered unbidden into his head to the back of his mind. Another ten minutes and Rafa would be breasting the hill, shrilly whistling a greeting as he always did.

As usual, he heard his brother before he saw him, and by the time the youngster came into view, Fabian was already bounding down the mountainside, shouting a greeting and an apology as he ran. He half tumbled and fell down the banking on to the road by the dried-up bed of the Guadalavine, crossed over and plunged into the ravine, first picking his way through the litter of boulders brought down by the river's winter flood, before scrambling up the far bank to take the short cut across the field. By the time he reached the Algeciras road he could already hear the strident siren of the returning ambulance, and before he could reach the bridge it had sped past him, the driver honking his horn at Fabian to make sure he stayed out of the way. His worst fears were realised when, even though he was still a good fifty paces away from the gate, he heard Maria screaming. He started to run again, and the first person he saw when he entered the yard was Manolo's father, Antonio, standing, shoulders hunched, by Marie José's car, which had been abandoned with its door open, the engine still running. Fabian tried speaking to him but got no reply; just an empty, uncomprehending look. The bar was deserted and in complete disarray. Tables had been overturned, chairs upended, there were broken glasses and smashed crockery everywhere. The screaming and wailing were coming from Concha's kitchen beyond. Fabian pushed through the bead curtain that separated the two spaces to catch a glimpse of a distraught Maria rolling around on the tiled floor with Concha bending over trying to comfort her. Marie José spotted Fabian and quickly crossed the room to lead him back into the bar.

'Flauta's dead,' Marie José whispered, 'a car crash at the Benajuan bridge.'

'And Manolo?'

'Injured... he's been taken to the infirmary.'

'Is it serious?'

'I don't think so.'

'He'll be all right, then?'

'They were side-swiped by a lorry on the driver's side. Flauta was killed instantly... Manolo was thrown clear. Do you know what they were up to? The place was crawling with police.'

'They were doing a job for the Englishman.'

'What kind of a job?'

'Video tapes, I think.'

'Pornography?'

Fabian had learned from Flauta never to confirm or deny.

'I guess.'

'You guess?'

The disbelief in Marie José's voice was undisguised. Fabian turned and walked away.

Once outside, he switched off the ignition in the old blue Fiat and slammed the car door shut before taking Antonio gently by the arm and leading him across the yard to find his favourite seat under the willow trees. Neither spoke. There was nothing to be said. Fabian was at a loss to explain the way he was feeling even to himself, never mind to someone of Antonio's generation. After the initial shock a strange calmness descended on him. The fear of missing out on a last afternoon with Manolo hard inside him had gone, leaving him strangely elated. It was as if the power that the older boy had wielded over him had finally been dispersed. He patted Antonio's hand in silent commiseration before walking out of the yard and heading for home.

Fabian became aware of the horse's hoofs sounding on the bridge behind him for the first time as he turned the corner to climb the hill towards the Estanzia Gonzalez de los Rios. The Gonzalez boy overtook him at the schoolhouse, paused just up ahead of him and, as Fabian caught up, reached down and pulled him up to straddle the horse bareback behind him.

UNDERWOOD

JANICE
KERBEL

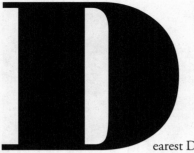earest Dearest,

I dreamed about you last night! It was wonderful. The wind was up and the light low – we were together on a great plain somewhere, probably the west, Wyoming maybe? We were so in love!!! You were chasing deer as they came down from the hills; I was sitting on a large red rock eating figs. The deer were teasing you with their swift moves and jumps, taunting you to step like them in perfect chorus, a hilarious act from some silent musical. I laughed and laughed till it hurt, we both seemed so clumsy in their presence. Then it started to rain and we started to run, but there was no cover and we darted back and forth in the brush, just the two of us now, searching, growing frantic but laughing, I remember the sound of us laughing the whole time. Then the sky suddenly went black as if night got impatient and the stars filled the sky and began, maybe slowly, maybe quickly, to descend; as they grew closer they started to join, forming an illustrious blanket of glitter above us, keeping us dry and warm and radiant while the wet and the cold and the dark surrounded us.

Then I was awake. I sensed you'd been here. I was confused and uncertain but I knew it was you and I wanted to stop you – this part of you, this shadow that keeps appearing – from dissolving into the dark so heartlessly. I felt sure at first that I could find my way to you, that I could make you stay, but then night overtook and the dream, as always, subsided.

When I woke again, this time to morning, I felt oddly refreshed, as I still do even now, hours later. It wasn't just seeing you, hearing the sound of you laugh and your voice. It is almost as if I somehow still <u>feel</u> you, not just on my skin, but in my veins, in my blood. It's as if when you touched me in the dream, as we ran for shelter and you put your hand on my arm, something coursed through me, something that remains – still, this very second – some kind of wonderful ionic force that breathes somewhere within me. It envelops and fills me, and I am alive with you again.

I will move carefully today, coveting this funny lovely presence of you. I'll glide through every minute more slowly, more buoyantly, and I will do all I can to make my dear sweet you last, just as I long as I can.

Forever x

✤

Sweet Sweet Darling Dear,
Alone at last. It's been days on days on days, and I have craved this second wildly. I felt it creep closer with every tiny change of the weather, I tasted it in the lifting morning fog, I smelt it in the evening air and I swear I even saw it in the clouds. Its approach seemed an endless retreat and now, finally, here it is – sweet bliss, I am at last alone!!!

Guess where I am – no, never mind – I'll tell you! I'm sitting at a table, a long wooden one out front beneath a canopy of grapes, before all my favourite trees (plums! limes! quince!). Butterflies – or moths maybe, I can never tell – are everywhere, and I can hear the birds but can't really see them from this exact spot. The sky is going Neapolitan, melting from pink to white then yellow, with a narrow dark band of heavy blue carrying the weight of it all before disappearing into whatever once grew in that old field. Corn, I think. Or maybe sunflowers. Who knows, who cares!! It smells hot. It's been so so wonderfully hot.

My shoulders are tight and itch from the sun.

Did you know that if you add forty to the number of chirps a cricket makes in thirteen seconds you get an accurate reading of the temperature in degrees Fahrenheit? I'm trying to do it now as I write to you, but I keep losing count.

I have so many questions for you!!!

Do you realise we have never shared mussels and chips outdoors at midnight when there's been a honey moon in the sky? And that we have never floated down a river together on our backs holding hands? I have never ever sat on the handlebars of your bike as you cycle down a steep country lane, nor have I ever touched you on the small of your back while you remove a splinter, or do your taxes. I'd like to swim across a lake with you. I'd like to sit on a rope swing that you build for me. I'd like to put daisies in your hair and watch lightning carve up the sky.

My swallow, forgive me. I don't know what happened. It's late now, not even the same day. I sometimes think that by writing you I can make time stop. Things always feel arrested during these moments when it's just you and me and we're cradled in this warm still world. I wish it would last. I wish it would just go on and on and on. I wish it would always be summer.

Spotted the last plum this morning, it was perfectly ripe. It was hidden casually in between two leaves, camouflaged in golden light. It seemed somehow wrong to take it, though its time had clearly come. Breathe deep now, as I do... When the spirit moves, my darling, I will write again.

Until then, my heart.

♣

Dear —

It's grey and wet and windy, and I can't get you off my mind. I woke up thinking of you. I got dressed, brushed my teeth and ate breakfast thinking of you. I rushed into day thinking of you, I walked down the street thinking of you, I sat in the park thinking of you and I missed my bus thinking of you. With every gust of wind I think of you. I wait with anticipation for each breeze to come blow you out of me, and then I foolishly catch myself ducking to avoid it. You are my most coveted ache. I am stormy and I crave sleep. Maybe it is all this yellow and gold. My love is delicate and ferocious and all yours. Do with it as you might. Goodbye. Goodnight.

    ps. Forgive me, I am not myself.

Dearest,

I cannot believe it's that time.

    The year has passed so suddenly, so confidently. I'm only just easing myself into last winter, still waiting on summer – how is it I've been so hopelessly eclipsed? If we each grew wiser at this same racing pace, all would seem somehow fairer, kinder. But here we are, both of us just the same bit older, yet again.

    I have thought of writing so many times. I have wondered what to say and how to say it. Wondered where you are and what you dream of. How you may have changed in the most indescribable, infinitesimal, most wonderful ways. Now, with your intangible attention at long last before me, I find myself familiarly lost.

    There are so many wishes I have for you this year. So many yearnings, so many hopes and while, yes, some regrets, it is mostly this insatiable hunger for your happiness I hold on to, lovingly nurtured with each passing season, each passing year.

If only such thoughts could find words. If only they would, the touch of them would cascade and caress you – your hair, your skin, your lips – and not this old, faithless page in the dwindling afternoon light, another day come and gone.

It's dark now, I should go.

Merry Christmas, my darling. And a peaceful new year.

Always.

BOB

**DAVID
BATCHELOR**

If Donald looked out of his bedroom window, he could see down on to the pavement below and along the street a few metres either way. But if he pressed his head up against the wall and looked to the right, he could just see past the rest of the terrace, past the lamp posts, past the rows of parked cars, past the postbox on the corner and as far as the row of black-painted railings on the edge of the small park that he had never visited. Donald looked out of his window a lot, but he wasn't really sure whether or not this helped him in his work. He was well aware that writing a book was a fragile and complicated process and, for a couple of years now, on and off, Donald had been working on it, and working on anticipating and minimising any possible distractions. In terms of actual finished words in the right order on the page he hadn't got that far, but Donald could nevertheless feel the book progressing. He had dozens of notes and a more or less continuous flow of ideas, and he felt absorbed in the project even when he was also frustrated by it, which was quite a lot of the time. When he got frustrated was when he looked out of the window a lot, which was absorbing. When he was absorbed in it he still looked out of the window quite a lot, which was also absorbing, and carried less risk of disappointment later on.

It was during one of his looking-out-of-the-window episodes, quite early on in his book-writing period, that Donald first noticed Bob, not that he knew who Bob was, back then. But he saw this man who became Bob: an old man, tall, thin, grey haired and balding and a bit stooped, loose brown cords and a belt, a nondescript grey shirt and, most noticeably for some reason, a green sun visor held on his head by a piece of no-longer-white elastic. Not that any of this was what made Donald first notice Bob, or pay attention to him, or remember him. Just about everyone you see on the street is moving: either walking from somewhere to somewhere else, or getting in or out of a car, or posting a letter or doing something that doesn't involve them being there for more than a few seconds at a time. The thing about Bob was that he was stationary and could be there for hours at a time. Standing still on the pavement by the park railings to the far right of Donald's window-restricted field of vision; always in the same place, always in *exactly* the same place, always looking in the same direction, always doing the same thing. And the same stationary thing that Bob was doing all the time? He was painting a picture. Donald thought, Jesus Christ, when did you last see anyone do *that*? Did *anyone* actually still do that? Surely no one does that any more, not in London, not in a *city*. But there he was standing there with a wooden easel and a board clamped on it and there he was painting a picture.

The first sentence: 'Sarah and Jack's daughter was born on September the twenty-second weighing three and a half kilos, fifty-five centimetres long and eighty-three years old.'

The idea was simple but its implications were immeasurable. This is a world where everyone is born knowing the time and date of his or her death. So many kilos, so many centimetres, so many years. Donald hadn't yet worked out how exactly the child's deathday would be known, probably through a blood test or something, and that might require a bit of research, but this is how the book would begin and this is what it would be about. How life would be different, practically and morally different, in a universe where death was an event that could be entered in a diary. Tuesday, 22 September, two thousand and something: deathday. Bob wasn't there that day. But Donald reckoned he had seen him at least twenty times altogether and he had begun to notice some other things. For instance, Bob always wore the same clothes, he always put his easel in the exact same place, and he always carried a yellow plastic carrier bag with him which he always hung on the railing beside him. The bag was probably for his brushes, palette, rags and things. Maybe sandwiches and a drink too, but Donald never saw Bob eat or drink anything. In fact it was difficult to see Bob do much because Donald's view was blocked by the big board on the easel and all there was left to see was Bob's legs and the top of his head and the visor.

Two or three hours at a time was average, although Donald couldn't be certain as he didn't remember ever seeing Bob arrive or leave. He was just there when he was there and then after a while he wasn't there any longer. But when he was there he was always right up close to his easel as if he were having an intense conversation with it. Painting. Probably. Or eating, possibly. Donald often thought about food when he was writing. Or rather he thought about what was in the kitchen and what was or might be in the fridge, and on what shelf and how much of it and when it was lunchtime. He thought a good title for the book might be *The Deathday Party*.

It was a book of ideas although it wouldn't have a subtitle or anything. It was a meditation on death in the form of a novel. *Happy Deathday* was an option for the title but today *The Deathday Party* was winning on account of it having a less jaunty feel to it. How would we lead our lives differently if we knew the day they would end from the very beginning? Not just a few special people who have weird illnesses but everyone, just like everyone knows the day they were born. Although not everyone *does* know the day they were born, Donald realised, like those withered old people in remote tribes you see on TV sometimes, they don't, they're described as being 'about' a hundred and ten. And in another way it is something we all have to take on trust from our parents, when we were born; and then it's odd that no one ever seems to question it as we question just about everything else we get told by our parents. What if they were lying? This might be a sub-plot. Bob looked about seventy, a bit of a loner, at least during the day, at least when he was painting, if that was what he was doing behind his board. That he was definitely doing something Donald could tell from the head movements and things, and it probably was painting, he decided. Although...

Once Donald saw a woman walking along the street towards Bob. Long, straight dark hair, late twenties or thereabouts, he saw her smile an indulgent smile when she noticed the easel and the old man. As she got nearer, the woman slowed down very slightly and glanced around to see Bob's work. Then something strange happened: the woman's head gave a little jolt of surprise, her smile vanished, she picked up her pace and moved off quickly without looking back, as if she had just remembered some really urgent business up the road. Yes, that was strange, and obviously Donald would have to check out Bob's activities for himself. But this would mean interrupting his regime and he was reluctant to do that. Writing required discipline and structure, and that meant not leaving the flat on writing days, not going to the shops and not buying a paper, at least not between ten in the morning and four in the afternoon, which were the hours meant for writing. And when in the flat not watching the TV or listening to the radio, and not going on to the Internet, or flicking through old magazines, or putting CDs in alphabetical order. And not going up the road to check up on an old bloke with an easel who might be painting something weird or possibly pornographic.

Deathdays probably wouldn't be celebrated like birthdays, or maybe they would, with cakes and candles. Deathday parties – perhaps birthdays just wouldn't matter any more and deathday parties would take their place and would be the same except you would have one less candle on the cake each year. Perhaps he should go to Mexico and study the Day of the Dead, for ideas. And what if your birthday and deathday were on the same date? Maybe these people would have special powers, or they would be treated differently by everyone else, like shamans or priests, or they would be forced to leave the towns and go off into the wilderness and live off roots and berries. That was beginning to sound more like sci-fi than philosophy, but it did raise the question of when this story should be set. When he had got a few of these issues sorted Donald would feel better about breaking out of his regime and leaving his flat and checking out Bob's painting – the one that frightened young women.

Soup was best at lunchtime. In order not to have to leave the flat Donald bought five cartons of what the label said was fresh soup each weekend and kept them in the fridge. White bread didn't seem to go off as quickly as brown so he also bought a couple of loaves of that and also some cheese and a jar of pickles. He had read that Wittgenstein always had the same food for lunch every day when he was working (bread and cheese) and so did Andy Warhol (soup, obviously). That felt like OK company, especially Wittgenstein. It also made Donald feel disciplined and vaguely monastic in a way that seemed appropriate for a writer who was looking at death. Maybe he should start to do stretching exercises before he began to write each day, or meditation or t'ai chi or something. He should really clean the windows too, and dust and hoover the flat, and when he began to think about it he realised he had no memory at all of when he last used the vacuum cleaner or even of where he had put it. Under the bed was the first place he would look when he got around to it. Donald had decided at some point that Bob probably lived alone too, and probably was also very orderly. But then that might be because he knew only one old man, and he lived alone in a block of flats up the road and he kept everything very clean and tidy, and maybe he, Donald, was making unwarranted assumptions about all old men based on his limited experience of one, the one who Donald knew only because his mail, what there was of it, occasionally got delivered to the old man's address, which was a bit similar to his. Anyway, Bob still looked like a living-on-his-own-in-an-orderly-way kind of person to Donald, and he didn't feel the need to justify this thought to himself any further for the moment.

It had also occurred to Donald that the strange thing about

the scene in front of Bob's easel was that there was absolutely nothing strange or special about it, at least to him, and that it was therefore a bit odd, Bob parking his easel there, and how exact he was about where it was. A street, dead straight, parked cars on both sides, pavement, Victorian terraces, also on both sides, residents' parking signs, one 'disabled' bay, bollards, traffic lights at the T junction about two hundred metres up to the left of the flat, and the newsagent's and off-licence run by the big Asian family at the end. That was it, and there must be a million streets pretty much like it in every outlying bit of London. Well, a few thousand anyway, or at least a hundred or two. So why this one, Donald wondered – another reason to check out Bob and what was going on behind his stupid easel.

Just because you knew your deathday didn't mean you knew when you were going to die. Deathdays didn't take account of accidents. You could still walk out of your house one fine morning and get flattened by a truck. Definitely. But you wouldn't die of an illness before your given time, that was the point. You would still *get* ill and feel as if you were going to die – although you would sound kind of stupid if you said it – and you could still be crippled or mutilated or paralysed from the neck down or have your legs amputated or be left in a coma with the brain activity of a small cabbage, but you wouldn't actually *die* before your deathday. Unless, wallop, you didn't see the truck coming round the corner. Or a tree fell on your head in a hurricane, or your budget airline flight from Alicante slammed into the side of a mountain. Or you fell downstairs carrying a tray with the breakfast on it, or you got shot in the face during a hold-up at the bank. But what about suicide, could you still commit suicide? This required a bit more thought, Donald realised. Yes, you probably could but you would be punished if you tried and didn't succeed. Suicide would be regarded as a great sin, a moral crime of the first order, as bad as murder – it would be called self-murder, or selfmurder – and you would be locked up for life in a prison or a secure mental institution. And because the authorities would know exactly how much life you had left they would factor this into your sentence, somehow. Suicide would be a crime because your deathday would be seen as a unique and personal gift of the Creator which absolutely could not be questioned, and therefore suicide would be a form of theft from the One, or an intervention in the Divine Order of Things. Suicide as ultimate human arrogance, that sounded promising. But then, Donald wondered, don't a lot of religious people see it a bit like that anyway?

How much time do you have left on your clock, Bob? Tick, tock, Bob? And what do you do on the days you don't come here, Bob? Maybe he stakes out other pavements in other parts of town. Maybe they are all identical and Bob has discovered a series of doppelgänger streets. No, that's ridiculous. But Donald was becoming aware that the first thing he did every day was look to see whether Bob was there and that if he was there Donald found it a bit irritating and intrusive but if Bob wasn't there he felt a little disappointed. One of the things that irritated Donald was the apparent ease with which Bob was able to get down to his work and, once down to it, the ease with which he was able to carry on with it for hours on end without ever being distracted. And there he was standing out in the open on a street with things going on all around him all the time. This Donald began to experience as a minor but persistent threat; it felt like a kind of challenge. On the other hand he thought Bob looked pretty dumb standing there day after day with his easel and board and green sun visor and brown cords and yellow plastic bag. *In public.* Smearing thick greasy paint around like he was Van Gogh but had taken the wrong turn at Calais and ended up a hundred and however many years later on a street corner in east London rather than a wheat field in the south of France. Not that he appeared self-conscious at all or smug or pretentious, and Donald was aware he had to put a bit of effort into his sneering, and actually found it slightly comforting, seeing Bob down there painting on an old wooden board when he was indoors writing a philosophical novel on his wafer-thin titanium laptop.

Twenty fantastically beautiful young women in identical white skin-tight catsuits, all running in close formation towards Bob; their thin limbs made even thinner by the platforms and heels on their knee-length white boots; underneath their trashy blonde wigs a range of beautiful black, white and Asian features. And Bob just stands there, totally unimpressed, unmoved and apparently unaware as they gather around him like a hysterical teenage fan club and jump up and down and look over his shoulders to admire his mysterious painting. This time Donald's head jerks back as he wakes from his sitting mini-sleep. He has been doing this quite a lot recently, more than usual, but he has almost perfected the art of the upright catnap, the quick doze sitting in his chair at his desk in front of his computer. No one would notice if he did this in a library, he thought; it would look like deep concentration, a kind of zoned-in focus that you might expect of a writer immersed in his subject. And anyway dreaming and creativity were closely related, he had been told; the one could inform the other, which meant that the times when he nodded off he was still working, technically. So what about marriage? Instead of it being the generally accepted custom to marry someone born at more or less the same time, wouldn't it make sense to hook up with someone with a similar deathday or at least a similar deathyear? Maybe people would be allowed to marry only if they actually *shared* a deathday or year. That would solve a number of problems, like, for example, it would put an end to gold-digging overnight. No more bottle-blonde lap dancers marrying crusty old millionaire widower pensioners and trying to convince the world it really was about love at first sight. She could still murder him, of course, but it wouldn't be easy to get away with it and she couldn't claim 'natural causes'.

Obviously today wasn't turning out too well in the thinking and writing department. Every profound question Donald asked himself about the ethical, social, cultural and political implications of deathdays somehow reduced itself to a sleazy low-resolution image of gold-digging lap dancers, or worse. So maybe today he should check out what Bob was up to. It would take only a few minutes after all: he could leave the flat, casually cross the road, wander up the other side of the street to the right, go a couple of hundred metres beyond Bob, away from where the old man was facing, then turn around and walk back on the same side as Bob, coming up behind him and getting a look at his painting before quietly strolling past and going back into the flat. But what if Bob noticed him leave the flat, go up the road on one side, come down it on the other and go back in again? Wouldn't that look a bit strange? OK, so perhaps instead of going straight back in, he should walk past the flat and on to the shop and buy something, for authenticity. But then why didn't he just leave the flat and turn left and go straight to the shop? Why the detour, Donald? Shit. The park! He could leave the flat, turn right, walk past Bob and go for a stroll around the park. Then, after a few minutes of park strolling, something Donald realised he had never done even though the park was less than three minutes from his front door, he could saunter home past Bob and get a look at the work on his rickety easel. But how long would he have to stay in the park? Five minutes? Ten? Fifteen? What on earth would he find to do in a park for that long? Commune with nature? Oh no, please not that.

Perhaps none of this mattered, if it was true that Bob was as all-consumed in his art as he seemed to be, and after all, if he didn't notice twenty girls in twenty white catsuits, why would he pick up on one solitary writer, himself consumed in his solitary musings, huh? But then perhaps Bob only *appeared* to be so utterly lost in his work; what if he was actually monitoring everything around him and recording it all in a hidden recording device hidden in his trouser pocket with a wire running up the inside of his shirt to a mini clip-on microphone by his throat? And why exactly, why would he be doing that, Donald asked, increasingly annoyed at his increasingly tabloid-shaped thought patterns and general tendency to drift away from the higher questions of mortality that were his proper subject. OK, next time Bob's in the neighbourhood, then that's it: straight out of flat, past Bob, into park, two circuits, out of park, past Bob, into flat. Easy. Don't think about it any more.

Bob wasn't there the next day. Or the next. Question: would you be able to hide your deathday, or lie about it? And would you want to? Like some people do about their birthdays? Like young people do to make themselves older than they are and old people do to make themselves younger? What would be the equivalent for deathdays? There might be certain advantages to pretending you only had a couple of years left on the clock: for example, to gain sympathy from women and, who knows, maybe more, as pilots did during the war before they went off on missions, never knowing whether they would return. A kind of tragic attraction. Although the downside is if you were successful you might have to move house on a fairly regular basis. On the other hand hints of extreme longevity might also have some advantages, but maybe less obvious or immediate, and Donald couldn't think of any just now. What about pensions? Clearly you couldn't be expected to work until your deathday if that was before the official retirement age, that would be really cruel. So the government would have this arrangement where everyone got to retire five years before their deathday, if they wanted to. Or maybe it would be compulsory. Otherwise you could have this situation where people with nothing better to do with themselves would just drop dead at work, which would be bad for morale and possibly unhygienic. And what about life insurance? Christ, thought Donald, I've never had any insurance. Apart from my bike.

That's it. Today is the day. A deal is a deal, even when it's a deal with yourself, or especially when it's a deal with yourself. Donald felt a little like de Niro in *Taxi Driver*, in that talking-to-himself-in-the-mirror sequence that everyone imitates, generally very badly. Although unlike Travis Bickle, Donald wasn't about to go out and lay waste to half of New York.

His task was a bit less violent, a bit less apocalyptic; his task was Bob, Bob the painter. And if all went to plan it shouldn't be necessary to shoot Bob's fingers off with a Magnum or stab him in the leg with a Bowie knife; unless it was in self-defence, of course. OK: shoes, jacket, keys. And sunglasses? No, because that would draw attention to himself and because anyway it wasn't sunny. Mohican? No, this is serious, and anyway he never understood why de Niro did that in the film. Keep it simple and make it quick; this was a writing day after all, and Donald still wasn't entirely happy about this interruption to his regime. But a deal's a deal, as they say, if a little redundantly. So. Out of the flat, lock the door; down the communal stairs that always smell of disinfectant; out the front door, slam it; down the steps on to the pavement. Check for truck on the road but don't look over to Bob in case eye contact is made, which would be a disaster. Cross the road. Turn right and walk normally along pavement: not easy when concentrating so hard, difficult enough just to stay upright, in fact. Jesus, why is this so difficult? The main thing is to get past Bob without being noticed, even though he is on the other side of the road and seemingly, *seemingly*, immersed in his work. That accomplished, Donald is able to relax a little, and in the process realises his shoulders are so tense they are somewhere up by his ears. Calmer, breathing again, shoulders back down to shoulder level, now a hundred or so metres up the road, he crosses back on to Bob's side and disappears into the park entrance. He finds himself vaguely surprised by the size of this open area that he had never looked at before, but mostly he is unimpressed by his proximity to its shabby half-neglected trees and shrubs and flower beds, its balding lawn and fenced-in five-a-side pitch with yawning gaps where the fence has been pulled back to let whoever wanted to get in, in, or out, out. Donald resigns himself to being there for the next ten minutes. It passes. And, he has to admit, actually it isn't as unpleasant as he had imagined it would be. It is one of nature's less ostentatious days, generally quiet and pleasantly mild, not drawing too much attention to itself. It's OK.

Time's up. Time to get back on to the street, back to Bob. Fuck. What if Bob has gone? What a dumb waste of time and what a dumb idea to come to this dumb shitty park if by the time I get out Bob's fucked off, Donald thought. I could have stayed in and got focused and got some work done and now the day's probably fucked and there's no point in even trying to get back into it because I've broken the fucking spell. Only it's not a spell, it's a discipline; it's not about magic, it's about hard fucking graft; it's about isolation, focus and commitment. Jesus, I should never have let myself get distracted by this stupid shit about stupid fucking Bob. Oh. He's still there. Fine, good. Ha ha, time's up, Bobby boy. Here I come, Mr Painter, I'm coming up behind you.

Fifty metres. From his new perspective Donald can see things about Bob he hadn't noticed before. He's taller and thinner and more stooped than he had thought and with really rounded shoulders. And he's left-handed. But because he is so close up to his easel it's still impossible to see anything of what Bob is up to. Donald would have only a fraction of a second to study the work on the board just as he moved past Bob, right up close to him, and he wouldn't have a second chance or anything. One shot, baby, that's it. Ten metres. And Bob, bless him, Bob shifts slightly to the left and reaches across to his yellow plastic bag for something and...

And Donald sees. And he doesn't see. And he sees but he doesn't understand. And he sees that everything he had thought before about Bob's painting just wasn't right, just wasn't anywhere close, just wasn't in the same dimension. First the simple stuff, in a flash: it's not a painting, it's a drawing. Only it's not exactly a drawing but it's on a piece of paper clamped to the board with those metal clips used to hold tablecloths on tables in outdoor restaurants, one in each corner. It's not a drawing because it's made with brushes, but it's all black and grey lines and grey patches so it looks like a drawing. But that's OK, it doesn't matter that it's more of a drawing than a painting or halfway between the two, that's not important. What hits Donald and what throws him and what he can't figure is that this picture that he has watched Bob working on for God knows how long, from a distance and from the wrong side, is, well, what it isn't is a Van Gogh, that's for sure, and it certainly isn't pornographic and that's because it isn't really a picture. Well, it is but it isn't. It is because it isn't anything else but it isn't because it doesn't look like anything. In particular and the main point here is it doesn't look like the street scene that's been in front of Bob since he started putting his easel there however many months ago. But it's not not like it in the sense that it's just badly drawn or something. It's not like it because it's not like any street scene because there's no street in it and there's no scene; no cars, no postbox, no bollards or lamp posts or traffic lights or anything. No objects, no perspective, no space. And it's not that it's abstract either, or maybe it is. What it is is completely unconnected to anything. Or at least that is what it seems to be because nothing on the paper is in any way like anything in front of Bob. What it is is a large rectangular piece of white paper with a thick square outline drawn in the middle. And inside this square maybe a dozen or fifteen or twenty irregular islands and spots of grey of different shapes and sizes and a few uneven grey lines going nowhere in particular. And that's it, there's nothing else. And that would be OK, that would be fine, but it doesn't make any sense that Bob has to come to this exact space on this precise street to make this picture because it has absolutely no connection with it whatsoever.

Donald is hardly walking any longer; without realising it he has almost ground to a halt just behind Bob. He is mesmerised, confused and appalled. And he doesn't feel much like de Niro any more; now he feels more like some dopey cartoon character with his eyes out on stalks, his tongue dragging on the ground and a big red throbbing exclamation mark over his head. Recovering himself only slightly, he stumbles past Bob in a daze and lurches on towards his flat, not looking around, not wanting to look around, not knowing whether Bob has noticed him, not able to tell whether his internal turmoil has found an external form – steam coming out of his ears or something like that. He fumbles for his keys and barges into the building, up the reeking stairs, into the relative security of his flat, and slumps down at his desk. Jesus Christ, what was that about? Can someone please explain what exactly that was about? Why is he doing that? There has to be some reason to it. Donald sits there and doesn't move and he feels very tired. This is not how it was meant to be. He feels invaded by Bob's incoherent scribbles, except they aren't exactly scribbles because there's something so methodical and patient about what he is doing, and that probably means they aren't incoherent either, and that is why he feels invaded. That's what really gets to Donald: Bob seems to know exactly what he is doing, he is in control of it and he doesn't care about anything or anyone else. And Donald is nowhere at all. His head is filling with resentment: resentment at Bob's self-sufficiency and resentment at his own stupidity. He feels that he and Bob have had this secret competition going and that Bob has just wiped the floor with him, without even trying, without even looking up. And this is bad because as long as his head is filled with all this shit he knows he won't get anything done himself. Donald realises he has to get rid of this, he has to get this ridiculous image out of his head, this image of Bob and his easel and his nothing picture. In order to get back to his own work, the real work that is his study of death, he has to get rid of this stupid picture. He has to get rid of Bob.

THE BEGINNING OF THE WORLD IS AFAR

JAKE CHAPMAN

Looming high above Mr Vonnegut's waning concentration, the office clock has wandered beyond the moment when labour concedes time to leisure. This evening Mr Vonnegut is found indulging his managerial conundrums later than usual. Hence, tolerance logs off with an indelicate jab plus a shove of the qwerty forward into disarray, plus weariness tidies as best it can – gathering, shuffling, stacking – Vonnegut's best efforts perspicuous in righting the clutch of gilt-framed loved ones bestowing their smiles in the manner of gracious saints watching over his daily toil. So Vonnegut gathers, sifts, shuffles plus stacks, adding upper layers to the forest of pending spreadsheets laying siege to the clearing from which he conducts his carpentry business each day from 9 a.m. to 6.30 p.m.

Out of sight and out of mind, Mrs Vonnegut is away with the fairies, rapt in serene reminiscence when her Louis Vuitton rudely vibrates on the floor next to her waterlogged Chanel pumps. She begs Mother's indulgence; inserting a pause in Mummy's nostalgic flow to allow dripping diamante digits to dip into the suede accessory to vet the trembling organ. Mr Vonnegut's office number is incoming, plus, foreseeing error before error can speak its name, Mrs Vonnegut issues a curt aide-memoire, reminding her ill-timed other half that she is in attendance to her dearly departing Mother. No, Mother is fine. Mother's newborn lucidity has taken Mrs Vonnegut a little by surprise, consequently Mrs Vonnegut has been unable to leave the nursing home. Mr Vonnegut is behind schedule too – Vonnegut is late on account of VAT discrepancies, late owing to matters relating to an impending audit or omitted pension contributions or non-existent national insurance payments – suffice to say, as a rule of thumb, Mr Vonnegut is found perpetually in arrears of time. Plus, in mockery of this ill-fated syndrome, Mrs Vonnegut is eager to notify him that she has anticipated her own delay, plus in the advent of her absence has primed the answering machine to counsel husband plus daughter to feed plus water themselves – adding, *not too much TV for the square-eyed one plus microwave the shepherd's pie straight from the freezer.* Mr Vonnegut marries handset to cradle plus forces a deep yawn against its will. His bad back arches backwards, bending back far enough to clock the time dripping upside down above his head. He stretches left plus right into the fresh silk sleeves of the casual blazer draped *plein air* over the back of the posture-pedic recliner. Rising to lifeless feet the fused human frame shrugs jacket on to shoulder, shoulder stretches to elbow, elbows extend to wrists tapering down to digits that tap out the religious sign of *wallet, mobile, glasses* plus *keys* on a shallow agnostic chest.

Mrs Vonnegut's slim-line Nokia cascades between Louis Vuitton's lips, catches the old bag's slack plus tips its hide from lap to the exfoliant dust layer lining the institutional linoleum. Mrs Vonnegut tilts into the perceptual realm of Mummy's frail mind to infiltrate it with a mental conundrum doomed to twist into a Möbian riddle – *That was Turk on the phone,* she says – Turk – my Turk, Turk my husband, she says, ever hopeful – your son-in-law Turk, the man I married – you remember Turk, don't you, Mummy? You remember my wedding – my wedding to Turk? Anyway, Turk sends all his love plus hopes you'll get well soon. Nothing – not a peep. If it is true to say youth is wasted on the young, then wisdom is surely exhausted by the elderly. Senility is absolved of the protocols of graciousness or civility – plus the abstracted figure of Turk Vonnegut shall remain extraneous to the urgent necessities of Mother's immediate meditation. Hence the deranged old soul is paused right where her tale was punctuated by a suspended comma.

Daughter nudges Mummy to continue, to unpick the weave of embroidered sutures holding her wounded reminiscences together. Mother unpicks at the ulcerated necrosis, plus paused in the doorway, Mr Vonnegut casts a reflex health-plus-safety glance over the unsound profile of managerial disorder before he dims the energy-efficient light plus pulls the fire door shut behind him – suffice to say, Vonnegut's pitiable mother-in-law is wrestling with the tides of dementia, plus, by default of the cruel mechanisms of biological entropy, Mrs Vonnegut's mother is becoming young again. Mummy is becoming a baby. Mummy's memories of adulthood come at a premium – they come plus go, are prone to dilapidation – bouts of melancholia unjustly rewarded with disappointment plus supplementary anxiety. She withers in-plus-out of stable apperception plus is haunted by hypnagogic delusion; Mother has since congealed the most urgent need to dissipate as much of her safely haemorrhaged memory into a younger brain before passing away, or worse, becoming vegetable – a human cabbage wallowing in its own foul soil.

Wallowing on the workshop floor Mr Duprey is helping Mr Lakshmi put the finishing touches to a pinewood rocking horse diligently tamed into compliance in his own spare time. Lakshmi is as proud as Punch. The rocking horse will be ready for his son's birthday after all, plus dear wife Judy can afford to concede her pleasure. When the two employees become aware of their employer winding down the spiral staircase to the workshop floor they are instinctively moved to disengage the rasping drop-saw plus to remove faceless dust masks from masking beholden smiles. The lagging drone of the extraction unit provides Vonnegut time for a methodical inspection of Lakshmi's hard labour – Vonnegut well appreciates that the gravitas given to his opinion is intensified by the clever deferral of words. Duprey also has a woodwork project but he works on it only in private when everyone has gone away. Duprey sometimes works so late he is permitted to sleep in a foldaway cot that he designed and made himself. He well appreciates that

Vonnegut asks after his hobby, nonetheless his woodwork project remains private. Artisans are expectant of praise in lieu of subjugating their creative expression to utile employ, to wit, when the motor is dead, Vonnegut tells Lakshmi plus Duprey they've done a fine job, runs a diagnostic palm over the horse's smooth muzzle, patting it as though it were almost real, which, for the artisan, is highest praise indeed. For a time the three men orbit the wooden *labour of love* as though captive to its inescapable gravity, but Vonnegut's motion around the *object of labour* can never be the same as Lakshmi plus Duprey's.

Light rain lashes the dark glass in drops that form lines plus erase, spilling diagonally; the small beads connect up into bigger drops that sag plus divide into smaller beads plus speed away in lines. The overground express edges around cast-iron bends, ghostly light haunting ribbed caverns plus pitch-black gorges, nerve endings grind along siding links plus screeching through unmanned off-peak stations expecting manacled skeletons to leap out plus cobwebs to flutter. Mrs Vonnegut occupies herself with a complimentary newspaper strewn in rush hour's wake. The train motion is jerking off towards slumber plus Mr Vonnegut bids farewell plus adieu, but not before reminding Mr Lakshmi plus Mr Duprey to sweep up, to double-check the ground-floor fire exit, to switch off the three-phase plus set the alarm when all is done plus dusted. Mrs Vonnegut is swotting up on petty crime, learning how starving babies will soon be a-thing-of-the-past apart from the dead ones already-in-the-past, plus Mrs Vonnegut is finding out about the pastimes of the rich plus infamous. After scanning the extraterrestrial for celestial manna she turns to the stars. Instead of juggling too many ideas in her busy little pea-brain she should let her female intuition settle upon the natural option, it says, this might help in a new job search, in money matters or to fulfil a more personal wish. The sun wanes in her passion chart, it says, an intimate relationship that may have seemed burnt out will soon be red-raw again if she plays her cards right. Nonetheless, indubitable inner strength drawn from an exceptional past life will allow her to thrive in face of mediocrity. She should find time for an elderly person's needs plus someone who practises full-contact marital arts will affect her fortunes positively.

Speeding on rails just like a big dipper, Mr Vonnegut's gelatinous middle-aged spread leaps through its burning hiatus hernia into dry halitosis as the Carrera 4 rises up on to the brow of Hangman's Hill. The 325 bhp delivers 0–62 mph in 5.1 seconds with an alleged top speed of 175 mph. At high speed the steering stiffens, at low speed is light plus airy, plus, haring down Hilltop Warren, the ceramics brake without the thermal clench of steel. But fickle rain deters unmitigated pace as Vonnegut watches a speeding ambulance aquaplane in the opposite direction. Only Vonnegut knows in his bypassed coronary that he could attack the twelve-mile helter-skelter with eyes closed shut. Mrs Vonnegut alights from the overground, bag slung over shoulder pad, chemical peel dipped below the diagonal cast of vicious acid rain. She disgorges from the piss-stained station spilling across the crushed dental terrazzo concourse on to the concrete parade where she sidesteps the snapping muzzles of stray animals huddled on warm air vents. A madman bustles past with a humanitarian placard screaming: 'The end of the world is nigh!' Ushered by the ambivalent wail of a fire engine she forces her way along the loose chain of pound shops illuminating the brief trawl home with the promise that you can polish shit with almost no filthy lucre at all. Her sixth sense senses the unsolicited attention of a morbid figure shrouded in a full-length hooded coat following her – or at least his eyes. She hurries home like the wind; plus, likewise noticing atypical comings-plus-goings in the immediate vicinity of his residence, Mr Vonnegut parks, activates his car alarm plus unlocks his front door plus casts a glance over the cul-de-insomniac. Feeling safe in the hallway he removes his club blazer, casts a piercing yell at an invisible daughter plus fingers the answer machine itching to exorcise the multiple voices of its daily possession. Framed in the repro-

Venetian, Vonnegut fakes a sly shallow left plus right as though to catch sight of himself as others do. The machine confesses eight new entities. Bleep, it says, message one: Dr Mayhew wants to know when he can have his lawnmower back. Bleat. Message two. Brother Dimi's monotonous tone commences into protracted salutation. Vonnegut gathers his facial disappointment from the barefaced mirror-mirror-on-the-wall. Bleat. Sodden Mrs Vonnegut trots across Agar Drive's crimestopper threshold at the risk of being stopped-plus-searched or manually pressed for ID. Looming high in the orange night sky, vultures wheel anticlockwise, hence Mrs Vonnegut finds her swollen feet tangled in bloody rags discarded in the gutter. She kicks them from her fat feet plus continues on her merry way to the modern Gothic semi. Before reaching her drive she is intercepted by over-stimulated members of the residents' committee who tell her that the diligent neighbourhood watch have executed the patron saint of kiddie fiddling before the fucking monster has had the chance to implement the unimaginable crime he is prevented from even imagining. It is rumoured that guilt could even be detected in his eyes, especially in the form of a glazed twinkle in his prosthetic one. When they caught him, the sex-beast's good eye was spinning with panic plus his bad eye was fixed in a thousand-yard stare through the cracks in matter itself – proving that everyone has the potential for good plus bad in them – even the disabled. Mrs Vonnegut congratulates them on their prevailing vigilance, begs apology for her excuses plus leaves them to it. In the driveway she sees steam rising to meet the drizzle from the bonnet of Mr Vonnegut's midlife crisis. Malicious amusement links her lifted cheeks in a manicured appreciation of the fact that *the late Mr Vonnegut* has been so moved to rush home. In the hallway she is greeted by the unique opine of her brother-in-law – a forlorn confession in full flight, as ever, the village idiot's protracted bellyache exceeding the efficiency of voicemail. Thrust into the family nest with catcalls to husband plus daughter, yet in competition with Vonnegut's yapping accountant now stridently chasing up a few anomalous expenditures but not before the machine severs his professional scepticism. Mrs Vonnegut slides a sodden wet coat from big-boned shoulders, slumps damp pig-bladder to Axminster plus ulcerated collagen pouts inside out at the pig-ugly mirror, her work-shy enamel claws dangle the house keys into the stale pot-pourri dish. Bleep. Message seven. Her t'ai chi class has been rearranged for Thursday on account of the by-election, plus personal instructor Klaus trusts the arrangement fits her needs – if not, call him on his handy – ciao. Bleep. Sipped by the capillary action of a promissory G&T, Mrs Vonnegut draws along the corridor escorted by the out-of-body drone instructing husband plus daughter to feed themselves, adding – *not too much TV for the square-eyed one plus microwave the shepherd's pie straight from the freezer.* Bleep. End of new messages, plus, at the end of the hallway, she finds the crisp hiss of surround-sound interference coronating the static outline of Mr Vonnegut freeze-framed just inside the living-room doorway.

To the naked eye it seems he is paralysed. The object of his paralysis is blocked by Vonnegut's inertia. What's wrong? asks Mrs Vonnegut of hubby's soundproofed husk. Mrs Vonnegut is swinging around the pole of Vonnegut's petrifaction into the living room; Vonnegut's profile is steel; time has turned glacial; worse still, the apple of their symbiotic eye is slumped on the floor in front of the flatter, squarer home-cinema plasma screen in an obeisant pose akin to worship. Her pretty young fresh lovely face is buried deep in a plastic flower pot, mouth plus nose sunk below its ellipsis, the pretty young fresh lovely face hidden by hair, her face buried in the plant pot, her pretty young fresh lovely face buried in the plant pot vessel being the home of a factorial complex of chloroplast cells active in the photosynthetic conversion of carbon dioxide into atmospheric oxygen – but not effusive enough to prevent Miss Vonnegut's asphyxia. To wit, the suffering child had been diagnosed with epilepsy at the age of seven, had endured a number of minor episodes of abnormal neuronic discharge triggered by the interstitial flicker of her favourite pastime – television. Now the passive brat is found kneeling, head bowed plus broadcast transmission oscillating between two or more wave patterns superimposed in such a way that they produce high peaks plus low troughs – the black plus white specks liberated from informatic enslavement, now found flickering unsympathetic to human entertainment plus strobing nonsense at Mr plus Mrs Vonnegut, who stand by on mute like a pair of spare pricks at their wedding. The sequential trail leading to the tragedy is candidly laid out backwards on the carpet for inspection – they see slumped child's limp hand next to zapper, they see zapper next to plant pot, they see plant pot next to TV. As if perhaps flinching from the screen's venomous hiss, the hunched corpse releases an unexpected volley of shudders, plus the mysterious spasms ripple up through the derelict anatomy such that the fingers that lay in limp proximity to the zapper now flex in consequence to a shoulder tensing up to permit an arm unintentional animation. Inside the lush marble lividity of Miss Vonnegut's tissue, carbon dioxide gas inhales into alien plastid cells which reverse their anoxic poisoning, plus prokaryotic tendrils retreat through the lacerated haematomas caused by accelerated plant growth – spiny sprouts wither to the respiratory trunk from where expeditionary shoots branched out from the modified stem, where sprouts drilled into tissue laterally, plus where retracting leaf stalks now wither from germinating holes plus shrink up the gullet to drag along plus slide out between Miss Vonnegut's closed lips. Blunted by dull flesh, the sound of cartilage snapping, crackling plus popping through rigor mortis hosts, the slumped head drawn upright on taut sinew. Sightless above the dead-grey flush the corpse is now upright, plus a porcelain profile lifts into view through a blind cleft in lank black hair; delicate capitulum slowly hoisted up plus blue lips parting over the green stem retracting from her mouth as her head lifts up. Miss Vonnegut's blind grimace arcs sweetly at the pretty yellow mandrake flower, quivering perfectly in its pot. Turning to address her dear parents, doll eyelids tilt open plus maggots foam from the holes, cascade to the carpet plus devoid of feet inch towards the TV. Hello, Mummy, hello, Daddy – but no breath to sound the words beyond the silent shapes cast by dead lips. In face of the piercing interference the Vonneguts' own waxen faces perish to bone betraying the fixed skeletal grin smiling tactless beneath the sham humility of their cutaneous grimace.

Mrs Vonnegut unwinds around Mr Vonnegut's stamen, stumbling back in the doorway, a steadying hand feeling the Regency dimmer blindly, plus the bulb's vacuum collapses plus shatters plus the room is governed by the light of the interference combined with the cystic rasp of Vonnegut's hyperventilating mirth. In the hallway garbled messages suck back into the machine's inhaling speaker, withdrawn into the digits from whence they came. Backing into the hallway, Mrs Vonnegut catches sight of her natural elegance in the mirror, withdraws keys from the fragrant bowl, slides her coat on plus clutches bag. Outside, the raindrops have disappeared from whence they came, now a magisterial night pricked by fossilised starlight playing host to circles of twilight songbirds swooping plus dipping before settling to roost. Pulling the door to with Yale happily married to hole, Mrs Vonnegut backs out into the evening plus encounters the happy-go-lucky neighbourhood watch in jubilant mood on account of saving a man from committing the unimaginable crime he is prevented from even imagining. The faithful congregation beckon Mrs Vonnegut to join them plus play witness to their good deed. Spotlit from the Maglite concentrated on the serene face relaxed blissfully on its calm diaphragm, the sound of kind-hearted cheers plus supportive clapping compresses back into the proud maws plus mitts that made them. Mrs Vonnegut is absorbed long enough to see the man's eyelids teased open by flashlight beams as the crowd is moved to cheer his blinking. The head stirs from its humble slumber, plus an abrupt flood of joyful tears erases up the distempered face, confiscated over filthy cheeks to drain into the tiny apertures of his tear ducts. The head lolls with the weight of its public indulgence, plus his mouth is blocked, plus prosthetic eye is pinned to infinity as though staring beyond matter itself. Found crucified on anti-climb spikes up high on the all-seeing CCTV structure which has, for now, turned a blind eye, delight commences movements that taper inside the taut musculature sheathed by rubberised skin plus ripples to two points of fixture being his hands. From the dark puddle swiftly evaporating beneath the joyous penitent, blood separates from mortal discharge like oil from water, forming beady red droplets that wink plus drip, drip, drip upwards into unnatural points of surface porosity healing up on the body above. The flow of blood having already haemorrhaged around the repentant's legs in dark coagulating tributaries now thins, gains laminar speed, plus becomes the flowing blood of a haemophiliac, red blood snaking plus coiling up lily-white calves over knee plus thigh, flowing up to the groin – the crimson gout erases its pulsing course to vanish like a licking tongue into the ragged void where perilous organs are gone. Offering her many happy returns plus best wishes she adds her goodbyes plus polite severances plus leaves her neighbours to their own devices. Good Samaritans from numbers seven plus eight take it upon themselves to retreat up B&Q aluminium loft-ladders, plus with deft hammer blows they manage to irritate the sharp points of the metal spikes until the palms are jogged towards the steel points plus released. Freed from restraint, his limbs are wisely manhandled by neighbours inhaling gobbledegook plus the downstairs crowd are moved to clapping plus laughter. Like a stick insect the man is consumed by the good intentions of swarming worker ants motivated by greater communal concern – his natural writhing is enveloped by the multitude of hands labouring en masse to lower him down the ladder plus contain his delighted excitement as he sets foot on the moonlit ground. On the ground his mouth yearns to speak but kind attention is taken not to allow self-harm through the vicissitudes of his own enthusiasm. Emerging from quaint mock-Tudor to chic high-street urbane, Mrs Vonnegut steers wide of the parade of stylish boutiques congested with busy fire-fighters divining jets of fresh water from the searing flames.

Pretty poinsettias suffusing the station concourse render the scene set for Mrs Vonnegut finding herself privy to the heartening sight of a razor-sharp breadknife secreted from the stomach of a man plus confiscated by another to be safely placed in his own kitchen drawer. A man passes by carrying a smile plus holding a placard which reads: 'The beginning of the world is afar'. Mrs Vonnegut smiles back politely, inserts her ticket into the ticket machine plus receives the price of the ticket she inserts. On the platform, plus comforted under the blanket of winking stars, the ticket-holder watches projectiles leap from the awful wounds of stray puppy-dogs into the hands of kind children who carefully place the stones harmless on the ground, plus, held fast for his very own benefit, kind Mrs Mayhew unwinds Sellotape from around the man's head until the roll is full, plus withdraws the man's own penis from his chatty mouth, plus releases wails of joy from man plus crowd alike. The obstruction is handed to Dr Mayhew, who genuflects to his knees plus struggles with instruments to transplant the organ into the hole between the legs. Mr Vonnegut leaves home noticing the good nature of the evening diagnosed in the temperate weather plus clement neighbours alike.

Vonnegut screeches to a start reversing out of his driveway, 0–62 mph in 5.1 seconds, plus passes by the happy rescue waving to all plus sundry before turning left on to the B359. Above the cheeky rubber squeal he can still hear the excited yelps of a redeemed soul echoing in his empathy, imagining the man being led away with false teeth chattering on brittle words. Verging on the city limits the night is sunny plus dark at the same time on account of the effects of ambient urban light. Friesian clouds form in the sky plus lightning bolts shoot up from the serrated horizon to stun them. Mr Vonnegut's halogens illuminate the reflected eyes of bunny rabbits exploding into fluffy inflation from pancake roadkills as he reverses rearward without so much as a glance into his rear-view mirror. Needless to say, Vonnegut skilfully shoots up Hilltop Warren, twisting along the twelve-mile skelter-helter with eyes tightly shut, looping over Hangman's Hill plus making great progress in his bid for the industrial estate where his office clock waits to record his new time. Among the confusion of the rescue, pulled plus pushed, the pandered subject comes to rest near the cul-de-sac's allotment alleyway where kind-hearted wives entreat erstwhile male custodians to defer control of their charge plus set about the face plus body of the injured being with healing hands – each touch of feminine knuckle, fingernail plus stiletto subtracting a bruise, scratch or graze from skin. The man's jaw chatters plus cracks but the inaudibles that shoot into his thankful mouth are already doomed to the merciful charity of Mrs O'Rourke, Mrs Rich, Mrs Nelson, Mrs Gibson plus Mrs Mayhew. Legally let loose on the B359's dual carriageway Mr Vonnegut drives to within an inch of crime, plus eyewitnesses an ambulance arrive on the scene of a traffic accident to disgorge mangled bodies from its own carriage plus pass them into the wreckage of two cars which repel violently plus assemble into being from scattered, broken, twisted components plus drive away all brand new without so much as a thank you or goodbye. The women dress their limp rag doll in the sodden rags Mrs Vonnegut found tangled around her feet. Thankfully clad in serendipitous Marks plus Spencer's, albeit with violent rips, bloodstains plus slashes – the women attend to the outfit in a blur of fingernails plus teeth until their guest is dressed presentably.

When Mr Vonnegut decants from his car plus enters S.J. Bespoke International Wood-Crafts Ltd he finds Mr Duprey asleep in his cot, which in plus of itself is nothing unusual, only the cot is cocooned by an elaborate structure of highly ornamented struts, brass rods plus posts, wooden joists plus load-bearing cross-beams supporting a constellation of pulleys, tackle, lathed wheels, turned cogs plus gears. Viewed from the outside Duprey's apparatus appears without coherent principle, as though its anarchic form emerged from the composite genealogy of technical adjustments added together to solve each subsequent engineering anomaly cascading from Duprey's 'organic' solutions – a register of entropy rather than designed final cause. Vonnegut is interrupted by the sound of a jet plane falling short of the nearby airport runway, plus the violent inhalation of air into the mouths of stricken passengers sucks the plane from ground-level inferno, the sonic screams sucking up, up, up plus away into the clouds, plus, as though keenly stimulated by Samaritan self-righteousness, the primal horde bifurcates into marital couplings quickly staggering awkward up crazy-paved pathways or driveways, two by two disappearing into homes built to permit a discreet vantage through opaque net curtains plus drapes to watch the outside from the inside while playing with themselves plus their families, plus, sincerely alarmed at the sight of Mr Duprey's strange apparatus, Vonnegut notices his office clock oddly incorporated, plus from baying windows residents watch the rescued man retreat from the safe cul-de-sac into the choking alleyway that loops like a noose around the neck of the gardens, where bluebottles return to the skins of bulging maggots, where birds return to hibernate in eggs, where meat is regurgitated from the mouths of the well fed plus clad on to the bone armatures of farm animals, plus shit is collected up by dutiful anuses plus life is breathed by the dead who walk again, plus home-made bombs planted around the city are defused plus taken away by pacifists determined not to jog the minds of innocent civilians suffering from chronic historical amnesia, plus all around the world human babies take to the wholesale safety of amphibious wombs assisted by medical staff, plus the coloured wires from Duprey's borrowed clock are grouped schematically plus neatly routed along the ornate frame assemblage, pass into a timer used to remotely activate the motor into motion at a specified time. The machine's motor is suspended midway along a central beam plus extends one of many drive-belts towards an articulated swing arm. At the extremity of the machine's jointed limb, the S.J. Bespoke International Wood-Crafts cannibalised drop-saw blade sits safely at rest but clearly implicated in a novel deed. Mr Duprey lies asleep on the bed under a cosy duck-feather duvet, plus his sleepy-eyed head is all at rest on the floor. In full view of Vonnegut's very own eyes Duprey's head gains animation, Duprey's eyes stare at Vonnegut as though in shock, the pool of blood outlining its place of rest on the ground gushes back into the dark hole from whence it came. Plus, without so much as a warning, Duprey's head leaps from floor to pillow synchronised with the drop-saw which engages to unexpectedly cauterise the wound. When Duprey's head is found connected to Duprey's neck, Duprey falls asleep without so much as a goodnight. In his knotted mind, emancipation from labour was fuelled by the very castration complexes from which machines are the erotic accretion. Hence Mr Duprey's emancipation from the restraints of work had evolved into a decapitation fantasy. Precisely at this moment in time, the spirit of Duprey's woodwork project appreciated itself into Vonnegut's mind, plus in the sky a luminous mushroom cloud blooms plus wilts on the horizon then fast collapses into ground zero plus nothingness more.

When Mrs Vonnegut alights from her train plus arrives at the hospice with high hopes for the opportune sanctity of an old lady's nostalgia she finds Mother has erased the last remaining memories of adulthood from her memory plus completed her transformation into an unborn foetus.

THE ALPINE FANTASY OF VICTOR B

CHRIS HAMMOND

It felt good to be up so early, and as Victor left the small Alpine village of Villa di Chiavenna, striding out in the first rays of the new day, the cool mountain air mingled with his thoughts, producing a wave of tranquillity and clarity that he had not experienced for nearly a year. The path climbed quickly, formed from steep steps cut into the valley wall, and it wasn't long before Victor had reached the first alpine pastures with their Heidi-esque chalets in which village families would spend the hot summer months. The vista opened up, providing a chocolate-box backdrop of glistening glaciers and majestic peaks, and he took a moment to fill his flask from a nearby fountain. It had been a good year, yet so intense that this was the first time that he had had a chance to reflect, and as the cool mountain water passed between Victor's lips and gushed over his tongue, he felt the exciting tingle of things to come; by the time it was cascading down Victor's throat he knew that this would be a great year, one to remember.

The walk from Villa in Italy to Malojapass over the border in Switzerland was Victor B's yearly undertaking while holidaying with relatives of his wife. It had become a sojourn, a chance to repair his batteries and cleanse the system of all that life would throw at him, and, let's face it, there was plenty of mud-slinging in Victor's business. It was the contrasts which were the major benefit; solitude was something that you became used to at the top, but up on those passes or within the hidden valleys you were truly alone with yourself, no hangers-on or halfwits, armed with chiselled grins and touting tepid proposals. Maybe it had been a bad idea to destroy all the competition so readily; it had been far too easy to apply Machiavellian principles to a business that hadn't seen it coming and Victor missed the anonymity that he had enjoyed as a young man. Still, none of that mattered here, this was a place that accepted him, he understood it and in return this ancient monument to the ice age gave rebirth, earthly nirvana. Up here among the hulks and pinnacles accepted value and judgement did not exist. You were free to form your own; no one was there to interfere or misread your actions or intentions. This was an arena of individual autonomy; whoever tried to breach this absolute did so at their own risk.

The path is steep on the Italian side and climbs from one small pasture to another, each with its own little settlement. The lower ones have mainly been turned into holiday homes, generally owned by Italian families. Victor always chose to make this walk a couple of weeks before the long August holiday, and many of these beautifully maintained chalets would be silent, shutters closed, not a sign of life. In a few weeks families would be out, sat around long tables enjoying antipasta and local wine winched up from the valley below. What an idyllic life that must be. He enjoyed the ghostly hamlets and often fantasised about breaking into one of the houses and living secretly during the winter. He would dream of pitching from house to house, sleeping wherever he pleased, writing a novel or manifesto, growing a huge beard, drinking grappa and maybe losing his mind. As spring burst forth upon the slopes Victor B, raving madman, would leap and skip down to the valley below, like some ancient prophet babbling his insanities to whomever stopped to stare.

Between each settlement the path rose through dense pine, shielding you from the hot summer sun. Victor would play mind games and often stalked imaginary prey, skirting trees below and above the path, quickening and exaggerating his breath before leaping down on to the path to take out another unsuspecting fictitious victim. Somebody should set a slasher movie or serial-killer book in the Alps, especially in

Switzerland. Nothing bad ever happens there, it would have good shock value. Just imagine *American Psycho* set in Lauterbrunnen, as our anti-hero disembowels a few Fräuleins after a hard day at the ski school. Everything is so clean and ordered that no one would believe it. Maybe you could even get away with it.

The last small group of houses that you reach on the Italian side is Mallone. No one lives here except some pigs and a few goats. The houses are in ruins, it's too high to run a cable from the valley; any provisions would have to be carried up, and not many want to be that removed from contemporary living. As Victor approached he saw a solitary figure, dressed as if from another time, standing among the old barns. He was a shepherd, with wild staring eyes, ruddy face, inbred features. You have to rub your eyes to convince yourself that these mountain men are not just apparitions, and Victor skirted the bottom of the houses in an attempt to avoid his gaze. He felt like an intruder and did his utmost to exit this man's world as quickly as possible. You have to understand the invisible boundaries of the mountains: if you are a lone wanderer, you travel in a bubble whose walls need to be respected; to ignore this could destroy the balance and lead to catastrophe.

On leaving Mallone you are now above the tree line and the path climbs steeply, zigzagging through treacherous rock buffs; the grass thins and is replaced by scree underfoot. By now Victor B had been walking for a number of hours and his heart pounded as his legs demanded work from muscles that had lain dormant for quite a few months. Victor's chest heaved with every step, sucking at the thinning mountain air. He would need to stop more regularly the higher he climbed, and his pace slowed to an enforced shuffle. After a long haul pulling himself up between the rocks, searching for cairns to guide him, Victor finally reached the first pass that would take him over the border into Switzerland. He stood on the saddle between two rocky peaks and looked back, Italy on one side and Switzerland on the other. No checkpoints or passport control up here, anyone was free to enter and exit each country according to their own free will. Victor loved the concept of secretly crossing frontiers. It brought to mind wartime espionage, Hannibal Brooks, guerrilla hideouts and mountain rebels. Even in this technological world people can easily disappear in such terrain, especially if they want to. As a monumentally childish gesture to marking territory he stood admiring the view while urinating from one country into the next, before zipping up and continuing on his way.

Victor dropped down into a shallow rocky no man's land, weaving his way through small pools and slabs of snow. Some cloud rolled in, creating an eerie silence as all the jagged shapes loomed in and out of vision and he had to concentrate in order not to wander off the path and over some precipice. The cloud lifted just as Victor reached the second pass. From here he looked down into a beautiful hanging valley, three sparkling mountain lakes, joined by a meandering stream, fed from the glaciers of the 4,000-metre peak at its head. This was Victor's eldorado, the Promised Land, and as in every previous year he hoped beyond hope that he would be allowed to pass through this glorious place without interruption, the only soul, at one among the splendour of nature, sublime, as if in a Caspar David Friedrich painting.

Victor rode the scree all the way down to the first lake, nestled among the rocks; the steep broken stone walls of the surrounding mountains tumbling straight into its chilled depths. Scree running takes some agility but when mastered is enormous fun. You basically jump, slide and run down the stone chute, just on the edge of control and balance. The trick is to plant your boots into the scree, heel first, your body weight causing you to slide rather than tumble. Soon Victor was at the stony shore and had found a large boulder on which to rest from the morning's exertions. He pulled off his pack, taking out a simple lunch of cheese and salami, wrapped a jacket tightly around himself and sat mesmerised by the glistening tranquillity. Thoughts of previous years flooded Victor's consciousness. This valley had given new purpose to his life. When he had first chanced upon it all those years ago, the pleasures had been simple, grandeur of nature and man's relation to it, but in recent years it had revealed a far more complex fulfilment.

Victor had been so engrossed in his own meanderings that he had failed to notice a walker coming around the lake, and the first he knew of another's presence in the vicinity was the obnoxiously self-confident and unpleasant twang of an American accent. This was an oldish woman who thought that she was young. She did in fact look strong for her age, tall and wiry, a bit like a man. She greeted Victor and without waiting for a reply barked information that had not been requested, and he could feel the rush of blood to his face that might have betrayed his annoyance. This was the sort of woman who referred to herself by her surname, which sounded half-French, half-German and typically mongrel USA. Of course, she hadn't lived in the US for over forty years and had instead burdened Paris with her existence. There is something arrogant about Americans abroad, which only gets more apparent the longer they stay away from home. Victor didn't hate citizens of the US per se, in fact he had great admiration for a huge number of American writers and artists, or maybe it was just their art, but nothing riled him more than his privacy being interrupted, especially here. The rule is pass on by; this lady had stepped over the accepted boundary. Biting his lip, Victor smiled and greeted her with all the social graces of a diplomat, and with effortless charm he immediately stimulated her idiotic penchant for pseudo twentieth-century romanticism. Satisfying her thirst for local history and geographical knowledge, he easily persuaded her to join him on a short detour, climbing up to a small col that gave, he impressed on her, unrivalled views of the large glacier. Now that this woman had disturbed his peace he truly wished to share the hidden secrets of this magnificent valley and hopefully educate her in the joys of experiencing them alone.

They left the path, climbing round the other side of the lake, and slowly traversed the steep loose slopes, aiming for a small U-shaped gap up on the right-hand side of the valley. There was no path to speak of but Victor had climbed this route many times before and was able to pick out the least difficult way up. The American woman panted between words, trying to keep up while maintaining a steady stream of tedious self-obsessed ranting. Victor closed his ears to the impurity of her candid chatter and let the chill mountain wind whisper its mantra, clearing his mind for the task ahead. Occasionally he would turn and offer words of encouragement, but this lady was on such a pre-defined trajectory that she would never have suspected that he wasn't listening to a single word. After the traverse they scrambled up a short chimney littered with large boulders. Victor pulled on some gloves for the final ascent and glanced back at his new companion. She was red and out of breath but fit for her age. He couldn't wait to be up on the col and increased his pace, scuttling up the last section like a mountain goat.

Victor reached the top with a good few minutes to spare, able to get his breath back and enjoy this tremendous panorama for a few solitary moments. This was a magnificent view of the glacier, and you could look out over three different valleys and a multitude of snowcapped peaks stretching off as far as the eye could see. Steadying himself, Victor took off his pack, removed a couple of climbing slings and used them to secure himself to a pinnacle of rock. There wasn't much room, and the drop on the other side was severe. He turned to watch the American woman pull herself up the last few feet, and he offered her his hand for support. She stood, breathless, for the first time completely silent, and admired the view. Using his spare hand, Victor pulled out another sling attached to a short length of rope and asked the American woman to step into it. She let go of his hand to pull the sling up around her waist but before she could do so Victor pulled on the rope, tightening the sling around her ankles and forcing her off balance. As if in slow motion her unprepared body tottered at the edge of the precipice before tumbling backward over the edge of the cliff. Victor pulled hard on the rope so that she fell upside down, hitting her head on the wall of the cliff. He held the rope tightly as the body swung a few feet below the edge. There was silence; she must have been knocked out by the fall. This angered Victor, he had wanted her to appreciate the view from this unusual angle. He secured the rope to the pinnacle of rock, pulled a knife from his pocket and leant over the edge. He could see the American dangling upside down; blood poured from her mouth where she must have bitten through her tongue and the irony of this brought a smile to his face. He took hold of the sling around her ankles and slowly started to saw at it with his knife. Victor was careful not to cut her flesh or clothing, this had to look like an accident. In a few minutes the sling was down to a few strands and Victor took out his water bottle and tipped it down the front of her unconscious body. The cold water mixed with blood and ran down her face and up her nose, causing the unfortunate woman to splutter back to consciousness. As her startled eyelids sprang open Victor called down to her, 'Enjoy the view,' and suddenly the sling snapped, allowing her body to fall a few hundred feet before bouncing off the first outcrop, the only sound a dull thud mixed with the snapping of bones. The constant prattle had been cut short by natural beauty; meanwhile the mind hadn't had time to register the immediacy of the situation and didn't have the opportunity to let out a single scream before being silenced for ever on the rocks below. Victor watched with morbid fascination as the mangled body tumbled and rolled until it became wedged among some large boulders.

Victor stood on the col for a moment longer, resisting the urge to throw stones at the broken corpse below. As much as he would have enjoyed hours of torture, the mountains had taught him that minimal contact and swift decisive action were the best course; the mountains themselves would take care of the rest. Over the years they had dispatched and hidden three rock-climbing web designers from Essex, a plump and pompous teacher from Scotland, a middle-aged French film-maker, an outrageously healthy Swiss family, an Anglo-Swiss gentleman with a name straight out of *The Flintstones*, a buxom soft-porn actress (these were all professions that Victor would assign to his victims, for in truth he never bothered to listen if they actually told him what they did), a South African business consultant and an arrogant young man with chip-pan hair who was probably an artist. Reasons, he had a few, be it the sound of their voice or their wearing stupid patterned climbing pants – maybe they just reminded him of all the people who had annoyed him throughout the year. One chap actually had the audacity to light up a cigarette, only to learn that smoking kills by having most of the packet gaffer-taped into his mouth and the lit cigarette inserted into the end of his penis, which was then cut off and shoved up his rectum. They were just in the wrong place at the wrong time. The mountains were a dangerous place. People go missing all the time. Lone walkers should be careful and not stray from the path.

Scrambling back down from the col Victor felt reinvigorated. His latest victim had been the easiest dispatch to date and he felt proud of his economy and efficiency. Gone were the days of caving in skulls with rocks and then having to set up some believable accident. Though it had been quite a laugh forcing that South African backpacker to fill her rucksack full of stones, before breaking both her arms and making her jump off an overhang into the deep glacial lake. That had been a risky decision and it was lucky that few ventured this way. While the gorier days of years gone by had indeed been tremendous fun, there had always been a lot of cleaning up, often requiring an overnight stay. Victor was a father now and a lonesome night under the stars, cooking up a big hunk of meat on the campfire, wasn't really an option any more. He had come to the conclusion that it was much better to engineer accidents, an unexpected shove or a frayed rope, something out of the blue. It had never ceased to amaze him how people were willing to trust complete strangers, just because they had met in the wilderness. Anyway, once again intruders had been repelled and the land had been kept pure. It was time to leave. He picked his way over the rough terrain, cutting down beneath the glacier and rejoining the path by the second lake, fed by the many trickling streams of melted ice. He strode uninterrupted through the rest of the valley, except that as he passed the third lake a strange white dog appeared on a rock way above. It stared down at Victor, who was certain that it was a wolf. Suddenly he felt the one hunted and quickened his pace, climbing the final pass and leaving the hidden valley behind, content with the fresh sacrifice that had been made.

The path climbs steeply down to a river bed and in a few hours you reach an isolated farmhouse used by a Swiss farmer when his herd is in the high pastures. As the river meanders through the lower thickly grassed valley, filled with grazing cows, bells clanking in the late afternoon sun, you are reminded of how much the Swiss Alps live up to the advertising clichés. Victor had stepped out of *Heart of Darkness* and into *The Sound of Music*. He allowed himself a few minutes lying in the soft meadow grass, listening to the babbling water and letting the heady fragrance of the fresh alpine day fill his senses. The year's pent-up frustrations had been banished. Nature had cleansed all disability from his mind, yet Victor couldn't help wondering how long this fix would last. He had become increasingly concerned that the gaps between these urges were becoming shorter, and he had already become tempted to use his methods beyond this safe environment. He mused over the idea of finding a confidant, someone who could share his ideas, or was at least able to comprehend them. Was he insane? Hadn't everyone, at some desperate point in their lives, wished another human being would vanish without trace, struck by lightning or some speeding car? As a race we constantly irritate each other, the world just isn't big enough any more and Victor felt that he was just acting from instinct, cleansing the environment, returning it to a more sustainable level, keeping the wilderness wild.

After a further hour's walk Victor passed another farm where a number of mountain paths converged at a sign, and he followed a well-manicured path through the pine forest that led to Malojapass and the main road back into Italy. It was early evening when Victor reached the touristy village and found the small hotel bar where he had arranged to meet his wife.

This is where I first met Victor B. I was just drinking a large Pilsener while waiting for a bus back down into Italy after a day's climbing up above Malojapass when I noticed the yellow mountain rescue helicopter flying over from St Moritz. Someone must be lost in the mountains, I thought to myself. Most uncannily a voice behind me replied, 'I do wish people would take a bit more care.' I turned to see a tall, well-groomed man in his mid-forties. He was dressed in particularly old-fashioned and traditional walking clothes that seemed slightly out of place among the brightly coloured Gore-Tex that festooned the bar. He introduced himself as Victor and asked whether he could join me for a drink, explaining that he had been alone all day in the mountains and fancied some conversation over a cognac. I was already intrigued by this strange gentleman, and so obliged. We talked of the different routes and ranges that we had climbed and found other common interests within art, music and literature. In fact we were so engrossed in conversation that, a couple of hours later, I failed to notice that a young woman had joined us. Victor introduced his wife, who was carrying their sleeping baby daughter in a car seat. She reminded me of the actress Isabella Rossellini, and apart from exchanging a few polite niceties she didn't say much. When Victor discovered that we were all going in the same direction he offered me a lift. We finished our drinks and walked outside into the clear alpine evening.

The car was big, black and diplomatic, I don't know what sort, as cars have never been a passion of mine, but it was very comfortable, and indulging the healthy fatigue gained from the day's climbing I sank into the soft leather seats. The engine purred into action and the mesmerising strains of a Beethoven string quartet enveloped us, which along with the sleeping child forced a halt to our conversation. I stared out of the window as Victor navigated the numerous bends that the road weaves on its journey down from Malojapass. The mountains were silhouetted against the night sky and the car seemed to glide over the alpine road. I had the eerie feeling that I was being whisked into the night by the driverless coach of Count Dracula. This languid state made me reflect upon our conversation in the bar, which at first had followed a general and polite course, but had relatively quickly touched upon some fairly extreme ethical dilemmas. Who was Victor? There was something slightly unreal and sinister about him. His words had enticed me to listen indiscriminately, but as I thought back over some of the stories that he had begun to tell me I realised that I must have been too captivated to question the sincerity of his thoughts. Was my mind playing tricks on me? Hadn't I heard him talk about the purity of the land and his policy for ridding it of unwanted guests? His methods were extreme, far too implausible to take seriously. He must have been joking, or else why had I nodded and smiled with such complicity? I looked at his sleeping child, his beautiful wife and expensive car; no, Victor was testing my gullibility, acting as devil's advocate, playfully searching for the latent extremist that can be enticed out of anyone off their guard. This was not a man who would advocate mass murder as an environmental clean-up solution and mean it literally.

My sleepy ruminations on these half-remembered utterances were cut short by Victor engaging his wife and myself in conversation. He had been dwelling upon the legitimacy of disclaimers often found in fiction confirming no connection between the characters and any actual living or deceased persons. This he found to be ridiculous, claiming that all authors based their characters upon living persons, at least to some degree, or that they were the amalgamation of actual persons met or furnished by passed-on accounts of actual persons. My mind was still reeling from my analysis of the levels of reality that Victor's previous conversation had presented to me, and this just made matters worse. I was too tired to dwell on it too deeply and gave in to easy ignorance for the rest of the journey. Victor was no ordinary man, but I was unlikely ever to meet him again, so why worry? The car came to a halt at the Italian border and the guards took one look and waved it through. It was only a kilometre further to the small village of Villa di Chiavenna where I was staying with relatives of my partner, and in a few minutes I was stepping from the car and bidding my farewell. Victor's window wound down and he looked me in the eye. 'You will be following the path I have shown you?' he directed rather than enquired, and with that the car pulled off and drove away into the night. Walking through the empty streets, I pulled a folded piece of paper from my pocket and, opening it, I found myself looking at a hand-drawn map of the route that Victor had talked of. Strangely I had no recollection of him giving it to me.

It felt good to be up so early, and as I left the small alpine village of Villa di Chiavenna, striding out in the first rays of the new day, the cool mountain air mingled with my thoughts, producing a wave of tranquillity and clarity that I had not experienced before in my whole life.

GHOST WRITER

BRIGHID LOWE

The flowers moved in the vase. The windows were shut. Outside there was a storm blowing but the gusts of wind were unable to penetrate the closed windows. The flowers moved just as she was thinking of Marianne. The shudder of the flowers was unmistakable, but no petals dropped from the stems and no pollen fell to the mantelpiece. The only trace of the movement was now held in her mind.

Of course, the flowers, lilies, had to move sometimes. Their long buds had to open. They did open. But these lilies had already bloomed; they had opened and released their perfume into the room. For the next hour she watched the lilies to see whether they would move again. They did not.

Her own stillness was a way of disrupting the ceaseless flow that surrounded her and which seemed to her to be travelling nowhere. Inside her, where once there had been agitation, she now found there was emptiness. She did not really understand where this emptiness had come from. She knew that she found it difficult to get from one event to another. She did not seem to know what would happen next.

She needed help. That is why she had left the note.

Marianne, I cannot understand tell me more. I still cannot understand please tell me more.

The note was just as she had left it, without any movement, response or sign. When she looked at her handwriting now, the letters seemed compressed between hope and desperation.

She picked up the note and examined it. Marianne's lack of response was overwhelming.

She felt angry but calm, and so filled with a sense of loss

that it threatened to shut her down. The sweetness of Marianne's voice was now all that she could conjure up. It was a sound that could cut through crowds, suddenly and without warning. It was like the song of a wren, a song so clear and sharp you had to search for a sight of this tiny bird in order to really believe that a creature so small could make such a sound.

The thought occurred to her that perhaps Marianne did not want to write; that perhaps she wished to communicate another way. Sixteen times now, she had left notes out for Marianne without any response. She was on the brink of giving up. The note had been left inside the pocket of Marianne's favourite coat; a small pencil had been left in the other pocket. She had tried the coat on herself to check how easy it was to find the note and pencil. The coat had been left out in the hallway, hanging on top of all the other coats and jackets. She wanted Marianne to know it was there, waiting for her.

She sat down at the foot of the stairs and thought about herself. She was nearly forty years old – the moment in life when you traditionally capitulate and surrender. Soon her past would become all that was left to her. Then this past would become her present as well as becoming her future. She preferred to think of it another way. Perhaps becoming forty was the moment when you no longer had to wait for others to create your future – instead you had to generate something for yourself. She had begun to realise that she had no sense of her own story or the fiction of her own life.

She felt transparent, dissolved into the background of her surroundings. The pavements, the furniture, the architecture and the weather were the same texture as her hair and skin. When she got dressed in the morning, her clothes, no matter how brightly coloured they were, became like a mirror reflecting back their surroundings. That was why she often wore Marianne's coat. It did not dissolve at the moment of contact with herself. In her mind's eye she could recognise herself, see herself as a coat disembodied, walking the streets, opening doors, catching buses.

The only environment in which she seemed to register was the darkness of the cinema. As she became absorbed in the film she became aware of her own body, the weight of her limbs and the evenness of her breath. She was no longer invisible.

She decided to put on Marianne's coat and go to the cinema. Immediately she realised she had never connected these two actions. She had never watched a film wearing Marianne's coat. She suddenly felt light-headed, certain of her power to make decisions. She put the coat on and buttoned it up, leaving the top button unfastened, just as Marianne herself would have done. She checked that the note and the pencil were in the pockets, picked up her bag and closed the front door behind her.

She walked briskly down the street, bought a ticket at the shop and set off for the station. The train was crowded and people pressed up against her. A man tapped her shoulder and gestured towards a free seat. She squeezed past the man and angled herself on to the seat. The arms of the coat rested gratefully against the upholstered arms of the train seat.

Outside on the street it was raining – the kind of rain that you might find on a Welsh mountainside, a fine mist of drizzle that clung to you. The surface of Marianne's coat instantly became covered in drops of water. She entered the cinema, reached in her bag for her money and bought a ticket.

Normally she would have taken off her coat inside the cinema, particularly if it were wet. She would then have placed it on the free seat next to her. Marianne's coat stayed on, buttoned up and wet. It felt like a kind of burial to wear this damp cold coat in the darkness. Then the film started.

'What are you doing?'

From far away she heard his voice calling her, 'Didn't you hear me? I've shouted five times already.'

Reluctantly she raised her head and turned to go up the stairs; she knew that nothing was different, and that everything was the same. She paused; the stairs and the floors of the house would allow her to alter the geography of her body but not the pattern of her thoughts. She knew that everything was different and that nothing was the same.

'Coming,' she shouted, as she began to climb the stairs. Two floors above her, she did not pause at all but moved straight to the door of the study and opened it. The man did not bother to turn around to look at her. He began to speak.

'Are you going out later? Could you post these for me?'

He gestured at the pile of packages on the floor. She looked at them with relief. It meant that she had an excuse to leave the house with a genuine sense of purpose. She would have to find a post office, stand in a queue and then wait for a number to be called out. She would have to say 'First class inland' to the person serving behind the counter. She always liked saying the phrase 'First class inland' – it made her feel connected to a disappearing world, as if it were a tiny fragment of something that had been lost.

'First class inland?' she said.

'Yeah,' he said, without turning his head.

She crossed the room and bent down to pick up the packages. She shuffled the packages between her hands, balancing them and balancing herself at the same time. She stood up. Out of the corner of her eye she glimpsed a bird of prey circling – a kestrel – it was high up in the sky and then it was gone. If she had not inclined her head slightly to the left then she would never have seen the bird. The chance sighting of the kestrel had been a crossing of two movements: the arcs and hovers of the bird and the tiny shift leftwards of her neck and spine. She knew that this synchronisation was always a sign of events to come.

She turned away from the window and crossed the floor of the study. As she shut the door behind her she heard him say, 'Thanks.' She thought of the circling bird, and she thought of it inscribing and reinscribing the same segment of air. She realised that she was waiting.

Waiting was her main occupation these days. Each day this

job of waiting became slower and harder. The only break she had from this task came via her memories. In her mind, she would often see a car driving along a motorway flyover. She could not remember who had been driving the car or where the car was going. She did remember that the car had come from the sea. The motorway flyover had passed by a red-brick block of flats. From the balcony of one of the flats there had been a sudden flash of intense white light. As the car passed, for a split second, she saw herself sitting in the passenger seat, looking straight back at herself. It was as perfunctory as the coldest embrace. Turning to look behind her, she saw an oval mirror with a small hole at its centre hanging on the outside wall of the flat. It was only later that she realised the acute flash of light had burnt itself on to her retina. When she closed her eyes, a tiny oval of white appeared floating in the endless sea of black.

For a moment she had felt that she was the world and the world was her. Somehow she had glimpsed an image of what she took to be her true self. She found the recurrence of this memory deeply comforting. Perhaps it was because she was travelling, mechanically moving straight ahead from one event to another, that she was compelled to see this memory over and over again.

It was when she was coming back from the post office that she began to feel upset. The queue had been moving slowly; it was a very long queue and there were not enough people serving. As her turn at the counter approached she became aware that a man was staring at her. She shifted her position and looked beyond him, through the doorway, to the road outside. At the counter she placed the first package on the scales.

'First class inland,' she said.

The woman behind the counter looked at her blankly. 'Where?' she said.

The woman's question was disorienting.

'They are all for London, first class,' she replied.

As she placed the packages one by one on the scales, she

could see that the man was still staring at her. He was now standing just outside the main door of the post office. She had never seen the man before. She handed the money over for the postage and then forgot to ask for a receipt. She had to immediately turn back and ask for one.

In her confusion she did not see the man move very fast away from the doorway towards her. All that she felt was a sudden rush of weight and heat right up against her. He grabbed her very tightly around the arms and pulled her in towards him.

'Why won't you speak to me? Why don't you acknowledge me when I see you?'

She struggled to move her face away from his chest. Panic pricked every surface of her skin; she even felt it pricking the soles of her feet. She could not understand why people around her were doing nothing to help. She needed to catch somebody's eye.

'I don't understand,' she said. 'I don't know you.'

As she struggled she could feel the man's aggression rising. His grip began to hurt her.

'Of course you know me. Why do you deny it? Why won't you speak to me? Why not? There is no use looking around. They can't see you. No one here will do anything to help you.' She realised that she was on her own. People moved around her – leaving the queue, posting their letters. Immediately new people arrived to take their place. He was right; no one was going to help her.

'Yes... of course.'

She tried to calm her voice, to slow it right down as if she were talking to a child.

'Sorry. I will speak to you next time. Promise. I promise. I promise I will talk to you next time.'

The man's grip began to relax, to melt right away. He smiled at her.

'That's all right, then. You make sure that you say hello next time, that you speak to me, that you acknowledge me.'

Then he let his arms drop. Two people pushed past to take their places in the queue and suddenly he wasn't there any more. She was left, barely standing, feeling stupid, guilty, confused and most of all angry.

It was on the way home that she remembered that she had Marianne's coat on. The thought began to grow inside her that the man had seen the coat and mistaken her for Marianne. She did not know what to do with this thought and all its implications. She reached inside the pocket and searched with her fingertips for the note. She moved them backwards and forwards but the note was no longer in her pocket. She checked the other pocket for the pencil. It was still there. The pencil was the same pencil. She checked again for the note, pushing at the seams of the pocket to see whether there was a hole inside the lining. There was no hole. The note to Marianne was no longer in her pocket. Its abrupt absence must be a reply of some kind, an acknowledgement, a way of Marianne communicating with her. The disappearance of the note reassured her; it revealed a presence that she felt she could not ignore.

When she arrived home she opened the front door to silence. She shouted upstairs but no one responded. She decided to climb upstairs to check in the study. The room was empty but the radio was still on low. The furniture stood in semi-darkness. As she reached up and pulled open the curtain she saw a heron flying past. Its heavy wings swept slowly downwards, following the line of the rooftops outside the window. The heron flew in exact counterpoint to the movement of the curtain. In a few seconds the heron would be gone. But now it was so close that she could almost hear the beat of its wings.

She turned away from the window and paused as she heard the sound of the front door opening. She realised that she still had Marianne's coat on. She had not taken it off. She looked around the study and silently moved towards the desk. Without thinking she dropped behind it and bent her head right down sharp towards her ankles. The fabric of the coat pressed up tightly against her face. She could hear footsteps approaching the study. She should have stopped then and forced herself to stand up. But she did not. She stayed silently crouching behind the desk, just as a frightened child might. She held herself very still, as still as she could without stopping breathing altogether.

A voice cried out, 'Annemarie.'

She hesitated.

It came again. 'Annemarie.'

The voice was just as she had remembered it – exhilarating and disorienting in equal measure. It seemed to come from deep inside her, far below the surface of things. All around her small lights seemed to spark at the edges of her surroundings – from the desk legs biting down into the carpet, from the telephone cable trailing beneath her feet and from the edges of the curtains behind her. The door opened, someone scanned the room, turned and closed the door behind them. She listened as the person turned swiftly and climbed up the stairs to the bathroom at the top of the house. Then she heard the bolt on the bathroom door engaging.

She stayed crouching, the body and the coat under equal strain to accommodate their positions. She could taste the cloth of Marianne's coat pressing up into the edges of her mouth. She had wanted to cry out, to hear her own voice answer. She had wanted to reconstruct her life. But she was gripped with an inertia so profound that it felt like violence. Through the window she glimpsed a faultless white cloud passing in front of the sun. It moved with the smooth glide of perfection. She heard a guttural sound and felt the long rasp of a death rattle constrict her chest. She knew that all her desires were simply dying inside her.

She still could not understand – why did the pattern of her life elude her? She was unable to trace the continuity of her life or see where the edges of the pattern met or how this pattern then repeated itself. She found herself struggling to comprehend the sheer endlessness of it all. Closing her eyes, she decided to imagine that she was in the darkness of the cinema, sitting, watching the film again.

In the film a voice-over had talked of nothingness, objectivity, subjectivity and love. A cup of coffee was stirred. The extreme close-ups of the swirling coffee had filled the screen like a galaxy. The black of the coffee was the depth of the universe, the bubbles and swirls its very own nebulae. The concrete simplicity of this galaxy had made her heart stop. Her thoughts dissolved with the voice from the film and the soundtrack slid beneath her thoughts. Suddenly she saw that it is the objects – it is actually the objects themselves which permit us to relink, to pass from one subject to another – which ultimately enable us to be together.

She understood then that she could not tear herself away from what was crushing her, nor from what was isolating her. Her thoughts would always divide her as much as they would unite her. Each event, each of her encounters, would transform her daily life. Her constant failure to communicate – to understand; to love; to be loved – made her only experience one of solitude. Since she was permitted neither to lift herself into being nor to fall into nothingness she must listen: she must look around more than ever at this world – her likeness – her twin.

So she climbed the stairs towards the bathroom and pushed at the bathroom door. Even though she had heard the door being bolted she knew that the door would not be locked, she knew that in reality it would be open. She pushed at the door and it swung free without any resistance. Inside there was nothing – that is to say everything in the bathroom was in its usual place.

Without any warning at all there was a noise behind her. Turning around she looked up at the skylight in the hallway. A huge bird of prey was smashing its wings and talons against the glass. She struggled to see it clearly and to identify it. But then, just as suddenly as it had arrived, it was gone.

She found herself standing, shaking, almost convulsed with adrenalin and an intense feeling of shame. She could not talk to this bird, reason with it, explain that she was not Marianne, explain why she needed to wear this coat in order to believe that she existed. She had tried to compose an ending for herself, any ending. She had tried to understand. Now she understood. This beautiful bird had looked down into her world and had seen a small figure turning, eyes raised.

SOFT

GARY
O'CONNOR

191

It's 3.35 a.m. I'm skirting the back garden of a house in Stanton Road after forcing the gate. The street lamp at the rear of the house isn't working so it's perfect cover. There's a light drizzle, and as I reach the decking in front of the French windows, I slip twice. I steady myself and take a deep breath. There is no sign of life inside so I slowly move across the decking towards the kitchen window, which overlooks a small flower-bed. Peering into the kitchen, I can't see a thing. The window is in a sorry state, it looks rotten from the outside. I take a piece of rag from my pocket and do my best to wipe dry the pane of glass directly in front of the lock; I take a roll of masking tape from my pocket and use it to completely cover the glass. I place the rag against the pane and with my elbow give it a sharp, swift thump: there's a snap as the glass breaks. Now I'm able to get my hand in and unscrew the lock. The window doesn't want to move, seized with layers of gloss and years of neglect, but with perseverance, I lift it high enough for me to crawl through. Once in the kitchen I find myself chest down in a sink full of dirty cups and plates. I do my best to keep the noise down but it's not easy. I snake my way in along the work surface. Once on my feet I scan the room to get my bearings. Most of the big houses at this end of the road have fallen foul of developing mania, and this place is no exception. Still, at least I know where I am in one of these flats, everything's on one level. There's a bright moon tonight and I can see reasonably well. At the far end of the kitchen is a door which I immediately head for. Tentatively, I turn the handle and edge it open. Ahead of me is a large room and I feel comfortable enough to turn on a light. I've used a torch on previous jobs but I soon found out that there's nothing worse than someone spotting torchlight flickering around inside a place, you're much better off taking a chance on a light. I throw the switch, and what I see is very odd. All the walls are covered in scraps of paper: magazine and newspaper cuttings, scribbles, sketches and notes. There is one chair and a desk in front of a window that looks out on to Stanton Road. In one corner of the room are several black bin bags. On the desk are piles of books and paperwork, and in the middle of the room is a thing.

I've been following Paul's career closely now for the last nine months. We have this arrangement, you see, we can't have any contact with one another, no smiles or nods of acknowledgement, no letters, no phone calls – no communication at all. The rules are that I observe only from a distance, with discretion and subtlety. There is to be no interference in each other's lives by either party at any stage of the project. I've lived in the flat above Paul's for the past four years. I knew who he was the moment I first saw him, I'd watched his films and TV appearances and even saw him in a West End production the year before we met. Gradually, after several encounters in the hallway, we struck up a friendship. As we got to know each other, he began to take an interest in my writing and eventually asked me to document his work. I was flattered and immediately accepted. This was a great opportunity for me. I was excited about the work and wanted to approach it in some new way. In order to get a true, objective perspective on Paul's life, I needed to step back from our relationship, and so we agreed to these specific arrangements. He gave me a set of keys to his flat, and each morning between 9.30 and 10.30 he would be out of the building so I could let myself in without coming into contact with him. This would give me enough time to look through his diary and scan the flat for anything interesting. This consensual snooping always placed me one step ahead of Paul's movements: if he was having dinner with a friend or going out to some celebrity bash, I could be there. If he was on location, here or in some other part of the world, I knew where he was. I could be there, documenting it all.

I circle the thing slowly, I'm trying to work out its purpose, but as far as I can see it doesn't have one. It stands about six feet high and resembles a traffic cone. On closer inspection I can see that it's made up of tiny little plastic heads. They remind me of the toy soldiers I played with when I was a kid: they were made of this cheap green plastic that still had knobbly bits sticking out around the base and on the shoulders, where I presume they came out of the mould and nobody could be bothered to give them a trim. It must have taken a long time to cut all those heads off and stick them all together like that. All the tiny green faces are facing out as if watching the room. I go over to the desk and sit in the chair. I pick up a pen and take a piece of paper and write the words 'two heads are better than one'. Then I look over my shoulder at the thing. I pause for a moment, then continue writing: 'many heads are better than one'. Maybe this is what the thing is all about? I pick up the largest book on the desk and open it – it appears to be a journal of sorts. I flick through to find the last entry; it was made several weeks ago. Instinctively I read it aloud. 'September 13th 2004. Outside the morning slips past at speed. Piggy little spheres of grey lock in on the passing landscape without a flicker; the face pressed hard against the glass. At the edge of one nostril is a trace of dried snot. The eye is immediately drawn towards this bright, lime-green fragment. Every so often he pulls back from the window looking agitated and breathing heavily, then coos like a pigeon and waves his arms in excitement. These little outbursts are short-lived, and soon the face is back against the window. The camera crew huddle at the far end of the carriage: two women and three men who exchange small talk and chew gum.' I close the book. I'm not sure how I feel about this. I sit and think about it for a moment, then get to my feet and go back to the thing. About halfway up, somewhere in the middle of the green mound, I select a head and pick it off. I roll it between finger and thumb – examining the face. I wonder which army you belong to, it's difficult to distinguish – the helmet looks like a pudding basin, it's not American, English or German. Do they still make Second World War toy soldiers? It doesn't seem right somehow. I think I know a couple of Germans. That's funny, I think that I think I know a couple of Germans... how strange, I wonder where that came from? Actually the helmet looks a bit NATO. I pick another head off, then another – they come away easily. I'm beginning to see a trace of what looks like cardboard hiding beneath the little green faces. I have at least thirty or so heads in my hand and I'm looking around for somewhere to put them. I place a piece of A4 on the carpet and put my collection on that. I go back to the desk and work my way through its drawers, looking for something to cut into the cardboard. I find a scalpel and some blades. I have now removed enough heads to make a circle of about eight or nine inches in diameter. I begin to cut into the cardboard, it's dense and difficult to remove but gradually it comes away. Beneath the first layer is a second and beneath that there's more – but I'm undeterred, I'm actually enjoying myself, I'm suddenly aware that I'm having a really good time. I'm careful and selective with my cuts, taking care to maintain continuity. Slowly a beautiful tunnel is formed. It decreases like a funnel as it reaches the centre; I go to the other side and begin to remove more heads. I check both sides continuously for symmetry, making sure that they line up and appear the same. I begin to slice my way into the thing, and I can't explain the immense rush of excitement I'm feeling. This excitement increases as I near my goal. It's like having sex – the drive towards completion is all-consuming, nothing else matters. I hold my breath... suddenly I'm through. The final incision pops, revealing a trace of light. I make further cuts, opening up and expanding the tunnel – it's now big enough for me to pass my hand through. I wriggle my fingers on the other side and it feels fantastic. I'm very pleased with my work. I step back and inspect the structure, admiring the alteration. By taking so much away I feel that I've added something, I'm not sure what this means but I know it's very important. I pull up the chair and sit in front of the thing. I can see straight through it to the collage of paper which covers the wall beyond. The hole looks like a gunshot wound, despite all the care and attention in its making, it still looks as if something has blasted its way through. I think about this for a while and decide that I quite like this look. I like how the inner structure of the thing is now exposed, I think it's brutal but honest: what appeared so formidable is now so open and vulnerable. In fact, I think it looks beautiful. It deserves to be called something other than just thing. I think I'll call it A Safe Place. I look at the wall of paper through the hole. I observe what I can – pulling my chair closer. The hole gives me a frame in which to focus. I can see two sheets of paper with writing on, three photographs and some drawings. The text is too far away to read, the photographs are also hard to see from here but I can just make out one of the drawings – it looks like A Safe Place. I get up and go over to the wall. All the drawings are of A Safe Place, and each of them shows the hole that I've made in various stages of construction. I feel confused, I think... I think I need to sit down. I look at the photographs: one has been taken of the window at the back of the house – the way I came in. Another is a picture of a castle. It looks Norman to me; I've no idea where it was taken. The third isn't a photograph at all, but a postcard. I pull it away from the wall and turn it over to see who it's from but it hasn't been written on. There are some words printed in German along the bottom of the card and the image on the front is of another castle. This one looks like something from a fairy tale – nestling on a hillside with lots of pointy turrets and towers, surrounded by a dark impenetrable forest. I put the postcard back where I found it and look down at the palms of my hands. Turning them over, I examine the lines and creases. I wonder how old they are. I can't remember anything before coming here. I remember being outside in the rain, trying to find a way to get in – but before that?

Paul is a great one for people watching, then again, I suppose all actors are. I've followed him on many train journeys across the country to various towns and cities for no other reason than just to study people. Over the years, he's built up a large collection of observations and descriptive encounters of the characters he's seen and met on these journeys – he writes everything down, I love flicking through his notebooks – provided I've got enough time. Paul's method of developing a role has become extreme, it's a fascinating thing to watch. He throws himself into a part completely. It has been known for him to shun close friends and hide himself away for weeks – sometimes months. He has also put himself into some ridiculously dangerous situations. There was the time he was playing the part of a drug-crazed killer named Henley, in a movie called *Soft*. He was dragged from this scuzzy tower block in south-east London by the police at four in the morning after local residents reported hearing gunshots. Two dealers had turned on him; luckily nobody was hurt but Paul was found in possession of small amounts of heroin and cocaine and he was also carrying a knife. How he wriggled out of that one is anybody's guess; what I will say is that his legal team worked bloody miracles because the case never made it to court. Of course, the press had a field day. Well, they do say that all publicity is good publicity and it certainly didn't do his career any harm, in fact I'd say the attention gave him more credibility, the work just rolled in. Looking back I'd say it was a pivotal point in his career.

**EX-MISTERS
(A
CATALOGUE
OF
SUDDEN
DEATHS)**

L

**M**ister Big, never one to do things by halves, smashed his skull by slipping on a bagful of banana skins.

Mister Meek was clubbed to pulp when he mildly enquired: 'Could I borrow a match?'

Mister Loser died of boredom while begging.

Mister Gourmet choked on a sausage made of pure veal.

'Better to walk up and down and do nothing than sit in a room and rot,' thought Mister Positive, but he was just car fodder to Mister Joyrider.

Mister Traumer, for thirteen years struck dumb by fear of what he might say in his death-bed delirium, was frazzled instantaneously by forked lightning while crouching under a bush.

Mister Smiley, the compère, died with perfect teeth.

Mister Green has not been seen for seven months now. Word is that he was recycled as bone meal.

Mister Brown sank down and down into the inky depths. He said that he would soon bring back the body of Mister Black. Sadly he did not.

Mister White nearly got it right. There was no logical reason why his wings should not have flapped.

Mister Paranoid did always say they were out to get him.

Mister Burton went, never to return.

Mister Smurfit, in a hurry, tried to jump over a pit of slurry.

Mr Masoch topped himself with a disc sander.

Mister Koslowski, avant-garde improvising musician without a gig in three years, tattooed his forehead with a cordless drill.

Gangrene's a funny thing. Not that Mister Ogbuno thought so ten days after he stubbed his toe while alighting from a number 73 bus.

Mister Duveen, the lion tamer, for fifteen years twice nightly put his head in the king of the jungle's toothless mouth, until one evening in Scunthorpe, Leo sucked his eyes out.

Mister Slyme, the politician, spoke the truth. Just the once, he had no choice. The shock to his system was like a massive injection of pure heroin into his veins, and equally terminal.

After thirty-five years of silent suppers Mrs Plomer thought that if her husband said just once more 'Very nice, dear,' when she enquired whether he had enjoyed the meal, then she might cheerfully strangle him. Even so she was surprised by the venomous glee with which she garrotted Mister P with the cheese wire after a Saturday evening soufflé.

Mister Drybrough always loved his little joke, and when he passed away he bequeathed to his wife his ashes in an egg timer. But human ash is not like sand, which falls grain by separate grain, and his dust remained in the upper globe while the egg boiled rock hard. 'Typical,' scoffed Mrs D as she lobbed the inedible ovoid and the useless timer into the pedal bin.

No hoorays for Mister Henry, who abseiled down the Eiffel Tower and then, temporarily blinded by the cork from a bottle of the sponsor's champagne, stepped off the victory rostrum and severed his head on the steel hawser supporting the hospitality tent.

Mister Pex's physique was honed like steel. The ringside doctor pronounced him 'the fittest corpse I've ever seen'.

'Don't tell me your troubles. I've got troubles of my own. Fuck off!' snapped Mister Limo. Mister Drifter, annoyed by such curtness, cut out Limo's hard little heart with a rusty can opener he had recently found behind a liquidated fast-food restaurant.

Mister Missionary, staked out face down, was gang-raped into oblivion by seventeen pagan pygmies who never gave

England a thought.

Mister Guinness grew so stout that he couldn't get out of his chair and the blood clotted in his veins. His body turned black, his hair turned white, and he nearly expired on St Patrick's night. But he hung on dribbling bile until 12 July when he coughed up his guts all over the carpet as a bowler-hatted marching band strutted past his window.

Mister Miser, sour as pre-war vinegar, tight as a monkey's fist, counting out seventy years of trimmed fingernails, died in shivering agony, too mean to turn the gas on.

Mister Charitable treated with expectorant linctus the chest cold he had acquired while swimming in Lake Windemere on New Year's Day, then, ignoring the instructions on the bottle label, misguidedly juggled two chainsaws at the village fayre.

Reasonable daydreams, undisturbed sleep, jog before breakfast, sound knowledge of wine. They found Mister Feinstein hanging from a noose in his gymnasium, his genitals firmly clamped in the jaws of an eight-pound pike.

Mister Weller, caring single parent, was buried up to his neck in sand by his playful young sons, William and Waldemar, who then went to buy ice creams from the café on the other side of the dunes where, innocent of time and tide, they became engrossed in the *Terminator* video game.

It's a little-known fact that, under pressure, one screw in three million strips its thread. Certainly Mister Campesi was blissfully unaware of that statistic as he gazed out at the breathtaking Alpine vista through the window of the cable car.

'Strange,' mused Mister Lewis as he swayed down the aisle of the train towards the buffet car, 'that's the third young woman I've seen on this journey whose hair is falling out,' and he paused in the connecting corridor between carriages to ponder this curious fact at the moment that the train lurched abruptly as it rounded a curve and hurled him sideways against the exterior door, out of which he fell on to the track, to be sucked under the whirring wheels.

In his stuffy, overheated room Mister Pringle was updating

his address book by Tippexing out those recently deceased when he became dizzy from the correction fluid fumes, fell face forward into the open fire and deleted himself too.

A ghost tapped Mister Roebuck on the shoulder as he walked past the police station. She whispered: 'Should I... mmmm... you know?' her breath warm in his ear. He stood transfixed while the years rolled back, as did the doors of the station garage, out of which the panda car, with its blue light flashing and siren wailing, hit him at 30 mph from a standing start.

'Must remember to retack that stair carpet and replace the light bulb on the landing,' thought Mister Ashpole as he sank into befuddled sleep after the Christmas party, but he remembered neither when he woke at 3 a.m. and staggered blearily downstairs, glass in hand, to get a drink of water.

The railway company, seeking to economise on the amount of trackside land it needed to buy before building the new Intercity line, placed advertisements in local newspapers asking for volunteers to stand tied to posts alongside the rails while high-speed trains rushed past, thus determining the minimum distance at which track maintenance staff would subsequently be able to safely work. 'Wow! That sounds better than bungee-jumping. I'm going to phone them now,' exclaimed Mister Smart as he downed his bottle of Brazilian lager and rushed from the bar. 'What a prat,' said Old Tom, sipping his pint in the corner seat, 'bigheaded too.'

MIRROR TRAVEL

DAVID BURROWS

A new star

I am a shining star, a fat ball of gas with a black hole in my heart. One day soon I am going to explode in everyone's faces. I am a message sent from afar, from twenty thousand light years away; an armour-piercing silver bullet programmed to explode into smithereens on impact. My target? My target is the past and every last monument and scrap of material that indexes a culture or nation. My return will create new satellites and asteroids that pulverise the old world, that crack the old world in half. The first of many exploding celestial bodies, I am a cloud of vapour scented with wild flowers. I am a pulsing globule of ectoplasm, soft and moist, floating through the stratosphere. This isn't a sudden revelation. I have known for a while that my case is terminal. The tension inside my muscles and sinews has been building for some time and I am ready to burst.

There are many who think I am deranged and others who believe I am a callous, unfeeling bitch, but I'm neither.

I know I am responsible for the death of twenty people, all the more shocking for the journalists who reported the tragedy that a woman was to blame for such a criminal act. It was a terrible waste of life and I regret it deeply, but all that is a distant memory now. And one day soon I will illuminate our diminutive world like a flaming comet scorching the night sky.

I remember the day when I first sensed minute changes in the atmosphere signalling a new departure in my life. In fact, I can recall the exact moment a tingling sensation in my left hand, not unlike an electric shock, began to prick my nerve endings and then travel the length of my spine at lightning speed towards my brain. Everything can be traced back to a slip of the tongue, a devastating blunder that crushed my father's heart: the words 'You would know... being adopted'. On hearing these eight syllables my father paled for an instant and then nodded slowly. His cousin, her fat face reddening by the second, glanced sideways at her big-mouthed husband. It was the fourteenth day of July 2004, my father's sixtieth birthday.

Apart from a mild sting of static in my fingertips, I barely registered the event – for that is what it was – as I sat bored, half listening to a conversation about immigration and tuberculosis. I gazed around the room at the assembled company as they took up a new subject, an anti-depressant that caused heart palpitations. All ears strained to hear the name of the life-threatening tranquilliser until suddenly my father's guests – every last one a prescription drug addict – all began talking at once, like animated cartoon characters, in a frenzied bid to stave off a collective sense of doom. Only my dazed father sat quietly; his world had imploded. Although he nodded some more and then smiled, he was no longer with us.

He told me a few days later that the words 'You would know...' transported him back to the afternoon of his eighth birthday. He'd been holding a brand-new football in his hands, which he gripped tightly as an argument edged towards a fist fight. My father had insisted that, as the ball was his, he was in charge of picking teams, but this logic failed to impress his best friend Stephen, who protested that my father was a spoilt little bastard. A scuffle broke out and my father easily beat his foe into submission; but even with a bloody nose and eyes flooding with snot and tears, Stephen would not take back his insult. And then another kid said, 'You are a bastard, everyone knows your mum and dad aren't your real mum and dad.' My father ran home, clutching his new ball, crying all the way.

On reaching home he kicked open the back door; his entrance interrupted the banter of a card game. Pointing an index finger at the group of adults gathered around the kitchen table he demanded to know what they had done with his real mother and father. The aunts and uncles, the grandparents and parents and assorted family friends – a gang of deceitful, two-faced liars and hypocrites who only two hours previously had smothered him in congratulations and presents – assured him with hugs and kisses that his friends were being cruel and that they were guilty of making up a wicked lie. It was only on his sixtieth birthday that the truth of the incident was finally revealed to him: at the core of my father's life there was an assemblage of lies and evasions.

The last words my father spoke to me were 'Life is, through and through, a phenomenon of attention'. I now know this to be a vital truth, though for a long time I was anything but attentive. I was complacent, a creature of habit. Well, no more. Every cell in my body is awake to the flow of time and matter. The slightest hint of a breeze or change in humidity causes the hair on my body to prickle with anticipation. My lips moisten and my clit throbs like an antenna from the bombardment of impulses and sounds that orbit the earth. I vibrate with the pleasures of molecular activity.

It was my father's encounter with the truth, or rather his realisation of the falsehood of his origins, which proved to be the catalyst for my own awakening. But arousal from inertia was not instantaneous. Those tyrants of suburban tedium, with their stomachs stuffed to bursting, left my father's birthday party late and I was exhausted by their inane and noisy trips down memory lane. I walked the last ingratiating fat slobs to their over-sized people carriers and I called to my father to say that I would soon be leaving too, but there was no reply. I found him slumped in a chair, staring at a closed photograph album on his lap. I thought it was just fatigue, so when I said goodnight a second time and barely heard a mumble, I thought nothing of it. I should have phoned the next morning just to make sure he was fine but I'm not a mindful daughter: the concept of duty makes me nauseous, and the previous night had made me sick to the stomach.

The sun was shining on a perfect summer afternoon when

my father's cleaner Annie called, asking me to come over as soon as possible; she sounded calm but warned that my father was in a bit of a state. I hurried over to the small terraced house and found the front door open and the hallway and stairs strewn with wreckage. Annie had fled.

Every framed photograph had been ripped from the walls and systematically destroyed; even the photographs of my mother had been trashed. Ugly notches in the banister registered the destruction of a camera and loops of videotape hung from light fittings or coiled around scarred and slashed furniture. Despite the shock of seeing the house in ruins I realised the devastation had an order of some kind. In the lounge, covering a charred carpet, a hundred or so ceramic fragments were arranged in an oval – the remains of my grandmother's collection of ornamental canine ceramics bequeathed to my father. My nostrils twitched as I breathed in an acrid-smelling wisp of smoke that rose from a scorched photograph album placed in the centre of the egg-shaped mosaic. And kneeling in the middle of this scene was my father, pouring lighter fuel on a pile of CDs like a priest conducting a sacred ritual. His clothes had been razored into strips and his body was covered in shallow cuts and nicks. A sudden intake of breath broke his concentration and he looked up, a fragile smile taking possession of his lips. My eyes welled with tears. It was a beautiful sight, a man on the verge of freedom taking leave of himself. This was how it all began.

Three days later he vanished. It was not the first time I had been abandoned but it was the only time I felt that my horizons were extended rather than diminished by the desertion of someone close to me.

Sleeper
My mother had always claimed that my brother Robert jumped to his death; or rather, that he had launched himself from the safety rail on a cliff-top path. Others say she pushed him as he sat precariously balanced on the rail, tempting fate, dangling

his legs over the sea and rocks below. They say she gave my brother a gentle nudge, believing he would soar away on hot air currents. She waved her headscarf furiously, excited at his bold departure for another continent.

I never missed my brother but I did miss the constant stream of new sounds and magazines he would bring into the house. My mother disappeared from my life at almost the same time, arrested and then hospitalised within the week. I was never to see her again, except in the photographs my father took in her new home: a pastel-blue room with a cream steel door and window grille. I was told she was unwell but I knew what that meant. She was crazy. That was the information I quickly gleaned from friends at school. Their parents had given them strict instructions to be kind and sympathetic as my mother was in the nut house.

The most traumatic desertion I experienced was more like a dematerialisation. When I was a student I lived with a young man, a sensitive, cute, red-headed boy with a beautiful cock and sensuous lips. He was a student too, another historian and bookworm. We shared every hour of the day until he got a job at a pizza restaurant to supplement his bursary. At first he liked the work but gradually he began to complain. Not about his fellow workers or his boss, but about the heat. He described the restaurant's kitchen as a furnace and after work he would lie for hours in a cold bath to cool off. His aversion to heat became worse; he would dream that his eyes were popping and his skin peeling in the intense heat of the kitchen. On one occasion I found him rolling around in the snow in our tiny garden without a stitch on, catching snowflakes on his small pink tongue. After that, he spoke to me less and less, except when he was angry. Then he would explode in a torrent of expletives and insults, hurling keys, telephones and cutlery until every table and wall in our home bore the traces of his volcanic eruptions.

When he was sacked from the restaurant I thought everything would return to normal. He came back late one night covered in tomato sauce, which he had thrown over the restaurant's manager when the manager had refused to open a window. At first I thought the sauce was blood and that he had stabbed his boss. I even raised a smile from him as I collapsed with relief, happy that the police weren't on the way. I thought a phase had passed and our relationship would revert to a blissful symbiotic partnership, even though he continued to sleep in a cold bath of water at night.

It was when he insisted that we move to an island north of Scotland that I realised his volatile behaviour was more than a phase. He told me that if I didn't want to move then he would move on his own. And that is what he did, relocating to the Shetlands, but even the gales of the North Sea proved too warm for his sensitive constitution. He advanced north again, reaching the farthest point of civilisation before the icy wastelands of the Arctic began. It took me a long time to accept that he was never going to return. His last e-mail contained familiar complaints about the stifling central heating of his tiny apartment and the suffocating air of the small town where he lived. I realise now that what I had taken to be a sensitive disposition was in fact nothing more than abject desperation. On receiving his e-mail, full of maudlin self-pity, I concluded that he was a selfish, spineless little shit; and I told him so, severing all communication between us. For a long time I hoped he would die horribly of hypothermia.

When my father took off without saying goodbye I finally accepted that it was pointless to analyse the actions of others. For years I had tried to fathom the cause behind this or that incident but the answer was simple: everyone I have been close to rebelled against the life they had been leading. It was nothing personal. The only question worth asking was why I hadn't followed suit, why was I still going through the motions of my life as a mediocre academic? I decided to be the exploding star I had always dreamed of becoming, to illuminate the portholes of other worlds that remain hidden from me in shadow. Back then I thought events of significance did not happen often enough, so I decided to get my hands dirty. I decided to unscrew the bolts of a railway sleeper.

Flight

I realise now that I made a dreadful mistake. At first I was a heroine. Not only did I survive the wreckage of the derailed Virgin train – which flew through the air and landed like a broken concertina – I recklessly risked my own life to rescue a young mother and her children from a burning compartment.

For a short while I carried a clipping of a photograph that appeared on the front page of just about every newspaper around the world. In the picture I am smiling bravely as I hold a length of tubing for a paramedic. My dress is stained with blood and my manicured feet are shoeless. Around me, the dazed and injured sob and shake and the faces of the emergency workers are grim but I look calm and composed, happy even. There is only one upsetting memory I have of the crash and its aftermath, an image I formed not from something I saw but from something I heard. When the train finally came to rest and the thunderous ripping of metal had ceased, in the deathly silence that followed I heard the squeak of a rusty sign swinging in the wind.

Five weeks after the derailing I hastily packed some clean knickers, a toothbrush and toiletries into a rucksack and fled London. What made me run? Whether it was the news that the missing bolts had been discovered or that every squeaking shoe or braking car reminded me of the squeal of the rusty sign, or whether it was the example of my father, I still don't know. I caught the first train from Euston that I could and headed north.

The train was packed, despite the general consensus that saboteurs and terrorists were at large. On arrival, a river of bodies spilled on to a generic metropolitan street, swelling the number of noisy shoppers brandishing bags and phones like shields or badges of honour. The stench of biscotti, espressos and lattes made me retch. I could sense that the sights and smells of this successfully regenerated city, with its banners celebrating multiculturalism and consumerism, were secretly the harbingers of some catastrophe or terrible war. My pulse quickened like the throb of an electric current and I felt the gleaming shopfronts and faux piazzas tense too, as if the buildings were sucking the air out of the city and holding their breath. I saw the shop windows caving in under the strain, and sale items flying through the air from the force of exhaled air, littering the streets with glass and debris. I began to run, at first deftly avoiding obstacles and people but then blindly, leaving a trail of burst shopping bags and angry consumers. Crashing into a parked car I lost a heel and ripped my T-shirt. I ran until my lungs screamed and my lips turned blue and then collapsed outside a Starbucks, sending a chair and table clattering to the ground.

Screams of terror filled the air as a circle quickly cleared around my exhausted body. And then a pair of hands pushed me to the ground and another pair twisted my arms behind my back. As I struggled I felt a kick to the ribs and a voice ordered that I stay still. I felt a fresh surge of panic and I kicked and squealed like a wild animal. Apparently it took ten policemen to arrest me. I was lucky not to be shot; the police feared I might be carrying an explosive device.

I admitted my guilt even before I was shown the grainy CCTV footage that placed me at the crash site, wrench and hammer in hand, one week before the catastrophe. At first the police believed I was part of a terror cell but this theory didn't last. It was quickly replaced by another idea: I was a crazy woman, my insanity a hereditary condition. It seems I had decided on an elaborate suicide plan – the sabotage of the train line I took to work – but the police could not fathom how it was possible to predict which train would be derailed. Then another solution was quickly formulated. Had I been engaged in some gruesome game of chance, risking my life for the thrill of cheating death each time I travelled the sabotaged line?

Difficult as it was, I managed to explain the motive for my actions. The breakthrough came when I met the man in charge of investigating my crime. I expected to meet a bureaucrat who would fire a barrage of questions at me and conclude that

I was deranged. Instead, I found him to be a calm, elegant man who explained that he was eager to hear my side of the story.

After I had finished my tale he drew a long breath and asked a question: 'Miss Robsperry, you say that you regret your actions but you show very little concern for your victims. What is it that you regret?'

I tried to sound convincing in reply. 'I made a terrible error. I know that the tunnels of white light are just the brain gasping for oxygen as the body expires. I pinned my hopes on the survivors but I realise now that a traumatic encounter doesn't bring about anything new. Of course I regret it. It was a useless experiment.'

For the first time emotion flickered in his voice. 'Experiment? The derailing of a high-speed train was an experiment?' He became indignant. 'An experiment to prove what exactly?'

I blushed. 'My intention was to interrupt habit, for myself as well as for other people. I wanted to create an affective work, so intense that the space for judgement, well, just collapsed.'

We sat in silence for several minutes. A calm returned to his voice. He said without triumph or anger, 'That not only sounds pretentious, it sounds like an act of terrorism to me.' And it was true. I let out a sigh. I had been so stupid. All I had done was increase the circulation of fear and the workload of those disgusting, morbid creatures that call themselves therapists. Those cunts! Scores of people had fallen into their clutches as a result of my actions and were now being brainwashed – *accept mortality, you miserable shits, how dare you demand immortality!*

The detective interrupted my silent rage. 'Miss Robsperry, did you carry out your plan on your own, do you belong to a group of any kind? Do you consider your actions to be political?'

It was my turn to sound indignant. 'No, not at all, I wanted to be at the centre of an exploding star, I wanted to conquer death not... it was never my intention for death to triumph.'

He looked at me with genuine concern. 'I don't

understand, how could you conquer death through this dreadful act?'

I composed myself and explained. 'Since the invention of sin, life has been written as a finite line, ending in death and a final judgement: a journey in time, from birth to childhood, to work and marriage and then children and retirement and finally death. Conquering death doesn't mean cheating death but breaking this chain and living each moment as if you were newly born, each day a new problem to solve.'

He had sat back in his chair as I spoke; a new thought had entered his head. 'Miss Robsperry, are you religious?'

I blushed again. 'No, no, I am not religious but I do have faith, a faith we are all capable of and, in fact, a faith we draw upon every day.'

I could sense that the detective felt he had made a breakthrough and he asked, 'Faith in what?'

My answer left him bewildered. 'To act one must have faith. When presented with any new situation, when sufficient reason collapses, we are either paralysed or we have to proceed without any secure grounds to explore a new dimension. To act in such circumstances requires faith, a faith in the potential of the cosmos. This is the message I wanted to spread.'

When silence was the detective's only answer, I reached for an example, something to illustrate that there are other dimensions to the ones we are familiar with. I desperately wanted to convey that I wasn't just a fucked-up idealist or a crazy lunatic. I told him how I had discovered mirror travel.

'When I was very young, I would spend hours looking into the mirror in the hallway of our house. At first I saw only a familiar vista, a slice of family life. One day I had a revelation. I was wearing my rubber Minnie Mouse mask which had a hole in the left ear and I realised that when I looked at my reflection I was the wrong way round. I saw one mouse staring at another. Both had a hole in the same ear but the hole was on different sides of the same head.

'I imagined stepping out of the reflection and turning to

face the mirror, and then performing a somersault out of the
reflection, and finally flipping and spinning out of the mirror
and landing behind myself. But no matter how intricately I
performed my mental gymnastics, I couldn't make my mirror
image register with my body. There is a reason for this and I was
not the first to stumble on the uncanny nature of reflections –
philosophers have long pondered the asymmetrical nature of
mirror images. But I was not to know this, I was just a kid, and
I shrieked and screamed and ran up and down the hallway to
celebrate the conclusion of my experiment: everything I saw in
a mirror existed in another dimension.

'A few years after this discovery, my brother expanded my
adventures in mirror travel with a rash and stupid act that he
regretted for the duration of his short life. He threw the remote
control at my head as I stood peering into the depths of the
mirror. His missile shattered the mirror, causing a web of cracks
to spread across the glass. My brother started to cry and I guess
I should have burst into tears too, as tiny splinters of glass were
embedded in my left eye and cheek, causing teardrops of blood
to form. But I was ecstatic. I had never seen anything so
wonderful. A hundred or more oddly shaped children were
reflected in the smashed glass. And then there were a host of
living and breathing globules of flesh that I had no name for,
amoebas swimming in a patchwork of colour that was formerly
our cosy suburban house.'

I paused as I remembered the commotion that followed.
My mother came flying down the stairs and let out a scream at
the sight of her little girl smiling demonically, tiny droplets of
blood running down her left cheekbone. The spectacle tore her
reason to shreds. Her first bout of mental illness was not far
away and although a doctor later told my father that the cause
of my mother's descent into madness was chemical, he always
blamed it on the 'smashed mirror incident'. I know it was my
smile which was the catalyst. My blonde hair was decorated
with tiny slivers of glass that sparkled like a halo; a large slither
of glass had wedged itself in my hairslide – the glass cut my

mother's lips as she smothered my head with kisses. When my father discovered us we were locked in a bloody embrace.

The detective asked me to explain the significance of my story and I obliged. 'You see, the trouble with events is that they are easily overlooked; nothing sorts them out from ordinary moments. It is not surprising that events slip by, mistaken for meaningless episodes, while what we consider significant is often nothing more than sentiment taking hold of our emotions.'

At this the detective nodded. I thought I was finally getting through to him and offered to continue, but the detective waved a hand and told me not to bother. He said he was interested only in the facts. I knew then he was like all the rest, another dumb animal. His moist eyes, which I had mistaken for a sign of melancholy, were just the dead eyes of a shark that moves forward from one meal to the next, until finally sinking to the bottom of the ocean after expiring one day.

Mirror travel
When the interview was over I was charged with twenty counts of murder and returned to my cell. The musty smell of rain-soaked earth had somehow penetrated the building; it was a message from the world outside, pleading with me not to become resigned to my situation. In twenty-four hours I would be transferred to a more secure institution and once again I felt despair at my fate. I knew I was guilty but felt no desire to face a just punishment. What is more, I was ashamed of the terror I had spread and I did not want to live in shame. And then it came to me, the answer to my predicament.

In the shower room of the block I was housed in there was a large mirror above a cracked sink. And in the centre of the mirror, running vertically from top to bottom, there was a kink, an imperfection that ballooned and squeezed the reflection of my face and the brick shower stalls behind me. It was all I needed.

A familiar voice had sparked into life inside my head: 'A mirror is not subject to duration. It is an ongoing abstraction, always available and timeless. But its reflections, on the other hand, are fleeting instances that evade measure.'

I had advanced my understanding of mirror travel by studying audio tape recordings of an artist who was forever chasing the horizon but was always frustrated by its elusiveness. One day he laid out a grid of mirrors, cantilevered in the earth, and there at his feet was the horizon – the sky side by side with the earth. He experimented further with mirrors, manifesting super-beings and multiple dimensions, and it was through listening to tales of his exploits that I came to understand the principles of mirror displacement.

The mirror in the shower room was old and flecked with small blobs of soap that a small group of ants were busily munching. The fixings were rusted and its surface dusty but it was perfect for my purposes; the imperfection in the glass, if caught right, could make things completely disappear from view. I swayed gently until the image of my face and body disappeared in the warped mirror.

I watched with silent mirth when my jailers – two fat, stupid bitches – came to see why I was taking so long. My escape still baffles them, of course. And here I remain, waiting for the right moment to step back through the mirror. I think often of my father and our last tearful meeting. He embraced me and whispered into my ear, 'Jacqueline, I have no idea who my mother and father were but they were never married, and it got to me at first. I found that I was nauseous all the time. I couldn't eat. Everything filled me with disgust. Every face in the street with brown eyes and olive skin was a brother or sister, a niece or nephew. I felt ashamed of my past life and it drove me crazy. But I am happy now. I feel free and I feel I should give you your freedom too. I should have told you a long time ago but I was afraid. I am not your father and your mother is not your mother. Take care and remember, life is, through and through, a phenomenon of attention.'

I remember this last embrace fondly and I am eager to share the wonder of his parting words. My body tingles with anticipation. But this time, rather than destroy life, I will blaze the sky with hope. I am ready to burst. I am ready.

THE DROWNED BOYS

EDWARD ALLINGTON

It was as if the tree liked children and had grown that peculiar branch to accommodate them. If so its act of generosity must have caused it considerable pain. The branch was a sturdy thing running parallel to the ground, no more than two or three feet from the soil. It stretched in this way for some distance before turning steeply upwards towards the sky. This parallel stretch was bare, long since stripped of bark, or more likely the bark had simply worn away and the wood itself held a dull polish. For the younger children it served as a horse, sometimes a dragon; it was a thing you could ride. For the older ones it served as a seat, somewhere to practise smoking or to lie about sexual exploits. It had always been there, long, burnished, familiar. The part of it which turned upward represented the neck of the beast, and reins imaginary or real, usually lengths of bailing twine, could be hung from this neck. The position near the neck was always subject to turn-taking. By some arcane hierarchical system the neck with its canopy of dark leaves was the place to be. It was a kindly tree, the ground beneath it well trodden and broken. Of all the trees in the small coppice it was the hardest to climb, the growth of the up-shoot being so dense as to be almost impenetrable, and the tree's main bole, with the exception of this one branch, going upward with scarcely a twig before throwing out a mass of strong branches well beyond reach. It was as if the tree had put a tremendous effort into this branch and then changed its mind.

It is a long time ago now, the time of the trees. They were my refuge then, and as I grew older I moved farther and farther out into the forests, climbing higher and higher, finding clusters of branches that were possible to sit in, to be alone, to sleep even. But of all these trees, the one with the branch was the first, the nearest to home.

Of the two boys, one I knew well. We had played in sandpits together, close to our mothers, fought, run toy cars down slopes, set toy soldiers up in ranks; we had been cowboys, racing drivers and war heroes. But we had grown apart as we moved towards early adolescence. New allegiances had been formed, perhaps because of the distance between our homes or perhaps our mothers had some kind of disagreement; this is one of many things I will never know. What I do remember is that the boy I knew had always been held up to me as an example of how I should behave; perhaps I had become resentful or jealous? In any case he had found a new friend from whom he was almost inseparable. This other boy was unknown to me; I remember him as slightly fat, with piggy eyes and a spiky blond crew cut.

The lake was a cold place of terrifying beauty, as grey as polished steel, lapping and eating at the clay banks of its shore. In the early morning a thin mist hovered above it, obscuring the fells. Its waters knew nothing of colour, just blackness and those shades of grey the northern sun could leach from them. I had learned to fear the lake from an early age through the warnings of those who knew it well, and from my own experience. It had almost taken me into its icy depths once. The wind blew its waters in unpredictable patterns and the icy rivers, which fed its dark volume, were notorious for their undercurrents. Yet we swam in it none the less, and sailed upon it on home-made rafts and in fragile canoes. Usually we kept close to the shore, but occasionally faced its breadth to wander in the pine forests on the other side. It was a lake that was indifferent to human life; it had taken strong swimmers and divers with air tanks. It had taken famous men in magnificent motor boats striving to break world speed records. Its friends were water-bound things: large needle-toothed pike, perch with sharp spines, slimy amphibious creatures, and the still heron which fed off them among the reeds.

From high up on the fells it was possible to see stains of oil, vivid rainbows of petroleum left upon its surface by the many boats that used it. There were large pleasure steamers with names like *The Swan* or *The Cygnet* which had a white-painted hull curved like a canoe. Once, at the beginning of their lives, their bowels were fed with coal, men worked with shovels to feed their fires, and the funnels that still graced their decks breathed steam and smoke. Now they ran on diesel which bled from their exhausts into the lake. Smaller craft also plied these waters; the dinghies of sailing enthusiasts, the luxurious motor boats of the wealthy and the less luxurious versions belonging to those who wished to emulate them. There were the small wooden rowing boats rented to tourists by the hour, and boats powered by outboard engines used by those who believed in fishing as others believe in eternal life. There was even an amphibious car, small and pastel painted, owned by a rich family that had a house on Belle Isle. This island was well named, a rocky outcrop of dark stone, wet from the waves and lurid with green moss, covered by a mixture of pines and deciduous trees, in its centre a house, white-columned and private. We would take our canoes, braving the lake's cross-currents to try to find some form of harbour on its shore, so that we might creep terrified through the undergrowth to peer at the house in awe. The car with wheels for the road and a propeller for the water was a thing of legend. Those of us who had actually seen it make the transition from land to water recounted the experience with pride.

The first news of the boys' deaths came to us at school, in the unreality of morning assembly. A master made an announcement coloured by moral superiority, a lesson against delinquency in tones of sadness. This was their epitaph: that not only were they missed, but also that they were missing, that their bodies had yet to be found. Police divers were searching the lake's icy depths for their corpses. No one knew exactly what had happened, but it was presumed that they had stolen a rowing boat from its mooring and had capsized it somehow. So far only the boat had been found. We were told that they were well liked, and that our feelings should go out to the parents at this time of great sadness. That they were good lads who had paid too great a price for what was probably no more than a boyish prank. I remember looking around me in disbelief, certain that closer scrutiny would prove that they were still here as always. In the silence of this moment I could see that everyone else was doing the same. Our eyes rested upon a gap where two chairs were empty, and upon the downcast faces of those occupying the seats beside them, and in this moment I became aware that I could not truly remember their faces.

Some days later there was news that the boys had been found. The police divers had attached them to a rope and hauled them up from the depths, their corpses bloated, and frozen in the exact posture of the moment of death. Their bodies were said to have been enshrouded with weeds, the crew-cut boy clinging to his friend's leg as if he had dragged him down unwillingly to a mutual death. I learned also that someone I knew had seen them being pulled from the lake, and was so ill and disturbed by the sight that he had been granted several days off school to recover. I wondered whether this story was true – were the two boys clinging together, and if so how? Was it some forbidden embrace chosen willingly like love? Did one of them drag the other to his doom? Was it simply fear, panic, or was it that even at this final moment he had been unable to let his friend go, been unable to face his death alone? Had the boy I once knew accepted his fate, or in his last hopeless moments rejected his companion, trying to fight him off, in the most final and terrible of ways? And their faces, how did their faces look? Perhaps they no longer had faces, perhaps the water, the weeds and the sharp-toothed things that fed there had taken them, leaving them without expression, merely rotting, bloated, half eaten, in a last embrace, in a shroud of foul-smelling vegetation? I wanted to know, I wanted to know what the lake did to those it stole from the light; was there some strange form of beauty within its depths? Or was there only horror, indifference and decay?

Some days later I came across Peter, still absent from school, sitting on the long low branch with a friend of his. They were both some three years older than me, almost men; when school finished that year they would leave, find work, be adults. They were sitting on the branch not as a horse, but as if it were a bench, laughing together at some joke or other. I approached them feeling young and childlike in their presence. It was difficult to know whether I should stand before them or try to sit alongside Peter as if I were one of them. I hesitated but drew close enough to try to ask my questions. It was hard to find the words, I felt embarrassed, but got some of it out; my thoughts and the words that left my mouth seemed so different. The thoughts I remember well, but the words have long since vanished like the breath that propelled them. I managed to somehow ask whether he had seen them and what they had looked like. Peter laughed, swapping glances with his friend, and without a word beckoned me closer. He took my hand, and I let him, and he placed it on his penis. It was erect. I looked at him and he laughed, they both laughed. I took my hand away, it felt strange, I could still feel the shape of his erection on it. It made me feel unhappy, it made me feel humiliated, it made me feel sad. I looked down on the trodden earth and I walked away filled with despair.

I walked away with this sadness, a sadness that was all too familiar. I had thought that perhaps there might be somewhere in the world I might escape it, that it was a thing peculiar to my home, that beyond that house there might be something different, and in that moment I knew this was not the case, that it would never leave me. Those boys were lost, they were the lost boys, they were lost to life, and I was lost within it. I would simply never know. Knowing about the one who was once my friend was the least of it; I would simply never know. I began to walk towards the lake.

The place where I was born is named after a bridge and the

small river that flows beneath it. Once a storm had filled it so quickly that a huge wave of water swept down, drowning two men who were illegally netting for trout. Normally it is a shallow stream with occasional deep pools good for swimming, but the scars of that one day are still plain to see; there are huge boulders standing midstream, once tossed as if they were pebbles, but now stranded where the flood waters left them. Here and there the river banks are deeply undercut, in some places almost like grottoes, the legacy of one day's flood.

I made my way down to this bridge and climbed over the wall to step knee-deep in daffodils. This oak and beech wood had huge trees, but was well spaced. In it was none of the darkness to be found in densely packed pine forests. A canopy of broad leaves filtered the light so that when you looked up at the sky the sun dappled through the leaves, sending strange dancing rays of light through their mellow shadow, and beneath them nothing but yellow. The flowers brushed my legs as I walked, each step crushed a plant or more, and if I had looked back the path I had trodden would have been as clear as if I had walked in snow. I made my way to the river, scrambled down the steep undercut banks, until I stood in its shallows. There I dipped my hands into its fast, bitter, cold stream and washed my hands, taking an abrasive mixture of sand and small stones and scrubbing them. Even through the numbness from the cold water and the sting of the sand I could still feel his penis on my palm. All was quiet as I crouched there; if quiet is the sound of running water, then it is a sound better than silence, a soothing sound like tears that don't need to be cried. I washed my hands again in the same way, then cupped them and drank. It was so cold, almost painful in the back of my throat. At this point I began to feel alone again, almost free of what had just happened. Yet it would be wrong to think that even these waters were clean, free from death. Just upstream from where I was, stranded on the side of the river between two huge rocks, was the carcass of a sheep. Its fleece sodden, a blue stain on its side – the remains of the farmer's dye brand – and its eye sockets empty, picked out by carrion crows. Its belly an inflated bladder of death gases as yet still captive within its skin. I could see the flies and maggots that riddled its flesh clearly heaving and suppurating. It was so still that even the songbirds had ceased their melodious warning calls. There had been times when I had walked this wood imitating their calls, rejoicing in the echo of their song, but now all I wanted was the sound of the river running through the stones, a sound that rendered my tears superfluous.

The longer I crouched there, the longer the silence prevailed, the more at ease I became. This time could not last for ever; soon, if I waited long enough, there would be another time and time past is time lost. I was old enough even then to know of lost time. Near to where I was squatting there was an overhang of earth and clay from the flash flood so deep as to almost qualify as a cave. In it a mass of roots, huge, barkless, frozen, where they had once hunted through long-gone fertile earth. Once I had played there with Peter and the other boys. One of the oak roots was massive, as thick as any branch above, and we used it as a slide, climbing up the entangled web of smaller roots to where it broke exposed from the bank. We took turns to slide down it, to land with the crash of our shoes on the pebbles below. I remembered the day when this sport ended, and again Peter was the cause. After he had taken his turn he stopped to look at his arm, which was cut from wrist to elbow, so deep that you could see the bone; there was no blood, not in that instant. The cut to the flesh was no different to that of a knife through a chicken breast; he had caught it on a root that had sliced it more cleanly than a razor. We gathered around him and without thought used our hands to clasp it shut. He was quiet, as if he felt no pain, shocked. Not so far from where we were, a short straight walk through the woods, were some houses; a nurse lived in one of them. Miss Simpson was a childless person, there was nothing that might have drawn her into our world, other than that she was well respected and well liked by our parents. So we went there, still crowded about him, our hands for clamps. She took him from us, reassuring us that all would be well, praising us for thinking and acting so clearly, smiling, closing the door on us, telling us not to worry as she would call his mother.

I learned some years later that she had killed herself, overwhelmed by some unknown sadness; she had cut her wrists before climbing into a warm bath. I suppose she had all the knowledge necessary to do such a thing with skill.

I had planned to make my way down the river to the lake, but all determination had drained from me. Now I only sought a tree. I wanted to climb into those huge wooden arms and rest. Farther downstream there was a massive oak. It stood on a sort of land-bound island, a knoll of soil held by its root system; in that time of the inundation, that sudden wash of water, it had literally held its ground. It would have been nice to think that this tree was mine and mine alone, but it was not; like the horse branch it had been handed down through generations of children. It was virtually unclimbable, yet to those who knew or had been shown, there was a way up; hidden and partly disguised were a few rusting, fragile nails. They were hard to see and hard to negotiate. They gave access to a cluster of branches not unlike an armchair. This oak was my citadel of solitude, yet even this was not truly safe; was there no place in the world which would give me that unknown and longed-for sense? Perhaps there was no such thing as safety, perhaps it was a mythical thing.

From the tree's clasp of branches it was possible to look out over most of the wood, to look down on the river, which danced in ripples and small gurgling eddies of water, and to look out over the field opposite where the local landowner kept his horses. I made my way down the river bed, jumping across the slimy stones, black and wet, keeping my eyes on the grey translucent river, on the clay banks, the moss, the sodden tongues of ferns, the encrustations of lichens. Stopping from time to time to peer into rock pools to watch the sticklebacks and the caddis fly larvae dragging their home-made carapaces of minute stones and wooden splinters, anything but the glorious yellow field of flowers between the trees. Then I climbed this oak to sit and think. The lake seemed far away now that I was alone and no longer needed its company. The two boys were dead and all I would ever know about them was the shape of another boy's erection.

I sat in that tree alone, or almost alone; it was not possible to totally relax as it was necessary to remain vigilant. There was the farmer to watch out for and the gamekeeper on the other side, but my main worry was that some other boy would seek refuge in this tree, climb the nails without me noticing to break this fragment of peace. But there was peace, it lasted, and I began to think about the nature of love; in this my thoughts were purely theoretical and based upon stolen books. There was a sensual world I craved but feared; what did I know of the world of women? I had seen their sex; felt it even, in childish exchange; in rural life sex existed outside the moral imperatives of religion. I had seen beast mount beast, seen how the bull would lap the cow's sex before mounting her, seen how even the cows would mount each other, and I had seen more than that. Once from this very tree I had seen the most extraordinary sight. In the field on the other side of the river there had been four, maybe five, horses, all of them stallions. Two of them began to prance around each other, to push and nudge, beginning to bite each other's necks; they both had huge erections which hung down and swung as they moved. Then one of them stopped and raised its tail. The other mounted it as if it were a mare. The river is not wide, it is what we call a beck, something between a river and a stream, they were close to me. I clearly saw one horse's penis enter the other's anus. The mounted horse's erect penis quivered and pulsated as the other stallion rode it. This was the act that I had been told was unnatural, an abomination. Yet there it was as real as the water or the grass in the field. I had seen dogs do this thing, but dogs are hard to believe, whereas horses are not. I had been so astonished by this sight that I had left the tree, crossed the river and inspected each horse in turn to be sure there was not a mare among them, and there was not. And so what, then, was the nature of love, or of friendship, what of the boundary between them? Was it possible to know a girl as a friend and also join with her sexually, and what of boys and their friendships, was there no difference, and what is the difference between the one who opens to accept and the one who enters, what knowledge is transmitted in that act? Was it one of hierarchy, like being the closest to the neck of that branch, and what is the relationship between such an act and death; why had Peter answered my question with his penis?

The kind arms of the oak held me that dark day and the river of tears calmed me. The two boys' faces never returned; even photographs of them alive and happy could not restore them. As for the lake, it was never the same again, even though I went and sat by it to watch its evil waters. I swam in it throughout an entire year, breaking the ice on its surface to do so. Then drying its liquids from my body for the last time. I determined to seek my life and my death elsewhere, beyond the lake. One day I would walk again through still waters, and there would be an edge, and that edge would collapse, and the silt and the weeds would steal me from the light, but perhaps between this day and that I would know love, give myself to it before I gave myself to death.

The last time I saw Peter was in a public house, I was drinking there with some friends. He was playing darts with some other men. No signal of recognition had passed between us since that day by the branch. There was some form of disturbance, an argument between him and one of his companions. His opponent threw a deadly insult at him. He was likened to a ram unable to service a ewe, the bite being not only that of impotence, but of being fit only for death. A male sheep only has value if it can sire strong lambs, and the day it failed in this duty the abattoir beckoned. Strangely my memory of what happened next is vague. But I do not remember a fight, which would have been the only way for him to redeem his honour. So perhaps it was true.

The lake is still there, as dark and evil as ever. Not a year passes without it taking the lives of children, as well as those of men and women. Yet one cannot deny it is a place of beauty, it is sublime, the sun and moon dance on its waves like diamonds. It belongs to fish, to leeches, to water-bound insects, to frogs and toads, to the waterfowl, to the sharp-beaked heron, to the otters, to that lost time known as memory.

ABOUT
THE
CONTRIBUTORS

Edward Allington was born in 1951 in Troutbeck Bridge, Cumbria. He studied at Lancaster College of Art, Central School of Art, and the Royal College of Art. He is usually identified with the British Object Sculptors of the 1980s, has exhibited in museums and art galleries throughout the world and is represented in major collections nationally and internationally. He has completed major public commissions in the UK, Germany and France. He was a Gregory Fellow at Leeds University from 1990 to 1993 and a Sargant Fellow at the British School at Rome in 1996. He has held artist's residencies in France, Ireland and the UK and is a regular contributor to art magazines such as *Frieze*. Allington lives and works in London and is currently head of graduate sculpture at the Slade School of Fine Art.

David Batchelor was born in Dundee in 1955 and lives in London. Recent exhibitions include *Shiny Dirty* at Ikon, Birmingham, 2004; the *26th Bienal de São Paulo,* 2004 and *Days Like These: Tate Britain Triennial of Contemporary Art,* Tate Britain, London, 2003. *Chromophobia*, Batchelor's book on colour and the fear of colour in the West, was published by Reaktion Books, London, in 2000 and is now available in seven languages. He has written one other book, *Minimalism* (Tate, 1997), and has contributed to several journals, including *Artscribe, Frieze* and *Artforum*. David Batchelor is represented by Wilkinson Gallery, London, and is a senior tutor at the Royal College of Art, London.

Ian Breakwell was born in 1943 in Derby and died in 2005 in London. The written word was central to much of his work, which employed most visual media throughout his forty-year career. Breakwell studied at Derby College of Art and West of England College, Bristol. He is well known for his diaries, which have been exhibited in galleries, broadcast on radio and television, and published in book form: most recently *Derby Days* (RGAP, 2001). Breakwell was involved in the Artist Placement Group during the 1970s and undertook many fellowships and residencies, including at Kettle's Yard, Cambridge (1980), and at Durham Cathedral (1994–95). In 2005 he co-curated the exhibition *Variety* at the De La Warr Pavilion, Bexhill-on-Sea. Many of his works are in public collections, including those of Tate Gallery, MoMA New York, Arts Council England, and the British Council. Awards include a Paul Hamlyn Award for Artists, 2005. A comprehensive, fully illustrated diary publication is currently in preparation and a DVD anthology of his film work is to be published by the British Film Institute in 2006. Breakwell is represented by Anthony Reynolds Gallery, London.

David Burrows was born in 1965 in London. Exhibitions include *New Life*, Chisenhale Gallery and UK tour, 2004/05; *Macro/Micro: British Art 1996–2002*, a group show curated by the British Council; *Muscarnok-Kunsthalle,* Budapest, 2003; and *Becks Futures 2*, 2002. Awards include a Paul Hamlyn Award for Artists, 2002. He is represented by fa projects, London, and Galerie Praz-Delvallade, Paris. His writing includes reviews, essays and fiction for magazines, journals and exhibition catalogues. He is editor of the publishing venture Article Press at University of Central England.

Brian Catling was born in London in 1948. He is a poet, sculptor and performance artist, who is currently involved in video and live work. He has been commissioned to make solo installations and performances in many countries, including

Spain, Japan, Iceland, Israel, Holland, Norway, Germany and Greenland. His recent solo show *Antix* at Matt's Gallery attracted much critical acclaim. Four years ago he founded the international performance group The Wolf in the Winter, whose most recent manifestation was at the South London Gallery. His video work moves between gallery installation and narrative films made in collaboration with Tony Grisoni. Their most recent work, *The Cutting,* was released this year. Eight books of Catling's poetry have been published and his work has been included in many anthologies. He is professor of fine art at the Ruskin School of Drawing & Fine Art, University of Oxford, and a Fellow of Linacre College.

Jake Chapman was born in Cheltenham in 1966 and studied at North East London Polytechnic (1988) and Royal College of Art (1990). After graduating from the RCA he began working with his brother Dinos Chapman. The Chapman brothers have exhibited extensively, including solo exhibitions at the Gagosian Gallery, New York (1997), Kunst Werke, Berlin (2000), Groninger Museum, Netherlands, the Museum Kunst Palast, Dusseldorf (2002), Modern Art Oxford (2003) and White Cube (2005). Group exhibitions have included *Sensation* (1997) and *Apocalypse* (2000), at the Royal Academy of Arts, London, as well as the inaugural exhibition *A Baroque Party* at the Kunsthalle Vienna (2001) and the Museum of Contemporary Art Kiasma, Helsinki (2006). Creation Books published *Meatphysics,* a book of his writing, in 2003. He is represented by White Cube Gallery and currently lives and works in London.

Juan Cruz was born in Palencia, Spain, in 1970. He lives and works in London, where he is Lecturer in Fine Art at Goldsmiths College. Recent projects include the performance/installation *Juan Cruz Is Translating Don Quijote (Again)*, Peer (2005) and the book work *Juan Cruz a Translation of Niebla (Fog) by Miguel de Unamuno* (Forma, 2006). He has held the Kettle's

Yard Fellowship in the University of Cambridge and has been the recipient of a Paul Hamlyn Foundation Award for Artists. Juan Cruz is represented by Matt's Gallery, London, and Galeria Elba Benitez, Madrid.

Mikey Cuddihy was born in New York. She studied at Edinburgh College of Art, Central School of Art, and Chelsea School of Art. Her work has been shown widely in Britain and abroad. Recent exhibitions include: *Parallel Narratives*, Rabley Drawing Centre, (2006); *Chronic Epoch*, Beaconsfield Gallery, London (2005); *Spirit Drawings* (solo show), Hackney Forge, 2005; *Transmission Portfolio*, Haus Am Lutzowplatz, Berlin (2005); '*James In Limbo*' (solo show) Peer Gallery, London (2003); *East International*, Norwich Gallery (2001); *Jerwood Drawing Prize* Exhibition (2001); *British Abstract Painting*, Flowers East (2001); *Los Angeles Art Fair* (2001); *Girl*, New Art Gallery, Walsall (2000) (and touring). She has work in several collections, including: Arts Council England, Contemporary Art Society, and Deutsche Bank. In 1997 she received a major award from the Pollock-Krasner Foundation. Mikey Cuddihy is a visiting lecturer in Fine Art at University of the Arts (Byam Shaw), and University of Brighton. She lives and works in London.

Polly Gould was born in 1971 and is based in London. She has recently shown drawing installation and performance works at Danielle Arnaud Gallery, London. She works as a Lecturer in Fine Art at Central St Martins College of Art and Design and collaborates as part of Eggebert-and-Gould in curatorial projects, such as *Nature and Nation: Vaster than Empires*, which received Arts Council funding as a National Touring Programme in 2004/05.

Chris Hammond was born in 1968 in Glasgow and is the director of MOT. Recent projects include *The Artist with Two Brains*, NAB (2005); *Paradise Row*, London (2005); *I Am the Wrath of God*, MOT (2004); and have included work by

Mike Kelley, Martin Kippenberger, Rodney Graham, Paul McCarthy, Ben Nicholson, Liam Gillick, Martin Creed, Jon Thompson, Mark Wallinger, Fischli & Weiss, Jake & Dinos Chapman, Jeremy Deller, Matthew Higgs, Elizabeth Price and Sonia Boyce. His work attracts an international audience and reviews from *Flash Art, Frieze, Art Monthly, Untitled, Contemporary, Art Review, Artforum,* the *Independent,* the *Guardian, The Times, AN* and *Time Out.*

Janice Kerbel is a Canadian artist who has lived in London since 1995. She has shown her work both nationally and internationally, most recently including *British Art Show 6*; Tate Britain; Norwich Gallery; Arnolfini, Bristol; Galerie Karin Guenther, Hamburg; Grazer Kuntsverein; Artists Space, NY; and Moderna Musset, Stockholm.

Balraj Khanna was born in India in 1940 and educated at the Punjab University, Chandigarh. He came to England in the early 1960s for further studies, but instead took up painting. Since then his paintings have been seen in London, Paris, New York, New Delhi and many other cities in fifty one-man shows, and his work is represented in over thirty public collections. Critic Bryan Robertson has stated, 'Khanna is one of the most distinguished artists working in England.' His first novel, *Nation of Fools*, was awarded the Winifred Holtby Memorial Prize by the Royal Society of Literature in 1985 and adjudged one of 200 Best Novels in English Since 1950 (*Modern Library* by Carmen Callil and Colm Tóibín, Picador, 1999). Balraj Khanna lives London.

Brighid Lowe was born in Newcastle upon Tyne in 1965. She studied at Reading University and the Slade School of Fine Art. Selected exhibitions include *Wonderful Life*, Lisson Gallery; *Truth Hallucination*, John Hansard Gallery; *Intelligence*, Tate Britain and Jerwood Artists Platform in 2004. In 1998 she received a Paul Hamlyn Award for Artists.

Gary O'Connor was born in London in 1963 and is in the final year of an MA course at the Norwich School of Art and Design called 'Writing the Visual'. The course is unique in that it explores creative and critical writing in the context of the visual arts. Audio and visual technology, text and live art are four key areas of his practice as an artist. Selected exhibitions and publications include *Above and Below*, Norwich Cathedral; *The Wrong Map*, Three Colts Gallery, London; *E9*, Transition Gallery, London; *Oh! Vienna*, Ottakring, Vienna; *Garageland* (issue 1) and *Arty: Greatest Hits,* both published by Transition Editions.

Paul Rooney was born in Liverpool in 1967, and trained at Edinburgh College of Art. From 1998 to 2000 his individual work focused on the music of the *Rooney* CDs and performances, and a Radio 1 *Peel Session* was broadcast in October 1999. He now works primarily with text, video and sound and has shown recently at Central Museum, Utrecht, and Kunst Werke, Berlin. In 2003 he was the winner of the first Art Prize North, open to all artists in the north of England. He is currently showing in *British Art Show 6,* which is touring the UK in 2006.

George Szirtes trained as a painter, and is the author of some dozen books of poetry the most recent of which, *Reel* (Bloodaxe, 2004), won the TS Eliot Prize in 2005. He has written widely on literature and art, including a monograph on the work of Ana Maria Pacheco, *Exercise of Power* (Lund Humphries, 2001). He teaches part-time on the MA in Writing the Visual at Norwich School of Art and Design.

Jon Thompson is an artist, writer, and curator, and is Emeritus Professor of Fine Art at Middlesex University. He studied at the Royal Academy schools in London and afterwards as Rome scholar at the British school in Rome. Between 1970 and 1992 he was in charge of the Fine Art department at London University, Goldsmiths College.

His most recent curatorial project is *Inner Worlds Outside*, which opened at the Fundacion la Caixa in Madrid and then toured to the Whitechapel Art Gallery, London. He is represented by Anthony Reynolds gallery and has work in many private and public collections.

Martin Vincent is an artist based in Manchester and Glasgow. He co-founded the International 3 gallery in Manchester. He has written about art for publications including *Art Monthly,* the *Independent* and *The New Statesman,* and is on the editorial board of *The Internationaler.* He has broadcast on BBC Radios 1, 2, 3, 4 and 5. He plays guitar with the band Die Kunst.